Echoes
at
Dawn

by

Kathleen Ann Gallagher

ଔ

Decadent Publishing Company
www.decadentpublishing.com

Echoes at Dawn
Copyright 2011 by Kathleen Ann Gallagher
ISBN: 978-1-61333-093-7
Cover design by Dara England and Cribley Design

Published by Decadent Publishing Company, LLC

Look for us online at:
www.decadentpublishing.com

Printed in the United States of America

~DEDICATION~

This novel is dedicated to the memory of my loving parents, Richard and Catherine Lane.

With special thanks to my wonderful husband, Joseph, for believing in me, and understanding why I need time to work on my craft. I want to thank my fabulous children, Dina, Anthony, and Jake for their love and support. I offer a heartfelt thank you to John, for your kindness and patience. I also thank my son-in-law, Michael, my precious grandsons, Cole Michael, Lance Kelly, and Chase Jackson. I love all of you. I offer a special appreciation to the memory of my dearest mother in-law, Mary Gallagher. I could not have written this book without all of you by my side.

Thanks and appreciation to my editor, Dana. You were wonderful to work with.

I can't forget to thank everyone at Decadent publishing for taking a chance on a new writer. I will always be grateful for this opportunity.

Chapter One

Madeline

$\mathcal{T}$he radio in the family room blared as my friends and I left my house. "That's the second time it turned on by itself to 'My Heart Will Go On,' from *Titanic*," I said. *Am I out of my mind?* When I turned to go back inside, Anne stood behind me.

"Maybe you have it on a timer," Anne replied. She was the voice of reason. Her explanation about the radio made sense, so I felt better, and made a mental note to fiddle with it when I had more time. Anne and I became close in high school. She gave me emotional support when the stress of my home life became difficult to handle. Her positive attitude resulted in high achievements. Even when she didn't study, she got straight A's.

She flashed her pretty smile and flung her silky blonde hair to one side. "Come on, I'll go back inside with you," she said.

Anne possessed an interest in the arts, especially in photography. I could make her laugh, and I think that's what she liked about me the most. We grew up complete opposites. She played by all the rules, and I broke them all. The photo studio she recently opened kept her on the go. Her clientele consisted of mostly brides-to-be.

We raced back inside together. I turned to face her and

shrugged as I hit the off button on the clock radio.

Once a month my three friends and I set an afternoon aside, shut off our cell phones, and got together for girl talk, lunch, and whatever spelled fun. We made the agreement when we were in our early twenties. Most of the time we would meet at my house. There was enough room in my circular driveway for everyone, and they insisted I make my famous cinnamon rolls, which held us over until lunch. The girls chose me to be the designated driver, since everyone usually drank a glass or two of wine with their meal. I chose not to indulge.

"My flats are in my car," I said. Anne, Maggie, and Mara headed to the driveway, as I rushed ahead. I popped open my trunk.

Anne placed her hands on her hip. "May I ask why your shoes are in there?" she inquired.

I felt the heat on my cheeks. "I left them at Joe's house last week," I mumbled. I felt like a sneak and wanted to shrivel up in a little ball. I took off my uncomfortable heels, slipped into my ballerina flats, and felt instant relief. After I tossed my shoes inside, I closed the trunk. Anne stood with her legs apart, like a drill sergeant, next to my car.

"I thought you dumped him! How old is he?" Anne frowned as she moved closer to me. I knew her views on my dating younger men. I respected her opinion and valued the fact that she wanted me to find someone worthy of me.

"Don't worry, it was innocent." A soft tone and a shake of my head did not convince her.

"I don't believe you, but let's go." The sides of her mouth curled up into a grin.

It seemed funny that whenever we got together, we acted like junior high students again. We giggled as we got into my car. As I pulled out of my driveway, a young man jogged by. He winked at us and wore a playful grin. He looked pretty cute in his tight shorts, and he had a deep bronze tan.

"Mara, you can turn around in your seat now. Between the two of you, I don't know who's worse," Anne said. She wagged her hand like a mother scolding her children.

Mara could be a flirt. We liked to tease her about her dating habits. I think she went out with the entire football team during junior year. She settled down after she met her husband. Her four small children keep her busy, and she turned out to be a wonderful mom.

We usually avoided Martino's, the restaurant I worked at, for our get-togethers. Instead, we chose The Cheesecake Factory. It was somewhere where we could gossip in private. The late September afternoon felt like a summer day with its warm temperatures and clear sky. The roses in my front yard still held their color and aside from the start of changing leaves, it was still August to me. I held onto summer and allowed the warmer days to linger in my mind. The private time with the girls was a welcomed event.

As I listened to their chatter, I pulled into the mall lot and tried to find a place close to the door. A monstrous SUV took up two spaces nearest the entrance. I circled around and settled for a spot in the far corner. We arrived in time to beat the lunch crowd. The hostess escorted us to the corner booth with mirrors around the seats, which made it look sophisticated and chic. The gold Roman plaster on the walls created a Tuscan feel.

A male server, who wore a James Dean tie and a studded belt, greeted us. He smiled, as he introduced himself, and I nudged Anne under the table. He handed us the menus, and went over the specials, before he left to get the waters we requested.

"Cute, but I'm no cougar," I said. The corners of my mouth formed a sneaky grin. I wanted to meet someone closer to my age. It had been almost fourteen years since I lost my husband. My habit of dating the wrong men seemed second nature to me.

"Oh, you're not?" Anne said. "Who are you kidding, Madeline? What about Joe? He still lives with his parents."

Mara and Maggie pressed their lips together and looked at each other.

"Did you forget about Ken, the twenty-two year-old you met

last summer on the boardwalk?" Anne asked.

"My involvement with the twenty-two-year-old was purely professional." I straightened my posture. "Kenny needed advice on his career since he had aspirations in the culinary field," I assured her. "He wanted me to teach him about the ins and outs of how to be a successful chef."

"Sure he did." Anne gave a quick nod, and crossed her arms.

Her outburst seemed comical, especially since she held a straight face. I laughed so hard my eyes filled with tears. Maggie motioned to me and I opened my compact to fix my eyeliner.

The Brad Pitt look-alike waiter left to gather our drinks, while we made our selections. He took our orders when he returned. Another reason we liked this place was that the service was usually quick. We didn't want to spend all of our time dining. The mall tempted us with lots of new fall lines in the great shops.

"I went on another date last week," I admitted and rolled my eyes.

"How was it?" Maggie asked. Her concern was evident in her expression and the gentle tone of her voice. She was the girl who helped everyone back in school: a dog lover who started an organization for stray animals in senior year. She owned three pups of her own and still worked with rescue animals. Her busy life also included the roles of wife, mother, and office manager.

"He spent most of the night bragging about his knowledge of how to please a woman with his special abilities," I said. It puzzled me why I even dated anymore. "His sense of humor was perverted, and I almost vomited listening to him. Maybe he'll lose my number." I rolled my eyes and crossed my fingers.

"It's nearly impossible to find a decent guy, especially one who has a job, or doesn't treat his pet like a partner," Maggie said. "'My cousin found a man on a matchmaking service, and he brought his Pit bull on the date. How weird is that? You know I love dogs, but not on a first date. I'm glad I met my husband. He's my own little couch potato."

Our blond, blue-eyed waiter set our plates down and

engaged in small talk. *He's probably a model* To avoid any further comments, I sat back and behaved.

"That's it. I'm giving up on men." I sighed. "I never imagined I'd be dating at this age." I reached for a kabob. "Our lives have certainly changed."

"Yeah, instead of late hours in the night club scene, I'm back and forth to the bathroom instead," Mara admitted. "I'm too young to have a weak bladder."

"It might be from all your deliveries, especially one after the other," I said.

"Maybe you have a point there." Mara giggled. She was the disco queen and taught us to do the hustle. She kept her amazing shape, and never gained an ounce.

"I can't wait to see Clare in her gown," Maggie said. "I wonder what designer she uses. I know Vera Wang has a gorgeous new line." Maggie loved to follow the fashion trends.

"I'm glad he finally proposed," I said.

Clare was one of the girls from our graduating class. She relocated to Manhattan and recently gotten engaged. It was a big event since they had dated for ten years.

"Are you bringing a date?" Maggie asked. She moved closer to me.

"No, I think I'll go alone." I repositioned the cutlery on my place setting and tried to avoid eye contact.

Maggie put her hand on my shoulder, as if to comfort me, as our waiter handed out the dessert menus.

"I'll be fine." I hurried to change the subject. "I think I'll take one of each." I pointed to the pictures on the menu. "Oh, yes, and I'd like a hot chocolate with whipped cream. Make sure it's got shaved chocolate on top." The waiter smiled.

I took a sip of water. "It's great to be all together." I glanced at the mirror next to us. I hoped they didn't notice my recent weight gain. To jump from a size eight to a size twelve was no joke. I still had a decent figure, even with the added inches. Our waiter returned with our orders, and I tried not to stare. I knew they would make a comment, if I did.

My goal was to avoid the topic of the upcoming wedding. Despite my efforts to evade it, the event popped up in our conversation. It was obvious I would be the only one at the reception table without an escort. I was used to it. They all had their devoted husbands. The steady buzz of gossip formed a pattern at our table. The topic switched from complaints about our jobs, our children, and to the low-rise jeans we wished we could fit into.

"How's your mother?" Anne asked. Her tone of voice sounded soft and empathetic.

"She's fine. I may move her into my house, indefinitely."

Anne lifted her wine glass and opened her eyes wide. "So, it's your turn now. How will you manage?" My mother lived with my sister, Bonnie, and her husband, Mike. They agreed to take her in when she almost set her house on fire after she fell asleep with the candles lit.

"Somehow, I suppose," I replied. I took a bite of the last spring roll. The soy sauce hit my shirt, and I dipped my napkin in my water glass and wiped the spot. I knew my turn to take her would come, and my admission to my friends made me realize I had to face the inevitable.

"The last time we got together, you mentioned you wanted to open your own restaurant," Mara said. "Put any more thought into it?"

"It's in the back of my mind. Unfortunately, I don't know how I could pull it off financially right now. I've dealt with family issues recently, and I sometimes I put my life on hold." *Mark and Desiree, my older two children are fine.* I lowered my shoulders and felt a knot in my upper back. "Desiree's job at the television studio keeps her busy, especially since her promotion. She managed to save enough money to buy her own place."

"It doesn't surprise me. She's a bright and ambitious young woman," Mara said.

"Mark will graduate from nursing school by next summer." I clapped my hands with joy. "His interest is in Geriatrics. He makes me proud, and he tries to push Jeremy to study more, with no luck. He's out of school more then he's in," I admitted. I sighed and took a sip of my Diet Coke.

"Jeremy won't open up to anyone. I don't know what to do with him." I sat back and hoped it didn't sound like I complained too much.

"You're still the people pleaser, I see." Mara joined in. She stretched her neck to give me eye contact. "When is it time to take care of your needs?"

"Soon, real soon," I said. I gave her an appreciative nod.

"I hope so," Mara responded. Her tone let me know how much she cared. "Jeremy will get through this. Brian went through a rebellious stage until I refused to give him a loan for a car. He changed real quickly when he saw his father and I meant business." Brian was in his last year of college.

"I hope it's only a short-lived phase. I've tried to talk to him with no luck. It's like speaking to a wall. His attitude gets to me. That's enough complaints from me." I tapped my hand on the table. "How about everyone else? Is there anything new in your lives?"

"No, my household is pretty much the same. Everyone's okay," Mara commented.

"Is there anything new in your world, Maggie?" I asked.

"My life never changes." She took a forkful of her cheesecake. "It would be nice to have the house to myself once in a while. No dogs, kids, or husband to clean up after. But, only for a day." Maggie laughed, and I knew exactly what she meant.

Anne chimed in, "Anyone up for a day at a spa? I've had a hectic month and could use a break."

The three of us shook our heads in agreement.

"Let's check our calendars," Mara said. "I know the best spa in the area. I received a gift card from my sister for my birthday, and I loved it. Especially the Avocado facial, my skin glowed for weeks." She raised her hand to touch the side of her face.

"I haven't had a facial in years," I admitted.

Mara proposed a toast. "Here's to our beauty. Maybe we can get one of those spray-on tans."

"Count me in," Maggie said.

We touched on all the latest happenings in our lives, and I thought about how fast the years flew by. Yet when we got together, we were back in high school. The four of us gave each other our undivided attention. After lunch, we window-shopped and found a leather seating area to relax and sip a latte.

Later we stopped at the bookstore and gathered in front of the magazine rack. Anne pulled out the copy of *Bon Appetite*. "I have this copy at home. Madeline, this could be you if you decide to open your own place." She opened the centerfold to display a spread about a chef from New Jersey who specialized in Cuban food, and opened his own Cigar Bar in South Beach.

"Do you expect me to open a Cigar Bar?"

"No silly, your own restaurant." She laughed.

"It would be nice." I flipped through the magazine and thought *maybe one day*. Our date lasted longer than usual. Luckily, I took the whole day off. Inseparable during those impressionable years, we shared all our hopes and dreams of long-lasting love. We made a special pact to remain friends forever. Now, Maggie, Anne, and Mara lived the life we planned as teenagers, all in the same neighborhood. On graduation day, we stood on the football field and took pictures in our long gowns. We jumped around like we had the whole world to conquer. The years passed so quickly.

I hoped someday, I would stop dating losers and end the relationship when the flags went up. I thought about how fast my children grew up, and I knew I needed to think of my future.

I tried to pretend my going to our mutual friend's wedding alone did not bother me. Every time we got together, I was reminded of how different my life turned out. I made jokes about the younger men I dated. It seemed easier to hide my fear of abandonment. Maggie, Anne, and Mara were honor students and attended the same college. I did not follow along. Instead, I got married. We separated a few months before my husband, Sonny, was killed.

We arrived back at my house by late afternoon, and I waved goodbye as they drove away. As soon as I stepped inside, I heard a moan from my son Jeremy's room. I ran to check it out.

"Are you okay?" I shouted.

My sixteen-year-old son was slumped over in the chair with vomit on his shirt. I moved closer to shake him, and he reeked of alcohol. Since it was only three-thirty, I realized he must have skipped school again. The attendance clerk usually notified me if he was absent. The old trick of a friend to call him out worked in the past. Jeremy knew all of the ladies in the office would recognize my voice. I rushed to the bathroom and got a cold cloth. I patted his head to try to revive him.

He aroused as I frantically dialed for an ambulance.

Two burly men appeared with a stretcher, and I let them in. The ambulance waited out front with the back door wide open. A few elderly neighbors gathered on the sidewalk to gawk. My hands trembled as I led them to Jeremy's room. They immediately placed an oxygen mask over his face and a blood pressure cuff around his arm. Jeremy opened his eyes and struggled to remove the mask. I was relieved to see him wake up.

"His vitals are stable. We still advise a trip to the emergency room."

"Will he be okay?" My head spun as I glanced around for my keys.

"He should be seen by a doctor."

"Of course, you should get him to the hospital. I'll follow in my car." First, I had to locate my keys. I saw where I dropped them next to the bed. I snatched my keys and tagged behind.

It was awful to see my son in a stupor. I drove as fast as I could. It was a good thing the hospital was only a short distance. My head pounded, and I feared for my son's well being.

Harbor Bay had been the community hospital for a hundred years, and it was also the place my youngest son was born. I parked in the visitor lot and had a clear view as the back door of the ambulance opened. Jeremy squirmed around and used profanities when they carried the stretcher inside.

I was relieved, although still angry. Jeremy had come home with alcohol on his breath after a party at his friend's house once before. After a six-week session with the counselor at school, I hoped he'd be on a better track. I thought about how I hated the effect excessive alcohol had on a person. Flashbacks of the horrific times with my Grandfather Nolan popped into my mind, and I prayed Jeremy would not follow in his footsteps. After I ran inside, I grabbed a pamphlet from a display on the wall and looked over it while they took blood and urine samples. A patient representative assisted me to a waiting area and assured me he was in good hands. My anxiety level increased, as I read the handouts. The emergency room had a separate area for patients with drug or alcohol-related problems. My mind wandered to a time as a little girl, when my Grandfather slept in the room next to mine. He hollered in his sleep all night. Grandpa made us breakfast in the morning. He slammed the pots and pans and kept a whiskey bottle next to the stove. I hated it when he visited. As I closed my eyes, I said a prayer for Jeremy. The awful guilt of not spending enough time with him due to my work schedule tugged at my emotions. The air inside the area was stuffy, and I felt claustrophobic in the small space. It seemed like I would never receive an update on Jeremy's condition. My imagination took me to the worse case scenarios. The room was crowded, and I crossed my legs as I watched the clock. A young nurse finally appeared, and gave me a friendly smile. She bent down to my level, and patted me gently on the back.

"He wants to know how he got here," she said.

"Can I see him?" I asked. I felt responsible for what happened to Jeremy. I had doubts, and it was difficult to raise three children without their father. *Maybe I could have done more with Jeremy when he was younger*, I thought.

"In about five minutes. The nurse nodded, as she straightened her posture. "He needs an x-ray of his abdomen right now. A CT scan of his head was already done."

"What's wrong with his head?"

"The doctor found a small laceration on the back of his scalp. It's protocol when we suspect a fall."

"Oh, I didn't even notice." My head felt like it would burst. I never thought his drinking was this serious. Luckily, I carried a non-narcotic pain reliever in my purse for emergencies. I popped two and swallowed without water. A caffeine fix usually helped with a migraine.

I grabbed a couple of chocolate bars from the vending machine in the waiting area. As I juggled a can of soda and three Kit Kats, I put away my wallet. It had been a month without my favorite snack. Since my jean size went up, I decided to change my habit of the use of sweets to calm my nerves. *Oh well, I'll stop tomorrow.*

Jeremy vomited a couple more times, and they gave him a medication to settle his stomach. After two liters of intravenous fluids and a few sutures to his scalp, he was ready for release under my care. His blood test showed an alcohol level above 0.20. The only way the hospital staff would let him leave was with someone who accepted responsibility. When he was fully awake and able to tolerate a box lunch, the nurse came in to take out the IV line. The discharge papers included instructions for alcohol poisoning and included information on AA.

"Sorry, Mom," Jeremy said. He held his head down and sulked as we left the emergency room. I pulled him close to me, gave him a squeeze, and told myself I had to intervene quickly.

I retired to bed early and lifted my favorite chenille bedspread to my neck. After I made sure Jeremy was safe and sound in bed, I curled up on my side, and allowed my body a long deserved rest. Since I had a stress-filled afternoon and needed to get up early the next morning, I tried to unwind. The cup of tea I made earlier was still on my night table. I gulped it in an attempt to calm my nerves. It did little to help. Eventually I fell asleep, around two a.m.

As dawn approached, I opened my eyes when a blinding flash of light emerged through the window. I heard a loud shrill sound and I jumped up. First, I repositioned myself on my back, and tried not to make any noise. The high pitch was familiar, and I remembered hearing it before. A vision appeared in my room when I was sixteen. My mother told me it might have been from my fever of 103 degrees. I never told her about the other times.

A cool breeze swept across my face, and I detected a strong peppery odor. One of the pictures, which hung on my wall, fell to the floor, and a willowy vision materialized out of nowhere. A silhouette of a young woman hovered in front of my antique armoire. The room took on a resplendent glow in the area she appeared. She swayed back and forth in a rhythmic manner, as she spread her arms open to the sides. A thin circle of shiny glitter seemed to take shape around her eyes.

I thought I may have been in a dream, and I became mesmerized. My instinct was to cover my eyes since the light was so intense. The unusual ring became louder. It echoed as the figure moved. Slowly, I let my hands fall to my side, and found her at the foot of my bed. The fog surrounded her image and my eyes shifted toward the ceiling, where a cloud of smoke appeared out of nowhere.

I turned to face the door, and heard the thump of footsteps race down the hall. I had forgotten mother spent the night. My mother and my son Mark burst into my room. They must have heard the ringing.

Mother tripped on her long silk robe. Mark grabbed her arm to steady her before he flicked on the light.

They stopped, gazed around cautiously, and started toward me.

"Grandma, watch your step!" Mark shouted. He reached for

7

2

her.

"I'm just fine," she snapped. Mother pulled her arm away from Mark's hand with a jerky motion. She took out a flask from her pocket, and sprinkled drops of water to form a circle on my carpet. I never knew what to except from Mother since she was into unusual practices, but when the dementia set in, I hoped her antics would slow down.

Mother sat on the edge of my bed, and stroked the back of my hair. She looked up to the ceiling and called out her sister's name. "Mary, is that you?" Mary and Mother were identical. Her twin died suddenly at the age of fifteen. They had a close relationship as little girls. Their mother would make all their clothes herself. She adorned them in frilly lace dresses and placed bows in their curls. Grandma cut Mary's hair a shorter than Mom's, so she could tell them apart. Mary spent a brief time on this earth, and my Mother spoke of her as if she were still alive.

The ghostly figure swirled around and circled like a cyclone before she vanished. The hazy fog gradually thinned, and it was as if she never appeared. Mother reached inside her robe pocket, took out a five-pointed star necklace and a tiny charm that housed a photo of her twin sister Mary. She loved to keep her precious belongings close to her heart. She clutched the pendant tightly before she put it around her neck.

Mark sat next to her on the bed. He wrinkled his forehead and tightened his jaw.

The room seemed like it closed in on me, and it felt like there was a thin veil over my face. I struggled to breathe, and gasped for air. It took a few minutes before I could speak.

"Are you okay? What happened?" Mark's voice drummed in my ear.

As I shuddered, I pulled the coverlet over my shoulders. "I saw a ghostlike image, and I believe she gave me a command," I blurted. I held my hand up, and pressed my fingers against my mouth.

"What do you mean? Were you dreaming?" Mark shouted

and sprung from the edge of my bed.

"No, I was awake," I replied. I shook my head.

"Did she touch you?"

"She didn't come close enough."

"Did she come to rob us?" he screeched.

"I don't think so."

"The doors and windows are locked. How on earth did she get in?" he questioned.

"She appeared after a bright light," I responded and found it all hard to believe.

"Well, you're all right. That's all that counts," Mother added.

She moved over to the antique armoire, which was in our family for over a century. It was the only item salvaged from her own bedroom when she was a young girl. It had a mahogany finish with beautiful gold handles. Around the doors were carvings in the shape of vines. Mother ran her hand across the old relic and opened the bottom drawer. She adjusted it to reveal an extra space. I never knew there was a hidden area in the back. To my amazement, she lifted out a box of white candles before she advanced over to the mantel. Mother lit five candles and lowered her head. She moved over to the window, mumbled, in what sounded like a different language, and then returned to my bedside as calm as could be.

"She had on an old-fashioned dress with a lace, hoop skirt," I said. I closed my eyes for a moment and tried to remember more details. "It had a wide sash around the waist, and she wore high top shoes. She floated in mid-air." I moved to hang my legs over the bed.

"You must have been terrified," Mark said. "Was she someone you know?" Mark glanced around the room for clues.

"She looked like Aunt Mary." After I made an attempt to place her, I felt a chill. It became as cold as the outdoors in my room. "It was Aunt Mary!" I cupped my hand over my mouth.

Mother peeked over her shoulder and recited a strange chant.

Mark sat down again and put his arm around my shoulder.

"I'll make sure there's no one in the house."

"I'm all right. I just need a moment. I don't think she wanted to hurt me. She seemed to have a message for me."

"Go on."

"Smoky letters in the shape of clouds, appeared out of nowhere," I recalled. I looked up to the crown molding.

"When the door to my room opened, she vanished, and so did the letters," I said and waved my hand in the air.

"That's spooky," he said. Mark raised his shoulders with his mouth open. He gave a scowl. "I'll see if anyone's out front," he said. It might have been a burglar." Mark reached over to grab the lamp. "Let me get my hands on her!"

"I don't think you'll need that. She's gone." Mother rested her hand on her chin. "Did she mention me, my dear?" She took another glance around the room, while she placed her hand upon her necklace.

Her tone of voice carried a tranquility that managed to calm me down. She did not seem as concerned about the intrusion as Mark. Mother held her head high, and the look in her eye told me she understood exactly what happened.

"The words, 'Harbor Bay Hospital,' dangled in thin air," I said. "She didn't utter a word." As I tried to comprehend what happened, I shivered.

"They faded and left behind a faint echo," I said. "The sound reminded me of waves hitting the shore at high tide."

"She kept her promise," Mom muttered.

"What'd you say?"

"It doesn't matter."

Mother maintained a perfect posture and displayed an aloof grin.

"I saw another flickering light, and I heard another muffled sound from a distance right before you and Mark came into my room," I said. My gaze shifted to the window.

"Don't worry, I'll stay with you," she offered. Mother moved the goose down chair that I kept in the corner. "I'll be right next to you."

I had some knowledge of paranormal activity because of my mother's fascination with magic. She amused my friends when they came over for Saturday night sleepovers. I was reluctant to let anyone stay at my house. My bedroom was the only one that was large enough to accommodate all of us.

Before I closed my eyes again, I looked over the pamphlets from the emergency room crisis department. The message left behind by my apparition lingered in my mind. Jeremy's close call made me realize it was time to learn more about the disease of alcoholism. *Tomorrow, I'll call them about the volunteer position*, I pondered.

Chapter Two

Nathaniel

"What do you want me to do? It's five a.m.!" Nat shouted to no one and slammed down the phone next to his bed. He owned his own business, and it was starting to get to him. Sometimes he wanted to shut out the rest of the world. The hospital kept him busy, but it didn't pay the bills. It was the second day in a row that Marty, the foreman on his crew, woke him. Marty's car had over a hundred and fifty thousand miles on it, and he could not get it started. He expected Nat to pick him up and drive him to the job site. Nat advised him over a month ago to shop around for a reliable vehicle. He reminded him how it was his responsibility to get to work. Especially since Nat paid him top dollar and needed him to show up on time.

The recent customer was moving in two weeks, and they had no time to delay. Nat knew when it was finished, she'd love it. He would have picked Marty up himself if he had not already committed to speak at the hospital that day. Since the house was down the shore, he knew he'd never make it back in time.

Nat stayed in bed for a few more minutes. He stared at the ceiling, with his arms crossed. He wanted to throw the phone across the room. Marty was a great worker, despite the transportation issues. He was an expert carpenter, and customers raved over his work. For the past month or so, his neediness had increased and interrupted the work schedule.

He was annoyed to have a call this early. A strong cup of Starbucks instant coffee and a shower helped ease the pain. He lit a cigarette and desperately searched his cell phone for Geraldo's number. He took a puff and reminded himself it might be a good time to quit. A nagging morning cough made him feel like an old man. Nat gave Geraldo a job doing sheet rock, and he worked hard to earn the respect of the crew. He would offer to accommodate with no problem when someone needed a ride.

"Hey buddy, do me a favor and grab Marty this morning. I have a lecture, and I'll swing by later. I have to attend an afternoon meeting, too. I'll try to make it before four," Nat said. He took a quick shower and dressed. He hurried to gather his keys and wallet before he picked up his briefcase, and left the house. Nat was curious to know why Marty called him instead of Geraldo. *Nat will take care of it*, he thought. He knew that's what they would all say. "They're all misfits," he mumbled. He hopped into his sports car and headed to the hospital. He knew his crew was an odd bunch. Nevertheless, they were the best at what they did, so he put up with them.

Nat sped up to make the light on the corner of Grove and Beacon Hill Drive. The light turned red, and he had to stop. A new house stood on the corner where he grew up. He hated his old neighborhood. He tried to not to focus on the past, especially since he had moved on. At least, he thought he did. A brief thought of a change of residence to New Hampshire crossed his mind. He recalled their motto, "Live Free or Die." Nat knew he should have left the area years ago. Day after day, he couldn't figure out what kept him in town.

As he waited, Mr. Rosen, who was the last one left of the old neighbors, approached his car. When Nat delivered his newspaper as a ten-year-old, he would always encourage him to start his own business one day.

"Stand back, I'll pull over," Nat said. He nodded, and turned down the street.

After he parked, Mr. Rosen bent down, held onto the edge of the door and squinted. He must have been in his eighties by now. Yet he had a full head of snow-white hair and kept all of his own teeth, which were as yellow as a banana. The others had moved or died, and young families made up the community now.

"How are you?" he asked. His eyes opened wide. "I thought you moved away, young man."

Nat cleared his throat. "No, I'm still around."

"Where have you been hiding?" Mr. Rosen lifted the brim of his faded cap. "Your old man has been gone a long time now. It's sad what happened to your family, lad."

"How've you been Mr. Rosen?" Nat cringed. "You look good." He lied to the old man. Nat would never tell him how worn out he really looked.

"I can't complain," Mr. Rosen said. "You have to keep busy and walk every day." He slowly lifted his cane off of the ground. Mr. Rosen had dark circles and a face full of lines and creases.

"Stop over when you're in the area," Mr. Rosen said.

"Sure, Mr. Rosen," he responded. Nat nodded. He knew he would never keep his promise. Nat merely wanted to show respect.

"Take care," Nat said. He drove away, and wished he never ran into him.

The old man gave Nat the creeps, despite his efforts to be nice to Nat. Nat remembered Mr. Rosen and his father playing cards and drinking whiskey in the garage until late in the evening. Anytime he saw someone from his old neighborhood, it put him in a bad mood. He hit the accelerator and passed a slow-moving Chevy in the left lane. As he slouched in the seat to relieve the tension in his lower back, he gripped tight to the wheel.

Nat made a sharp turn into the parking lot of the hospital and made a mental note to make an appointment for a massage at the gym. He grabbed his briefcase, and took the back stairs. He moved quickly to avoid anyone. His office was locked, and the key was behind the nurse's desk. He thought his plan of avoidance would be impossible. Nat liked to clear his mind before a lecture. Sometimes the nurses would ask him a lot of personal questions, especially about his love life. It made him feel uneasy, and he was in no mood to deal with their comments. The desk area looked isolated except for the secretary. Nat realized after he checked the schedule that he had time to prepare for his talk. He planned one of his favorite topics, which was a definite crowd pleaser. It took a moment of meditation to get into the right frame of mind. He needed a clear mind to be reminded of the life he tried so desperately to forget. His father ruled the house with his quick temper and drank vodka from the bottle. The run-in with Mr. Rosen reminded him of his childhood. Nat sat back in his office chair, closed his eyes, and hoped to gain control of his emotions. The phone rang and broke his concentration. He reluctantly answered; surprised to hear from one of his friends he met in one of his counseling courses.

"Hey buddy. Sorry to bother you at work. I just got in town. Your cell was shut off, and I found this number in my contacts. I thought we could catch up later," Dean said.

Nat was happy to hear from Dean, but didn't have much time to talk. "When did you get in?" he asked. Dean's parents lived in Ocean County, about an hour drive from Nat.

"Last night and I'm only here for a few days. I have to help my parents with some repairs around the house. Are you free tonight? Maybe we could grab a beer," Dean suggested. Nat recalled the nights they crammed for exams while they attended a counseling program in Minnesota. *Those were the days*, he thought.

"Come on by at around seven. We'll hang out."

"I'll see you then," Dean said.

Nat regained his train of thought and focused on the preparation for his lecture. The class began in forty-five minutes, so he had time to prepare. He began his deep breathing exercises and let his thoughts slip away.

The time flew by. Nat closed his office door and headed to

the lecture hall. The techniques he learned from his Therapist helped, and he hoped he could make it down the hall without being seen. Nat relaxed his muscles as he took quick easy steps. He managed to escape the clutches of the nurses who usually bombarded him with a million questions. Once he entered the lecture hall, he systematically arranged his books across the desk. He placed a cup of water within reach. Public speaking held many challenges for Nat, although he pulled it off like a pro. He knew it would not be long before the room filled and the adrenaline rush would begin.

Nat loved to see the faces of the men and woman who entered the facility and tried to find peace from the grips of addiction. Many of them would find serenity and move on to have successful lives, rekindle relationships with family and friends. They would learn how to reenter society as respected members of their communities. It wasn't easy to ask for help, and Nat knew how difficult change could be.

He had a life filled with heartaches. His mother would cry at night as he lay in his bed, and he listened to her sobbing. One night he snuck out of his room, crawled into his parents' bed, and found his mother alone. He asked her why his father wasn't home yet. Something crashed in the kitchen, and she reached for him, pulling him close to her. They both rushed to the top of the stairs. Nat's father banged the pots and pans, as he tried to prepare a midnight snack. When he tiptoed down to see if he was okay, his father shouted to get back to bed or else he would get the belt. Nat dashed up the stairs and locked his bedroom door. He knew how violent his dad got when he was drunk, so Nat hid under his bed and stayed there for the whole night. To avoid the pain from the quick lash of the belt across his bottom, he tried never to answer back. Only once he lost it and spoke his mind, never to forget how painful the snap of belt felt against his buttocks. The wounds on his skin healed on the outside. They left a scar deeper than the eye could see. The bell rang, and the clients filed to take their seats. He greeted them with a confident nod, and hoped he could help each and every one of them.

Chapter Three

Madeline

As I drove up to the medical center and approached the parking area, a man stood on the corner. He looked about the same age as my twenty-two year old son Mark. The young man wore a tattered green army jacket and had an unkempt beard. Alongside of him was a crumpled brown paper bag. He pressed his hands against the window next to the bench with his knees buckled as if the zest for life slowly disintegrated from within.

When I called to ask about the volunteer position at the hospital, the head of the department asked me if the homeless would frighten me. I assured her I'd be willing to accept the clients without judging their situations. I recognized the young man on the corner from the day I interviewed. We left the intake area at the same time. He was warm and friendly; he even held the door open for me. It made me curious to learn the circumstances, which led to his destruction. I realized a hardship could happen to any one of us and throw our life in another direction. The decision to sign up to help at the recovery unit would hopefully benefit Jeremy while I learned about his disease. Although it frightened me to examine some of the facts I never wanted to face.

My plan was to gain insight on my family's afflictions. The arguments and disruptions in my family caused me a lot of pain. Grandpa's alcoholism had affected everyone in our family one way or the other. I feared what I would learn when I faced these emotions; nevertheless, Jeremy followed a path to destruction, so I had no choice. I thought about my decision and did not turn back. The elevator door opened, and I pushed the button that pointed upward. The ride to the fourth floor seemed like an eternity.

Unanticipated energy mounted deep inside of me. I found it difficult to concentrate, yet I remained determined. The locked unit was called Path to Life. The specialized division made groundbreaking progress in the field of addiction. Fortunately I would be able to spend a few days a month volunteering. I knew it was odd how my latest apparition involved a message about Harbor Bay. Since Aunt Mary came to visit me in my dreams and visions over the years, I dealt with it. When you have a mother who practices witchcraft, you learn how to cope with life out of the ordinary. Although Aunt Mary's appearances jarred me at times, her latest visit helped me find the courage to make a commitment to investigate the world of addiction. It was usual practice to push it to the back of my mind. Most of the time, I thought my visions were from too much coffee, lack of sleep, or from too many paranormal books. I began to realize how Jeremy's episode of intoxication could lead to much more, and it made me determined to get answers before it was too late.

A stop sign was pasted to the door, and it startled me when I stepped out of the elevator. There was a locked door with a window in the center. I pressed the button to announce myself. A raspy voice bellowed through the intercom, and asked me who I was and the reason I was there.

It startled me at first. "I'm the new volunteer, Madeline Young." My nerves caused the pit of my stomach to tighten, and I wished I had brought an antacid. My decision gave me a sense of pride, as my curiosity increased. The buzzer sounded again before the door opened. The entry slammed behind me with a loud click of the lock. The call bells at the desk lit up, three in a row.

It's a busy place, I thought, while I searched for someone to approach. To my surprise, no one greeted me. As I took a deep breath, I glanced over to the desk. I hesitated to approach anyone. The sound of the wheels on the dietary wagon screeched behind me. A young man handed out the breakfast trays, and I stood back to allow him to get around me.

The staff rushed around, apparently involved in their daily activities. As I moved cautiously, I passed a red cart with an orange locked box on top. I wondered what was inside. The drawers were fastened with the same device. A hospital unit was the last place I thought I would be. The area struck me as a professional place, and I hoped that someone would greet me. It concerned me when the staff in front of the entrance never acknowledged my presence. Two younger nurses sat behind a modern designed desk with three computers, swivel chairs, and color-coded charts. They focused on their documentation while an older nurse stood at the far corner and wrote in a large binder. It seemed like a good idea to investigate on my own.

When I made it to the center of the corridor, I saw a shadow move near a large window around a vent. A vision emerged, and it caught me off guard. A misty fog hung an inch or two down from the ceiling. As I shook my head, I told myself it must be the fluorescent lighting, along with poor housekeeping. A sudden chill came over me, and I pulled my arms close to my chest, in an attempt to warm up. I closed my eyes and took a deep breath. When I placed my hand next to my ear to stop the awful ringing, another image of Aunt Mary appeared. Her eyes glared at me from high up in the hazy area. This time only her face appeared. My heart sped up and my mouth became dry. Gradually, the image disappeared. It took a couple of minutes before I could move on. This was the first time my visions had happened outside of my own bedroom. I hoped I wasn't having a nervous breakdown. My mental state was stable in the past. Lately, I seemed unraveled.

The staff continued to ignore me, and I curiously tried to find the manager's office. My instincts told to find a clue about the real reason Aunt Mary sent me to Harbor Bay. Sure, our family was affected by alcoholism. Nevertheless, there had to be another reason for the urgency. I slowly advanced down the never-ending hallway, with my fingers clutched tightly onto my notepad. My hands trembled as I swallowed hard. The walls were painted a shade of pastel green with white trim. The sound of the heels on my shoes intensified on the waxed flooring. My anxiety increased, and I tried to remain focused. I read somewhere how the color green had a soothing effect. When I peeked into an envelope on a table in the waiting area, I felt like a secret agent. My goal was to find the missing piece to the puzzle. An announcement sounded through the intercom for the classes on the agenda. A large group of people filled into a classroom, one by one. As I approached, a lecturer began his session.

I paused outside and tried to sneak a look. Inside, a man stood with a book in front of him on the podium. I had to crane my neck to see through the tiny window. His face appeared flushed as he jolted back and forth. His enthusiasm fascinated me as he stood in front of a room full of people. He raised his hands in the air. I moved back, concerned I would distract him.

He spoke loud enough for me to hear bits and pieces of the lesson. The members of the class were people from various age groups. They sat with their mouths open, eyes wide, as quiet as if they were in church. When I turned around quickly, I almost collided with a woman who appeared next to me.

"Excuse me," I said, stepping aside. That's quite all right," she offered. She gave a nod.

The woman shook her head back and forth, and she wore a tiny grin. She looked polished and professional in a long plaid skirt with a red jacket.

I thought, *At least someone is friendly.*

The woman motioned for me to enter. "He won't mind go ahead take a seat." Her hand brushed up against my shoulder as if to guide me inside. Reluctantly, I tiptoed, and did not want to disturb the speaker. I slid into the first seat I saw in the front row. I fidgeted around in the folding chair, while I heard the others shuffle behind me. I looked up at the blackboard and mouthed the words that were written in large black letters, "You can change your life." It sparked my interest. I gave the speaker my undivided attention and became enthralled in the moment. His speech was extremely motivational, and it carried a positive message. He articulated with confidence when he explained how difficult it was with an alcoholic father. An important piece of information he focused on was how it was a family disease. At the end of the lecture, he opened up the floor for discussion.

The group interacted with each other for about thirty minutes before the session ended. Everyone formed into a circle to join hands. The young woman next to me reached her hands out to grab mine. Her voice was monotone, but she managed a smile. Her hair was jet black and pulled back with a hair band. She wore a nose ring and had tattoos on her arms. After the prayer, she handed me a meeting book with a list. There were handwritten phone numbers on the back of it.

"This is how it goes," she said. She motioned to a copy tacked to the wall. They recited a brief prayer and ended with a friendly exchange to the person who stood at either side. An atmosphere of hope surrounded each one of the participants in the group. Although some of the older members looked weary, they held their heads up. They looked proud and peacefully satisfied.

The room emptied quickly as I ambled towards the door. I moved leisurely, pleased with the positive message the meeting offered.

The lecturer gave me a welcoming smile and made his way over to me.

His demeanor took me by surprise, but I liked it. There was a familiarity about him. My mind quickly searched for information. If our paths crossed before, I could not remember where. *Maybe he reminds me of someone I know*. I shrugged.

"I'm a counselor here. My name is Nat Griffin. Miss Morris

told me we had a new rookie today," he asked. He held out his hand.

His eyes held a wisdom and confidence that instantly held my interest. I saw the top of a cigar in his shirt pocket. I hated them ever since I first took a whiff of the ones my Grandfather Nolan smoked. I would not hold that against Nat.

My palms felt sweaty as I reached to accept his offer of friendship. I cleared my throat before I answered. "I'm the new volunteer, Madeline Young." I forced a nervous smile when he swung open the door.

"How'd you like the meeting today?" he asked. He reached over to secure the security device on the classroom.

I shook my head in approval. "It was great. I found your message motivational." My arm hit up against his as we moved away from the door.

He parted his lips. "I'm sorry for my clumsiness," he admitted.

"That's okay. It was only a love tap," I said. I did not want to sound like a flirt. I pressed my lips together and took a breath.

"That's not a bad gesture," he added. He gave me the once over, as if he were checking me out.

As we continued our conversation, I still felt like we already knew one another. I tried to remember if I ran into him, or where I could have met him before. I searched my memory for answers.

The woman, who invited me into the classroom, started toward us. She came to a halt and positioned herself in front of me. Her manner was courteous, yet, she seemed surprised when she saw Nat and I involved in conversation. Miss Morris crossed her arms. She remained silent while she looked at him, then at me.

"I see you've already met Mr. Griffin." She turned around to face me. "He's one of our best counselors," she said. "He does catch the attention of our clients and many return to thank him. I'm the manager of the unit, Kelly Morris. You must be the new volunteer."

I nodded back. "Yes, I am. We spoke on the phone last week."

"You didn't show up at the in-service again, Nat," she said. She placed her hand on her hip while she tapped her foot.

"They're a waste of time," he said. Nat shrugged.

"Come with me to my office, and I'll get you started. Let's begin with a trip around the unit," she said. Miss Morris looked about forty-five with the fine lines around her mouth, which appeared through her makeup. She confided in me during our initial conversation that she put in sixty hours a week. I admired her devotion and respected her choice to work in an area many people frowned upon.

I reached into my bag for a pen before I began the tour. Unexpectedly, my notebook slipped out of my hands and onto the floor. The book fell apart with the handouts from the class adrift throughout the area. I felt my neck tighten, and the heat rise on my face. I bent down slowly and attempted to gather my belongings.

Nat promptly retrieved the scattered papers and calmly handed them to me. His caring nature became obvious in the way he assisted me in my awkwardness. He tilted his head, and it made his strong jawline noticeable.

"Here you go." He handed me my papers. "It was nice to meet you, Madeline. I look forward to working with you."

"I can't wait to start," I said.

I turned to join Miss Morris. My eyes followed him as he walked away, and I wondered if he noticed. Once again, it seemed to me like the events were a replay of a past encounter. Out of nowhere, a cold breeze blew through the corridor and stopped me in my tracks. The temperature's sudden drop made me curious. Before I tagged along with the head nurse, I took a deep breath.

A voice rang out from behind the nurse's desk. "Miss Morris, there's an important phone call from out of state in your office." Miss Morris turned around quickly, put her hand up, and appeared embarrassed by the interruption. She shook her head;

her brow tightened.

"I'll be right there," she said. She hurried to the desk.

Nat walked over to me and we waited side-by-side until she returned.

"I don't want to impose on you, Nat, but would you show Madeline how we operate?" she asked. "I have to take this call, if you don't mind."

"I'm sorry for the delay," she said. Miss Morris reached over to touch my arm. "Nat will have to be your guide today. You're in good hands. The recorder is in the lounge, and so is the orientation packet." Miss Morris hastened toward her office while Mr. Griffin took her place.

"No problem. I'd be glad to show you around," he said. Nat offered a proud grin.

His quick acceptance toward the change in plans put me at ease. He had a confidence apparent in his voice, yet he had an edge about him that puzzled me.

Nat raised his shoulders. "I usually greet the new volunteers anyway." He touched the cigar in his top pocket. "Does smoking bother you?" Nat tilted his head, as he waited for my reply.

"No, that's fine." I tried to be open-minded.

The unit had multi-colored carpets rich in color. The windows let in the light to make the area inviting. There was a large room with plenty of tables used for group meetings and lectures. The rules were displayed in every area along with the steps of the program. There were private offices where the addiction specialists spoke with their clients. We passed a giant calendar in the lounge with the day's events written in large print.

"The format introduces structure and guides the clients to take responsibility for their lives," Nat recited. "Our goal is for each person who enters this unit to learn how they're not alone and to accept their shortcomings. There's a need for an open mind and total honesty at any cost." He guided me over to the station, checked over his schedule, and snuck a quick peek at the nurses in the lounge. Nat turned quickly, and never made eye contact with his co-workers.

"Is anything wrong?" I asked.

"No, it's going smooth. It's so stuffy in here, that's all," he said. Nat took off his jacket. "Come on, I'll show you where we keep the supplies." He stood in place and waited for me to take the first step.

Nat spoke in a smooth tone, and his words flowed in a lyrical fashion. It was a pleasure to listen to him speak. His hair hung over his collar in the back, and I liked it. He motioned to a room off to the side, which had a closet with the supplies. It became difficult to concentrate.

He gave me a list of things to do on morning rounds. I finished all the orientation needed on my previous visit, so it was time for me to jump in. Volunteers only had one day of class before they assisted on the floor. I would be able to visit each room, bring toiletries if needed, and I could assist with the phones. Another duty was to pick up supplies and run errands for the nurses, and if needed, I would transport clients for tests. There was plenty to keep me busy. If someone needed to talk, I could simply offer a shoulder to lean on. There was a confidentiality tape, and a few others to watch for everyone who worked on the unit. After I finished the lessons, Nat handed me the hospital's welcome packet.

The scenarios I watched on the videos qualified me to begin with a resource person for assistance. It wasn't as difficult as I expected. A kind word or an errand could make a difference on a hectic unit.

"You could probably run the place; there's no big mystery to it," Nat said with a grin.

"Sure, let me use your office," I teased. "All kidding aside, thanks for taking the time to show me around." I jotted down the days I would be available. I handed them to him, and felt optimistic.

He accompanied me toward the door.

"See you tomorrow, Madeline," he said.

I shifted my hips back and forth. I hoped my eagerness

would not annoy him. "I look forward to working with you and your staff," I said.

"I think it's great to have you as a volunteer. We're glad to welcome a person who's willing to help out."

His friendly smile and kind manner put me at ease. The way he delivered his lecture sparked my curiosity. His eyes displayed an intensity and passion for his work.

He accompanied me part of the way. As we made our way through the unit, I looked around to see if Miss Morris was finished with her conference call. I wanted to thank her for the position. I did not see her at the desk, so I decided to be on my way. A peaceful mood came over me.

"I'll see you tomorrow." Nat closed his office door and left the area.

My serenity did not last long. As I was about to leave, a shrill scream rang through the air. I jumped back and checked behind me.

A young woman trembled in her doorway. Her face had a flushed appearance, and she sobbed uncontrollable.

Two nurses placed the girl into a nearby wheelchair, called to the desk to alert security, and assisted her to her bed. The girl continued to shake, and I heard them say she was having a seizure. The nurses did not restrain her; they applied an oxygen mask instead. Miss Morris rushed out of her office and quickly obtained a vial from a secure area behind the desk, which must have been the medication room.

"Can I help?" I asked. I wanted to offer assistance.

"We're okay, thanks anyway," Miss Morris said.

It saddened me to realize the girl could not have been more than twenty-years-old.

The head nurse glanced at me out of the corner of her eye and breathed a sigh of relief.

The young women settled down and appeared much better. Her eyes closed, and her respirations became regular and easy. I shivered, imagining the same happening to Jeremy. I knew I had to find the answers.

I counted the moments until my orientation at the medical center. I could not wait to learn what secret would unfold, or life changing experience waited for me inside the mysterious ward. At the time, my family and friends questioned why I wanted to spend time in a rehab center, since I already had a busy schedule. I was the executive chef at a waterfront restaurant and was the mother of three grown children. I never thought I would raise them without their father, but I did. You never realize how strong and capable you are, until you have no other option. After Jeremy's episode of alcohol poisoning, I sought answers.

My grandfather lost his self-respect and much more, because he was unable to stop his heavy intake of alcohol. When I was younger, I did not want to discuss my feelings since I believed our family was the only one with this problem. One Christmas Eve when I was around eleven, he knocked our tree down when he came over after a party. Grandpa stumbled around the house and made a mess of all the presents. He fell in the bathroom, and there was blood all over the floor. His behavior frightened me. My mother made excuses for his accidents and let him get away with his antics. The household was full of drama, so I stayed in my room most of Christmas Day. Everyone else on the outside seemed so normal.

It was time for me to leave; I saw enough for one day. I took a drink of water from the nearby fountain, left the area, and headed to the elevators. My knees weakened from the events I witnessed. I watched the numbers light up on the panel. Before the door opened, I heard the sound of footsteps from a distance, and I quickly held the entry.

The counselor appeared next to me. All at once, I found myself wobbly. I stood still, and tried not to appear overly anxious.

Nat turned to face me as he took a sip of his coffee. His gaze met mine. He tucked a lighter into his jacket. "I know it's a nasty habit," he offered. "How do you like our little corner of the world, Madeline? I think you'll fit right in."

I looked down first, then at him. "I think it's great that you can really make a difference in people's lives. That's what counts."

"I agree," he returned. "When we give what we've learned to others, the program works."

"Well spoken," I said.

I could see beyond his professional image into a place where he held his deepest emotions. We pushed our way through the lobby and made our way out front.

"Are you through for the day?" I asked. I wished we could talk more.

"I'm through here, but now I have to go to my other job. I run around like a mad man most of the time." Mr. Griffin took a deep breath and put on a tan, wide rim hat. He buttoned his jacket. "I'm usually on the run, busy life."

"I know what you mean. Thanks again, for showing me around this afternoon. I'll see you tomorrow. I placed my purse over my shoulder."

He nodded, and gave me a wide grin. "Anytime, have a great day."

I watched him cross the street.

He turned back, and gave a fast wave.

I experienced an excitement that sparked my interest. I left the hospital with renewed optimism and was thankful for small blessings. While I stood on the top deck, I looked around and tried to decide which vehicle belonged to him. I imagined Nat drove a fast, sporty vehicle. I laughed to myself. I felt a strong attraction towards a total stranger, and I struggled to remember where I parked my car.

The afternoon was beautiful; the sun was still out and the smell of fresh cut grass filled the air. The employees came off duty, scattered through the lot, and said their goodbyes for the day. They appeared to be a happy bunch. It was apparent to me at that moment; I made the right choice by volunteering at the hospital.

My mother's adages rang in my ear. *The events of our lives will flow into a circle of love. All events are mapped out ahead of time.*

Why was I so compelled to answer that article in the newspaper? I already had a busy schedule. I could not get the listing out of my mind. Was the message from Aunt Mary meant to lead me towards a life changing event? Why did I stumble into Mr. Griffin's lecture? Could my mother's proverbs have any significance? I knew it all sounded out of the ordinary, but I could not help but wonder.

Chapter Four

Madeline

I started my car as the morning events played over in my mind. When I rolled down the windows and opened the sunroof, I inhaled. Then, I closed my eyes and rested my head back. There was so much to think about. After a few abdominal breaths, I pulled out of the deck.

It was such a beautiful day. I decided to stop at the waterfront. Since it was still early, I took the scenic route. I needed time to unwind, before I went home. It was an ideal time to take advantage of the pleasant weather. The experience at the hospital held a lot of drama, although commotion was a usual occurrence at my house. I had to learn to adjust to turmoil quickly, when I was a young girl.

The dock was full of boats with people on benches alongside the walkway. I made my way through the parking lot, and enjoyed the sea air. The water was calming, and I routinely walked on the pier. You could see the bridge to New York City while you watched the sailboats in the bay. I found a dockside restaurant and chose the outside area to take in the view.

If I had time, I loved to try new places to eat. It was fun to compare their menu to ours. You'd say I had my own critique of the other eateries in the area. The water looked so beautiful, I stood at the railing and enjoyed the view. The sailboats formed a circle in the water. They had the appearance of a fleet of colors side by side.

There were a few young men on the dock, and they wore vests with stuffed pockets. They leaned on the rail while they fished. As I hiked by, I gave them a friendly smile. They gave me a nod as they steadied their stance. My heels wobbled in between the cracks on the planks, so I stopped at a nearby bench. I would have loved to stay all afternoon. It was exactly what I needed to unwind.

I could stay for hours, and gaze out across the water. It transported me to a serene and tranquil place. When I was a young girl, my parents brought me to the water. The dock had a long pier with massive private boats lined up in a row. We took a tour on a private party boat, anchored at the far end of the dock. You could rent the yacht for parties or take a dinner cruise on a Saturday night. At night, long strings of lights along the outside dining area, gave the whole area a festive feel. Sometimes after we came home from our outings, I had trouble falling asleep. A bright light would hover around my bedroom window. Due to my innocence, I thought it was from the streetlights. The light appeared again when Aunt Mary appeared in my room. Now, I could put together the pieces. I folded my arms and breathed in the salty scent of the water. It was the perfect place to reflect on the day. The time seemed to stand still before I realized I was hungry.

The menu featured numerous selections of delectable items. Silently, I knew it could not compare to ours. The servers wore white sailor suits. The uniforms added to the ambience, and it made their appearance fresh and poised. My thoughts traveled to earlier in the day and the intensity of the lecturer back at the hospital. Nat really held my interest with his talk about a way to find balance in your life.

I thought Nat looked sophisticated, yet stylish in pleated slacks with a tailored shirt. The formfitting shirt revealed his muscular physique. His eyes were an incredible shade of blue. He had thick brown hair with long bangs, which made his appearance youthful. His features were strong and classic. I found him fascinating, and I wanted to learn more about him. It became obvious how he liked to help others when he took the time to console a young man when he became upset in the classroom.

While I watched the tiny creatures, as they swam around near the dock, the water became a mirror. The events up to this moment seem to all fit together, as if there really was a divine intervention. I questioned if my mother was right all along. Mother held on to her prophecy that all I desired would take happen when the time was right. She assured me that when it was supposed to happen, I would find that special someone.

It was difficult to believe the right man would come into my life. Somehow, I learned to place a value in her predictions. She did have a record of being right most of the time.

On many occasions I pleaded with my mother. "Why can't he just stop?" I insisted, desperate for normalcy. I watched my mother suffer over the conflicts caused by my grandfather's drinking. Grandpa died when I was sixteen. Silently, I was glad. A sense of guilt about my reaction on the night he went to the hospital remained tucked inside my heart. It's not normal to feel happy, instead of sad when your Grandfather dies. Instead of tears, I applauded the news. I thought I must be an evil person to despise my own Grandfather. Luckily for me, I was able to free myself of blame after a Saturday confession. It wasn't enough to make a difference. The past still held me back. It became necessary to learn more about the man behind the bottle.

My grandfather's antics and the quirkiness of my mother's rituals embarrassed me, but I still adored my mother. "The events in your life happen for a reason; you are where you're supposed to be." She assured me whenever I doubted myself.

I wondered why she expressed such a confidence in her predictions. She seemed to have inside information, and I thought she was simply intuitive. My father's sister, Aunt Lilly, told me on my thirteenth birthday how my mother was able to stay in contact with her departed twin sister. I insisted she was a liar and a gossip, when she tried to spread rumors about my mother and her practices. Sure, she read tarot cards and told the neighbors their future. All in fun, I believed. But to be able to connect with the deceased was over the top. She kept a leather covered book called "Book of Shadows" in a locked drawer. I snuck in her room, browsed through it one night, and never told a soul about it. Special abilities, and a book of spells was not normal, and not what the other kid's mothers did. So, I forced the idea out of my mind. It would take time for this mystery to unfold.

When I got home, a note on the refrigerator reminded me I had a dinner date with my daughter, Desiree. She had recently moved into her own condo nearby which made it easy for both of us. I placed the mail and my purse on the counter.

I scurried around the kitchen to prepare her favorite meal. My house was an older one. When we moved in, I had the kitchen renovated, and chose a biscotti-colored island that had tons of drawers. The stove was the appliance I loved the most. It had a convection oven, a stove top grill, and an extra burner.

While I filled a large pot of water, I daydreamed about my conversation with Nat. After I prepared the sauce, I pulled the stepladder up to the counter, and reached for my Limoges plates. They belonged to my Grandmother, and I only used them for special occasions. Her mother left them to her, and they passed through three generations. When I ran a clean cloth over the dishes they sparkled. The plates had beautiful rosebuds in red and pink that kept their color as if they were brand new. A vintage linen tablecloth was the perfect touch to the setting. I arranged a fresh flower bouquet from my garden, and had time left to relax in a warm bath.

Desiree arrived a few minutes early, and when I opened the door, I was happy I had such a good relationship with my daughter. Desiree was an ambitious young woman. She had a busy schedule, and it was my time to have her all to myself. I moved a strand of her silky, black hair from her eye, as I welcomed her inside. She gave me a smile, and I felt such pride for the responsible young woman she had become.

"You look lovely today," I said. Her tiny little waist and curvaceous hips made even the simplest outfit look perfect

"I'm glad to see you," she said. She reached over to give me a hug and a kiss on the cheek. She placed a large bakery box on the kitchen counter and took off her jacket.

"Let's go inside," I said. We moved into the family room and sat on the coach.

"Before we eat, how's Jeremy?" She kept her tone low.

"He's better. He still has a long way to go."

"Is he going to school?"

"Yes and so far, no calls from the truant officer. At least now, I'm on my way to understanding more about addictive behavior. I started the volunteer position today."

"Is Jeremy still involved with those hoods?" she inquired. Desiree crossed her arms. "I told you those derelicts he hangs around with would be a bad influence. I could not believe he drank so much he had to be taken to the hospital. When I heard your message about what happened, I had to leave work early. Sorry, I didn't come to the hospital. It would have upset me to see him in such a state."

"You're so right. You would think an evening in the emergency room for alcohol poisoning would make him frightened, but it didn't," I said. "He acted like it was a normal day the following morning."

"I knew he was headed for trouble." Desiree clenched her jaw.

"A detective from the juvenile bureau paid me a visit with a warning about those hoods he hangs with," I said.

"Really?"

"They vandalized the school property, and this time it's serious. I don't know what to do with him, I've tried my best."

"I'll have a talk with him. He might listen to me. Maybe I can entice him to have a heart to heart, by promising to give him driving lessons," Desiree offered.

Her offer to help warmed my heart. I gave a sigh of relief. "Great idea! We have to stand by him."

"I agree," she added.

"I found a fantastic new bakery in town, and the cheesecake looked scrumptious," she said. Desiree's beautiful smile brightened up her face.

"Good choice, I'm in the mood for a sinful desert tonight. "

"What's wrong with you?" she said in a concerned tone. "You seem different tonight. Did you win the lottery or what?" She lifted her chin to stretch her neck forward.

I hesitated for a moment and stood up. "No, there's no problem, but I did have a wonderful experience today. I sat in on a lecture from a counselor at the medical center."

"He must have been amazing. You're blushing!"

"Let's go inside. Wait until you see what I prepared."

She got up, and I extended one arm to lead the way.

Desiree had a flare for design. She loved fine dining and a beautifully set table. Desiree stood in amazement, with her mouth open.

"The table looks stunning tonight," she said. She ran her hand over the tablecloth.

"I thought we would use the plates that great-grandma left me. What am I saving them for anyway?" I asked. I held back a dubious grin.

"It's about time you used them. The table looks elegant," she said. She straightened the napkins. Desiree turned her head to one side and squinted. "You look exceptionally pretty tonight. Is that a new shade of lipstick?"

"It is. I bought it at the spring cosmetic fair at the mall. It's a richer long lasting color."

My daughter had more wisdom than other girls her age. She

could read me like a book. She was the first-born and had to grow up fast. The kids at school teased her, and picked on her about being in a one parent household. Sometimes she became angry and had a hair-pulling match, not caring if she got in trouble. I regretted my dependency on her for support when she was far too young to understand my struggles. She had so many difficult times as a young girl, especially after her father died. Desiree persisted to make a good life for herself, no matter what.

She turned her leg out to the side and placed one hand on her hip. "What happened today at the medical center?" she asked. Desiree lowered her brows. "You must have really enjoyed the day. Come on, you cut fresh flowers and set the table with the fancy plates. You're acting different today. What's the occasion?"

"There's no occasion. Can't a mother make a fuss over a dinner date with her only daughter?"

"Sure, she can. Thanks for making the seafood pasta dish I love."

"How's work?" I asked. *I'm off the hook, for now.*

"The studio is busy with the change in the fall line-up. I have it under control," she said. Desiree shifted her weight. "Are you going to keep me guessing? What are you hiding?" Desiree persisted; both hands remained on her hips. She shifted from side to side, while she waited for me to answer. Her eyes held a curious glare.

I sat down, took a deep breath and waited before I spoke.

"All right, it's really not a big deal. I just want to spend a nice night with my daughter. Maybe I am more upbeat this evening. "I did meet a nice man, and I found him quite intriguing. There's a unique quality about him." I sat back and crossed my legs. "I'm not quite sure what it is yet, but I listened to him give a lecture and I was really impressed."

Desiree's jaw dropped. She sat down beside me, and looked directly at me.

"I knew it. I can tell when you're hiding something from me. Tell me, is he hot, and what's his name?" She tapped her hand on my leg.

Unexpectedly, I felt like a teenager with a secret crush. "His name is Nat Griffin. He's a counselor at the medical center. Yes, he happens to be, as you put it, hot. I think he's extremely handsome." I felt my senses overflow with excitement as I admitted the truth.

"Do you think you might like to date this guy?" she asked. She gave me a mischievous grin. "I hope he's over thirty."

"I didn't say I wanted to date him. I simply found him attractive," I answered. I could not believe I actually said those words, to my daughter, no less.

"The manager, Ms. Morris, acted strangely when she saw us together. He has some sort of issue with his co-workers," I said. "He tried to avoid them when he showed me around the unit." I hurried to change the subject, since I felt a little foolish.

"Ah-ha, why are your cheeks so pink?" she teased.

We enjoyed our meal together, and when we finished, I showed her a rough draft of the new winter menu. I asked for her advice on how to name the dishes, to shift the conversation away from my love life. Desiree stepped into the kitchen, and took out the ice cream. We brought it into the family room to sit next to the fireplace. She wore a smirk, and a look of I know a little secret, as we filled each other in on the week. We tried to catch up on all the latest happenings.

Desiree sat back, and adjusted the pillow behind her back. She crossed her legs. "How's Grandma?" she asked. "I meant to stop over at Aunt Bonnie's to see her."

"I worry about her over there," I said. I looked away briefly. "I know she's not happy with Bonnie and Mike. I'm planning to arrange a way to spend more time with her." I sighed, and felt a sense of guilt about the arrangement.

"Grandma's a strong woman. She still looks healthy, and her appetite is as good as ever," I said. "I stop over to see with her every week. It's so funny; whenever I visit, she serenades me with those silly songs from the twenties."

"Maybe we should buy her one of those tabletop organs. She

would probably enjoy it, and it could help her memory," Desiree said.

"That's a good idea. Bonnie told me her behavior is unpredictable. She talks aloud, when no one is in the room, and she's lighting candles again." I fidgeted in my seat. "She insists on using her Ouija board, too. Maybe it could be worse," I said.

"Are you still considering Grandma as a permanent houseguest?" Desiree asked.

"Yes, I am." I lifted one shoulder. "The boys would have to pitch in."

Mark assisted Mother with her household chores, when big jobs became too much for her. He loved visiting her and ran errands for her on many occasions, and never complained. The two of them would spend hours playing cards on the screened porch on Saturday evenings. She usually let him win, although he thought he was a champion at gin rummy. My oldest son would pack a bag when he was ten-years-old, and beg to spend the weekend at Grandma's.

"I'll have to work on convincing Jeremy to help," I said. The tension in my neck built. He was going through a tough phase. He seemed to rebel against anything that was good for him. My youngest son took his father's death the hardest.

"How was your date with that young man from your studio?" My daughter's smile disappeared into a frown.

"A disaster and I decided to keep our relationship purely professional. He's so immature. He likes to party to all hours and comes into work late," she added. "He tried to force his negative habits on me. He won't last long with my boss." Her eyes took on a look of certainty. "He turned out to be a real jerk. So many bright young people want to break into television. I bet he doesn't last another six months at the job." She chuckled. "I don't have time for a man who doesn't have his act together. I worked too hard to get where I am to let a creep hold me back. I'd rather stay alone than date him again."

There was such conviction in her words. She had graduated from Rutgers University top of her class. Desiree was determined to have a career before she settled down. Her judgment was so different from mine when I was her age. Desiree and I cuddled up on the sofa, and shared all the details of our week.

"How was your lunch date with your girlfriends from school?" Desiree asked. She reached for a pistachio.

As I moved next to my daughter, I slid my arm through hers and gave a heavy sigh. "It was really great to see the old gang. Each year it gets more and more discouraging for me," I disclosed. "Mara has been married to Jack for twenty-five years now." I paused. "Their children gave them a surprise anniversary party at the country club last month. When they asked me how I was, I don't let on how I really feel. I brag about my children's accomplishments, but I still feel like the odd one, because I'm the only one that's on my own. My habit of dating men who are losers has to stop. I wanted to set a good example for you and your brothers." I looked away. "I'm probably over sensitive." I sat back and put my hands on my lap.

Desiree placed her head on my shoulder with one arm around me.

She left at eight o'clock, and I sat up in bed to read a self-help book and sipped a chamomile tea. I was exhausted, and I dozed off before I reached the second chapter. Awake by midnight, I tossed and turned until three am. My room felt like an ice box, and I could not get warm. My terrycloth robe draped over me added no comfort at all. The nightmares with girls and boys running through a field with chains around their feet had returned and more vivid than ever.

Nathaniel

Nat straightened up the downstairs in his house. After he hid the old newspapers under the couch and placed the glasses in the dishwasher, he gathered the junk mail from the table. Nat wasn't a neat freak, or close to it. Lately, Nat had been preoccupied with work, and suffered from a lack of motivation when he got home at night. The little bit of energy he had left would get him through a few workouts at the gym. Nat ordered a couple of pizzas and grabbed extra sodas on the way home. When he heard a car pull up, he went to the front porch. Dean hopped out of a classic black sedan.

"Hey, how are you doing?" Nat gave Dean a friendly embrace. "It's great to see you." Nat noticed how old Dean looked. He remembered him to be about thirty pounds heavier, too.

"I'm okay, thanks for the invitation," Dean said. Nat wondered why his friend looked so drawn.

A couple of sodas and a half pie later, they covered a lot of what happened over the past few years. "You've probably noticed my weight loss," Dean said with a serious expression on his face.

"Well, now that you mentioned it, I did."

"I had a heart attack, and I had surgery to place a stent in one of my arteries."

"Wow, I had no idea. How are you now?" Nat asked, shocked over his friend's confession. "I hope a pizza is okay. Are you on a special low fat diet?"

"I'm better and have to follow up when I get back with my cardiologist. Sometimes I cheat on my diet, as long as I don't go crazy. What the hell, I'm on meds." Dean laughed.

Nat thought about how quick life can change, and realized he hadn't had a check-up in more than a year. He made a mental note to schedule an appointment.

"Remember the client we had in school who recovered from alcoholism and became diabetic after he celebrated one year clean?" Dean recalled.

"Oh, yeah, I do. I felt sorry for the poor guy." Nat tried to treat cheer Dean up. "There's a lot of success stories in Harbor Bay for people with heart disease."

"I have faith in my doctor, and I guess I'm lucky. My wife and kids are glad to have me still around." Dean said.

"You're going to be fine." He patted his friend on the back. They joked around about some of their antics in school, and the night took on a happier tone. Nat showed Dean his motorcycle and let him take it around the corner. As Dean took off down the street, Nat thought about the new volunteer and wondered if she was at home. He didn't pay much attention to women these days. After his last girlfriend left, he decided he didn't need a woman in his life. He had no idea why the brief encounter with a stranger lingered in his mind. Nat had a good sense of the kind of woman Madeline was from the time he spent with her on the unit.

Dean returned from his ride. The look on his face told Nat what a great time he had. They went inside, finished the pizza, and watched the end of the ball game. Dean left around ten and promised to keep in touch. Nat liked the weather when the temperature dropped enough to need a jacket. He inhaled and thought one of his neighbors had their fireplace lit. It made him think of the outdoors, and he wished he could sneak away for a trip.

When Nat took the empty pizza box and empty soda cans out back, he surprisingly wished he did not have to spend the night alone.

Chapter Five

Madeline

While I made my bed, I turned on the radio to find a piano solo of the same tune, I'd heard multiple times over the previous days. I stood still for a moment and shook my head, before I began to straighten up my room. An optimistic feeling came over me. I aligned my soft cream color quilt perfectly on both sides, and placed the pillows in lavender shams.

My schedule at the restaurant was Friday, Saturday, and Sunday, so I had plenty of days to myself. Since I wanted to look my best, I thought a professional classic outfit would be a good idea. After I selected my attire, I placed the ensemble on my bed and pulled my hair back in a clip, and zipped up my sweatshirt. The news predicted brighter skies later in the day. The sun hid behind the clouds, and the temperature was cooler than I liked, but I was still motivated. After I placed the dishes in the sink, I headed out for my morning walk. The telephone rang right as I was about to close front door. I hesitated at first and decided to rush back inside to answer it. *Who would call so early in the day?*

The voice on the other end was soft. At first, I could not make out a word.

"Are you almost ready? Have a pleasant day at the hospital."

"Mother, is that you?" I sat back, placed one hand on my forehead, and quietly laughed. I did not tell her my plans for the day. She never called this early. Mother usually needed extra time to take her meds and have her breakfast before she contacted anyone.

Her morning buzz surprised me. *Bonnie must have put her up to it.*

"How are you today?" I asked, still curious.

"I'm wonderful."

"Are you sure you're okay?" I asked, baffled by her offerings.

"I'm positively fine," she said. "I called to give you mine and Mary's blessings. Off you go. Now go and don't be late."

"Who's blessings?" I asked, afraid she was delusional.

"You'll have good fortune when you help others. We think you made the perfect choice," she boasted. "Mary and I hoped you would make that call, and help at the hospital. When I spoke to her last night she was happy to hear about the volunteer position. You will finally have what you desire."

"What do you mean? Are you at it again?" For whatever reason, I could not make the connection between Mother's call and Aunt Mary's appearance in my room. I did not want to make an attempt to figure it out. It was easier to belief I dreamed the scenario and made the choice on my own, since I was interested anyway.

I reached into my purse and opened a bag of peanut M & M's and popped a handful in my mouth. At the moment, I didn't care about my plan to stop my urge for sweets to soothe me whenever I became anxious.

The temperature suddenly dropped, and it made me wonder if the furnace was the problem. I checked the thermostat which read seventy. A dazzling light appeared out of nowhere, and a whistling sound filled the air. I headed over to the front door, to look outside, when a shadowy mist loomed around my porch.

"Hold on for a minute, I have to check the breaker box," I said. It seemed as if there was an electrical problem, somewhere in the house. As I hurried to the basement, I wondered if any of my neighbors had the same problem.

"What on earth is going on?" I spoke aloud.

It did amaze me at how mother still gave me support. I appreciated her encouragement. I got to the top of the stairs, still concerned. The electric turned out to be fine, and for the life of me, I could not figure out Mother's unusual statements. How could she know what I was about to come across? At the time, I guessed she merely had my best interest in mind.

Recollections of the day my mother visited her sister's grave came to mind. She carried a box of tiny figures to place on the headstone. She wore her locket with Mary's picture. It was a gloomy, rainy day, so she placed an umbrella over the grave, and stuck it into the wet earth. I wore my school shoes and the mud-stained my white socks. Mother made me kneel on the grass while she performed what seemed like a ceremony. She waved her arms around the grave and closed her eyes. I felt a hand on my shoulder and I jumped, and wondered if it was a spirit. I hoped it was my imagination. "Mary will watch over you, and she'll be there if you need her," Mother whispered. At the time, I never thought it would really happen.

"Are you still there?" I asked, slightly out of breath.

"All will be well, my dear," Mother said in a confident tone.

The peculiar glow and the noise slowly diminished.

"Talk to you later," I said. "I love you."

I knew how lucky I was to have one of my parents. My closest friends from school lost both their mother and father within a few years of one another. Fortunately, my mother survived, and she held the years she spent with Dad deep inside her heart.

I welcomed my mother's well wishes, yet I was still concerned about her outlandish comments. I needed exercise to help clear my mind, before I started the day. Every step I took moved me toward a season of change. The scent of the fresh air encircled my senses. My knees ached, as I pushed forward. I enjoyed the time outside, and I was able to make four laps around the neighborhood. The colorful floral arrangements in large planters, on the porches of the lovely homes, brightened the street, and the aroma of freshly brewed coffee greeted me as I passed the donut shop. The commuters who passed by gave a nod on their way to work. I walked for thirty minutes.

I returned from my sunrise outing feeling good. In the shower, I enjoyed the soft, rich feel of the crème brulee body wash. It made a difference to indulge in the pricy line. When I finished, I put on some make-up and got dressed.

As a child, my mother would tell me not to rush. Her words remained in my head, and I could hear each one of them loud and clear. When I was in need of her assistance, I took part in her idea of a celebration with select herbs and a ritualistic dance, right before I got passed my exit exam at culinary school. Maybe I was desperate at the time or sleep deprived, since I usually shunned her magical practices. I never believed that I would have such a successful career. Mother had faith that I would succeed. She encouraged me to hold on to my desire to find the right man. My instincts told me I should have listened to her when I was younger, instead of getting married at such a young age. She warned me about Sonny not being the marrying kind. Nevertheless, we had three children during our brief time together. I hated to admit how her analogies did seem to fall true, most of the time. The day felt different. I wondered if it was due to my age, and a change in hormone levels. There was a feeling in the air that told me my life was about to change.

Miss Morris greeted with a cordial smile. She arched her brows and widened her eyes when I appeared at her office door. She did not look as composed as she did the day before. Her collar was crooked, and her lipstick looked smeared. Nevertheless, she tried to maintain her professional tone. Her office reminded me of a principal's office in school, a room where business was the motto, not fashion or attention to detail.

"I'm glad to see you. It has been a hectic morning with two callouts already," she announced.

Miss Morris stood on her toes, reached up high, and struggled to reach the files on the top of her cabinet.

"Do you need help with those?"

"That's all right. I have them. Thanks anyway."

"I'll do my best to make it a little easier for you today. Where can I start?" I asked. I was optimistic.

"Here's your name tag, and the card that opens the door to the unit." The tension showed in her expression with the lines in her forehead prominent, as she handed me the items. The nurse manager seemed frazzled, and I could tell she struggled to keep her tone calm. She led me to the back of her office, and pushed a large supply wagon over to me. "The volunteers keep the cart with the toiletries and magazines in that area." She pointed to a large storage space. "When you're finished with rounds, please check with the nurses to see what they need," she added. She took a deep breath, as she straightened her back.

Miss Morris sighed, and I sensed she felt comforted by an extra person to help that day. Her expression took on a calmer look, as she handed me the checklist for the items.

"I better get started," I said. I reached for the cart. The clients waited in their room, while I stopped in front of each doorway, and entered only after I knocked. I gave out the toiletries, and a sense of well-being came over me. It felt good to help people in need. I counted my blessings. The insignificant complaints I had, seemed trivial. With morning rounds finished, I went back to the nursing station to check the schedule. I wanted to see if there was a lecture posted for the afternoon. My eyes quickly examined the lined paper. Nat had a class on the agenda. I was thrilled to see that he had an afternoon session posted. I looked forward to his newest lecture. I made a conscious note to make sure that I planned my day so I would be able to attend.

I hurried over to the nurse manager's office, and tapped gently on the door. I had a few minutes to spare in between rounds.

"Come in, Madeline," she offered.

I entered and stepped lightly. "Do you have a moment?"

"Sit down," she said. Miss Morris motioned to the chair. "What can I do for you?"

I looked at my watch in anticipation of Nat's afternoon speech. Miss Morris appeared more organized. She had rows of files lined up in front of her. She flashed a grin while she meticulously placed each stack into a folder.

I took the seat next to her desk.

"I'd like to attend the lecture this afternoon. Of course, if it's all right with you?" I rested my folded hands on my lap.

The manager put on her glasses. "Let's see," she said. She glanced at the calendar on her desk. "Yes, there is a lecture with Nat Griffin, this afternoon. I'm sure he would love to have you join them."

The tension built up from my neck and down my back. I took a deep breath, and was pleased with her reply.

"Nat really gets excited during his class," she said. "He loves what he does, especially when the clients come back after they've gotten their lives together. It's wonderful when you can share with someone, and see results. To give back to others is really the way this whole program works."

She moved closer to me, and whispered, "Don't let him scare you with his authority; he's a real softy inside. On Sunday morning, he picks up five men from the shelter, buys them breakfast, and takes them to a meeting." She placed one hand next to her mouth. "Don't expect him to discuss his personal life. He doesn't part with that information easily," she added.

"He seems friendly and open," I said. I wondered what she meant.

"Sure, that's what you think," she replied, firmly. "The girls have their way of finding out the latest from an inside source. He's top secret with his private life. Anyhow, don't let his standoffish attitude fool you; his ability to deliver is outstanding."

I could tell she regretted her words. Her eyes darted toward the floor as if she were embarrassed, so I did not add to the conversation. I stood up, excited for another opportunity to see him in action.

"Thanks, Miss Morris. I should get back to work."

"Welcome to the Path to Life Unit," she offered. She stretched out her arms.

I left her office with a tranquil feeling. This decision opened up a complete new area to me, and it made me curious. I was not sure where it would lead me, but I was certainly determined to find out.

It was time for a break before the next rounds, and since I only had fifteen minutes, I preferred to step outside. The stairs were nearby, so I decided to use them for the exercise. There was an area with a few tables in the center of a garden. It had lovely greenery and large potted plants. A light almond fragrance from the pink flowers filled the air. I enjoyed a snack I brought from home while I speculated on what Nat had planned for that afternoon. My thoughts returned to the counselor as I relaxed.

A young woman sat next to me and engaged in conversation.

"Nice day today," she offered. The woman gave me a friendly smile.

"Yes, it's wonderful," I replied, as I munched on my granola bar.

The employees were cordial and welcoming at the medical center. I knew the nurses were busy when I first arrived on the unit, but they warmed up when it finally settled down. They seemed like one big family. It was a usual occurrence for a staff member to greet you with a smile; along with a pleasant 'how are you?' After my break, I reapplied my lip gloss and hurried back upstairs.

The afternoon got busy. While I ran errands for the nurses, the time flew by. Already a quarter to two, it was time for the meeting. I took a seat in the back of the room, next to the blackboard and rested my arms on the desk.

Nat entered the room and glanced around with a quick sweep of his eyes. He wore a tan blazer and a pale yellow shirt. He had an unshaven face, with a five o'clock shadow, and I liked his rugged appearance. He still looked sophisticated and professional. He actually reminded me of a professor. He introduced himself to the class and wrote the day's topic on the board. It was entitled, "The Art of Balance." Nat took out a pad and a few books, and systematically arranged them on the desk. He took a drink of water and cleared his throat before he began.

I rested my elbow on the desk, propped my face on my hand, and listened attentively. His enthusiasm was evident when he spoke. He moved around the room with an easy stride. One of the girls up front started to cry. He stopped and brought her out into the hall, and remained with her until she composed herself. When Nat and the tearful client returned, he proceeded where he left off as if there was no delay. The topic of discussion seemed to suit me, especially since I felt like I had no balance in my own life. It really held my interest.

The group got excited about halfway through and passed comments in his favor. Their hands shot up in the air as soon as he opened up the room for discussion. It impressed me to see how the crowd eagerly participated. Nat snuck a fast look my way on a few occasions, and I felt myself blush. I felt the heat on my face, and quickly patted it with my powder puff. The session ended on a positive note. We formed a circle, and joined hands, once again. I found the whole experience fabulous.

Nat started toward me and my body began to quiver. I did not know why I felt unsteady. Maybe it was because I had not been around the opposite sex much, and anyway he was so cute.

He strutted across the room with a confident smile on his face. I took a deep breath when he held out his hand.

"How are you, Madeline? I'm glad you could make it today," he said.

"I wouldn't miss it. I appreciate you letting me join in," I said. I felt the strong grip of his handshake.

We moved toward the door together. I tried to think of what to say next.

"It's amazing how you can stay so calm when you speak in front of so many people."

He took out a handkerchief to wipe his forehead. Nat waited a moment before he responded. "You think I'm calm." He laughed. "Well, that's what I show you from the outside, inside I'm a basket case," he said. "I've struggled with public speaking. I actually addressed this in my counseling courses and practiced for years before I finally got it together. Once I get started I'm fine, but before I begin, I'm terrified." Nat put his pen in his pocket.

I straightened my back and felt honored that he would confide in me with such details.

He stopped to drop a large envelope into the outgoing mail slot, and turned to face me.

"What do you do for a living?" he asked in an upbeat tone.

"I'm a chef at a restaurant by the water," I replied, eager to engage in conversation.

"Really, that's awesome. Maybe you can teach me to be a better cook. Although, I have to warn you, I'm a slob in the kitchen."

"Sure, anytime," I replied.

"You must be very creative," he offered.

I usually became shy when given a compliment, but this time I felt self-assured.

"I suppose so. My daughter is my biggest fan, since I do try to come up with new and unusual recipes," I added.

"You're kidding, aren't you? Did you say your daughter?" His eyes opened wide.

"I have three children: a daughter and two sons."

"That's cool. I would never have guessed you were the mother of three kids."

He squinted, as he took a step back.

"Well, I started young."

"I never had any children. I'm still a kid myself," he said. Nat gave a chuckle and placed his books under his arm. He stared at me, and I liked the attention.

I straightened my belt as I attempted to remain professional.

"I'm not married," he said in a more serious tone.

"I was, but it didn't work out, and ended very quickly," I divulged. *Oops, I should not have said that. Oh well, it's too late.*

"I'm sorry to hear that," Nat said, in a soft tone. He kept his eyes on me, and moved his lips to the side.

"My husband left us, and a short time later, he passed away," I openly disclosed. *Okay, I did it again.*

Nat looked away, and waited a few seconds, before he spoke again.

"Are you all right?"

"You bet," he said. "Tell me, Madeline, what made you want to volunteer on a unit like this?" he asked. Nat crinkled his forehead.

I wanted to be completely honest.

"My grandfather had a difficult time his whole life with alcoholism, and I watched my mother suffer over it," I replied. "I felt so sorry for her. I've read so many books in an attempt to figure out the reason behind addiction. I have a strong interest in people who try to change. I believe it's never too late to improve your life."

Nat listened attentively. "My dad's alcoholism was the reason I became a counselor. It looks like we have a lot in common," he said. He gave a fast shake of his head.

He sounded confident and at ease with our conversation, but his eyes saddened when he confided in me about his father. I spoke with him as if he were a trusted friend. As we continued on our way, the nurses whispered to one another. I sensed that they were talking about us. Nat and I kept up our discussion as we passed the desk. Before I knew it, we were next to his office.

Nat held the door open. His invitation was all I needed to agree.

"Check it out." He grinned. "I don't bite. I'll give you the grand tour of my office."

Above his desk, there were pictures of buffalos which I found interesting. I entered slowly, as Nat led the way. I stepped closer to the wall, studied each one, and felt his eyes on me. The room was small, with diplomas in frames, on the opposite side.

"I love your winter scenes," I said. I ran my hand across the glass and turned to face him.

"I took them myself," he said. Nat straightened his posture. "When I became interested in photos of wildlife, I gained an interest in hiking, too. It was really cool to start a hobby." A light color of red appeared on his cheeks, and I thought he looked adorable.

Nat sounded excited to discuss the topic. His expression brightened, as his eyes met mine.

"There's snow on their faces, it must have been freezing," I said. "They're marvelous. It looks like a professional took them. They really capture the sense of wild life."

"This one is my favorite," he said, as he picked up the frame. "I had some great times while I was there."

He stood next to me, and I felt a strong physical attraction to him. "Is that you?" I asked. Then I put my hand to my mouth, and giggled. "You look like a rocker."

"I wore my hair longer back then. Most girls liked guys with long hair, but I bet you liked jocks," he said. Nat winked one eye.

"Sure I did. I adored big and strong football players." I snickered. "Who's that?" I pointed to the person next to him.

"That's my buddy, Dean. He stopped in town last night, and we hung out at my place. He's a lot of fun." Nat placed his hand on his forehead. "Maybe I shouldn't have stayed up so late, although it was good to see him."

As he sat down and flung his arms around the desk, the

candy dish flew to the other side. His desk had a dark finish and a leather swivel chair which looked comfy with the thick padded armrests. The setting reminded me of an old English study. There was wainscoting on the bottom and taupe wallpaper with a touch of gold specks on top. The matching maroon lampshades added a nice contrast. The space had a welcoming feel. His office was cheery and comforting, yet professional. Along the wall, across from the photos, he had a bookshelf, filled with literature on recovery. In between two gorgeous pewter bookends, there was a stack of textbooks on the human body. Next to his desk, he had another chair, I presumed for clients. I laughed, and enjoyed his company. I sensed a similarity in our lives and loved the way he gave me direct eye contact. He seemed interested in whatever I had to say.

Nat got up with a confident stride and closed the door.

I lowered my voice, and tried not to disturb the nurses. I could not remember when I had such fun.

He sat back down, and placed his hands behind his head. "I've worked here long enough, to know how the nurses love to gossip. It doesn't bother me at all. They don't mean any harm."

I looked up to a typed copy of an agreement. I stood up and strained to read it.

"That's a copy of a roast I had at counseling school," he said.

"It's all supposed to be just for fun. One of the counselors I became close with gave me a list or rules to obey."

He looked at the framed copy and began to recite it. "The first rule was to lose my unrepentant New Jersey attitude. Another objective they gave me was to identify a more appropriate way to express my anger, instead of the F word. The other suggestions were: to talk to a wolf at least once a day, discuss the urge to run outside, scream with my peers, and most importantly, be sure to go to a shrink!"

"That sounds like a tall order," I said in amazement. I held my lips together and tried not to laugh.

"I don't know." He looked down.

By the way he opened up to me, I sensed he felt at ease.

"Sometimes I still lose it." He held his chin out. "I've changed a lot since those days," he admitted.

"It sounds like you were quite a handful," I assumed.

"Yeah, you could say that. That's my spoof on my days in school," he said and grinned. "It's cool that you accepted the volunteer position. Most people stay away from a place like this. You did the opposite." He leaned forward, and raised his thumb up.

I could tell we were close in age by the era he referenced, and I guessed he was a few years older than me, but not much.

I glanced down on his desk, and noticed he had patchouli incense. The container had a peace sign on it. "You're just an old hippy," I said with a chuckle. It puzzled me how I never saw him around town. When I sat back down, I crossed my legs.

Nat clapped his hands together and moved his chair in a half circle.

"Absolutely, I would love to take a ride to the country like in the old days, just for a weekend and sleep in the woods," he admitted. "It would be great to sit around the fire, play guitar, and smoke pot. Those were the good old days. The photo in the corner is my mother, who lives part of the year in Florida." His eyes took on a blank stare.

I noticed an uneasy tone in his voice, when he mentioned his mother. He moved around in the chair, and seemed on edge. His tone of voice sounded almost frightened when he mentioned her. Nat repeatedly twisted the bracelet on his arm around in circles.

Oh well, maybe it's none of my business. When I asked him if he had any brothers or sisters, he really got flustered. The corners of his mouth began to twitch. I felt it was better not to pry.

The two of us chatted like old friends. We learned so much about each other in a short time. It was if I was the right person to open up to. The time flew by so quickly. The rest of the world seemed to disappear while we were together. I've heard when the right person comes along, the music plays in your head, and your heart thumps out of your chest. Sparks and rockets might explode deep inside. I did have a sense that Nat and I knew each other for our whole life. I wondered if this was just a fluke. On the other hand, was he the one that I was destined to meet? Maybe I was simply naïve, but I didn't care.

"Tell me about your job as a chef," Nat said. He held my gaze as his head tilted slightly. His expression showed interest.

"What do you want to know?"

"What kind of restaurant is it and where is it?" Nat crossed his arms and continued to pay attention to my every word. *I like the way he listens to me....*

"Well, I work at Martino's, a seafood restaurant on the water. My boss, Tony, has been wonderful, and he has the patience of a saint. I really owe him for the tips he gave me about the business. It's a family owned establishment and opened over seventy-five years ago."

"Sounds like my kind of place," Nat said.

"It really has a lot of character. There's dark wood beamed ceilings, with huge round chandeliers and authentic fishing supplies scattered around. The wall displays are actually from the 1800's. In the foyer stands a gorgeous antique clock."

"Fresh seafood is the best, and I can tell you stories about my fishing trips miles out into the ocean." He rolled his eyes and gave me a grin.

"Tell me, what's so funny?"

"The trip from hell came to my mind. We all got sick, spent three hours below, and missed out on the catch of the day. I'll tell you the story another time." Nat flicked the top of a pen. "Do you work all week?"

"I do three shifts, Friday through Sunday. We hired a great assistant, and he has an experienced staff. You should come in sometime," I said. I hoped I wasn't being pushy.

"Maybe I will," Nat said. His slowly reached into his jacket, and I watched his hand slide across his chest. I knew I fell spellbound to his stories of adventure.

I found it unusual when Miss Morris mentioned how Nat

was secretive about his life, especially at work. He told me details and personal information about his past with enthusiasm. I speculated if she had an ulterior motive to scare me away from Nat. I guessed he probably felt comfortable with me, since we both had families affected by alcoholism.

I stood up slowly, and turned toward the door. Although a part of me wanted to stay longer. Nat had a special gift for making a story come to life. It seemed as if time stood still. The vertical blinds were open enough to allow the sun in. The brightness drew me in as I moved closer to the window.

"I've really enjoyed our visit, and I loved hearing about your travels," I said. I stared down at my feet, and became bashful after our personal disclosures.

After all, we were practically strangers. His enthusiasm for adventure intrigued me. Time stood still as I listened to him speak. I never met anyone like him before. There seemed to be a side of me that longed for the spontaneity he displayed in his voyages. Our lives appeared strangely linked together. Nat spoke of travel as a way to soothe the anguish in his heart, and I used reading as a chance to find peace from my troubled past.

My late afternoon appointment popped into my mind. I glanced at my watch and noticed the time. I had to hurry, or I would be late for the meeting.

"Well Nat, thanks for the tour." I laughed nervously as I fumbled with my handbag. "I've enjoyed our conversation. I have to meet with my boss this afternoon."

Nat moved closer to me. He flashed a boyish grin and gave a playful chuckle. He looked into my eyes, took a deep breath, and parted his lips. He took another step toward me, and I anticipated his next move.

"Thanks for listening to me go on. Would you like a piece of gum?" he asked.

When I reached for it, our hands touched briefly. I shivered. An immediate rush of pleasure flooded through my body. I tried to ignore it, and quickly put the gum in my mouth. My heart raced as he walked me to the door. Pleased about our conversation, I left for the day.

Chapter Six

Nathaniel

"Sorry I'm late," Nat said. He bolted inside the outpatient center. The main office had an odor of fresh brewed coffee, piles of literature, meeting books, and other drug and alcohol related support options, scattered around the waiting area.

The receptionist, Connie, welcomed Nat with her pleasant smile.

"It's okay, Nat. Your client's not here yet," she said. "Is there a lot of traffic?"

"No, I left later than usual." Nat made it a practice to be early to appointments, and it wasn't like him to arrive last minute. He opened the door to the small space he used for his counseling sessions, and Nat realized why he left the hospital late. He didn't want to make a new friend and certainly not with a woman. It puzzled him how he could not get her out of his mind.

Anthony Lancer was Nat's first appointment. He was an alcoholic who started to drink as a teenager. He recently did a stint in an eighteen month program, but relapsed the first week out. Anthony moved cautiously as he reached for the arm of the chair.

"How's it going?" Nat asked. He thought about how the

revolving door to relapse and recovery might slam in his face one day, and pitied him.

Anthony held his head down and did not make eye contact.

Nat forgot to turn off his cell phone, and the Jimi Hendrix song he used for the ringtone played.

Anthony looked up and laughed. Nat was glad for the interruption. After one hour, Nat gave him a book on relapse and patted him on the back. "It's time to take the blame off of yourself and move forward," he said. Nat felt like he had no right to preach.

"Thanks, Mr. Griffin, I feel better after our sessions. Catch you next week," he said.

"Okay, have a good day," Nat said.

Alone with his fears, Nat locked the door, sat down, and closed his eyes. His thoughts made him dizzy, and he realized he let his guard down. The knock on the door broke his concentration.

"I need a favor," Connie said. "Can you stay and answer the phones while I pick my car up? I'll be back, before you know it," she said in a desperate tone.

"Sure, go ahead."

"Wait a minute." She lowered her voice. "Is there a problem?"

"I'm okay," Nat said. His eyes held a dull stare.

"Oh no, you're not. I can tell. What is it?"

Connie and Nat would talk, since he helped her a year previously with a family crisis. He knew she was not the type to blab his business to everyone. Connie conducted herself professionally and he felt like she could be trusted.

"There's a new volunteer at the hospital and she's really friendly. I think I told her too much about my life," Nat said.

"You like her, I can tell." Connie slid a chair next to his desk and sat down. She moved closer to him. "It's time to let someone into your life."

"I know, you're right, but...." He tapped his fingers on the desk.

"Never mind, you're not getting any younger. Go for it, before it's too late," Connie urged.

He knew this girl was different. She had an honest appeal unlike anyone he met before. Yet, he had his doubts. He sat at the front desk, and scribbled on the calendar. Nat wondered why he felt like such a jerk.

He hadn't dated anyone seriously for over two years. His last girlfriend, JoAnne, lived in New York City and would stay over Nat's on weekends. She wanted commitment, but Nat could not bring himself to propose. JoAnne gave him an ultimatum, kept her word, and eventually met someone else. Nat received an invite to her wedding. He attended and even became friends with her husband. For some reason he felt trapped whenever a woman got too close to him. His independence was threatened every time he let someone into his life. Yet, he was attracted to the new volunteer, and he knew it would be hard to resist her charm.

The switchboard lit up, Nat answered and directed each call to the appropriate place. He realized how Connie's knack at being able to zero in on his emotions, made him squirm. He tried to free his mind from further concern, as he did his work. His head buzzed with the endless complaints from the callers. The hotline flashed, and he took the call. The sound of panic rang through the receiver and all of a sudden all else stood still.

"I've had enough of this world." A hysterical young man on the other end said.

"I'm here to help you, stay on the line." Nat sat straight up in his chair and listened first. Then he proceeded to calm the frantic caller down, and convinced him to seek help. Nat was able to hold him on the line long enough to have an ambulance and the police respond to the call. He knew the caller needed immediate assistance and acted quickly to his plea. Sometimes a caller would be in need of outpatient counseling or addiction treatment referrals, but when a life was at risk, a red flag went up.

Connie returned, and Nat rushed to the emergency room to

assist with the intake of the despondent man. After he waited at the ridiculously long light next to the hospital, he finally made it inside. He spent two additional hours with calls to locate an accepting facility for him. The reason Nat became a counselor was to help someone in need. Despite his reluctance to share his past with some of his nosey co-workers, they did work together to help people when they were down and out and that's what counted.

Nat stopped for a quick bite to eat at a local diner. He sat at the counter and ordered a cheeseburger and side salad. The waitress winked at him when she placed the platter down in front of him. They chatted about the weather and he felt pretty good about the day. He knew his refrigerator had only a few sodas, a container of leftover Chinese food, cold pizza and a half-full container of orange juice, so he ordered extra salad to go. All around him in the booths sat mostly elderly couples. The dinner hour ran specials regularly. He wondered if he would spend the rest of his life at the counter alone. Nat knew it would be his choice to remain isolated, yet the thought of what it would be like to grow old with someone crossed his mind.

He drove home and thought about his conversation with Madeline. Their instant connection seemed scary, and he feared what might happen if he let her get close to him. Yet, in a corner of his heart, he found her fascinating.

Chapter Seven

Madeline

I promised my sons I would be home in time to make dinner. Unfortunately, I stayed longer at the restaurant than I hoped to. They knew how to survive without me, even if it was on cereal or junk food. We loved our home, especially since the great room remodel. There was never a dull moment, since most of the time Mark and Jeremy invited the whole neighborhood. Their friends would usually gather on the patio, listen to music, or hang out in the family room to watch the latest craze on reality TV. Fortunately, I found a builder who had a custom home with a tiny place in the back, he added for his in-laws. The basic design had a closed feel, and I wanted an open floor plan, so I changed the lay out. The price we settled with gave me enough left over to play with. The sellers relocated to California, and they needed a quick closing. It was a great opportunity for me to get what I wanted.

The boys were in the family room when I got home. I bent down and gave them each a hug, like I did every night since they were little. They were great kids, most of the time.

Jeremy's recent change in behavior concerned me. His grades had dropped way below average, and the drinking made me fear for his health. His mood would change from easy to temperamental and angry, at any moment. I never realized how difficult it was to raise young men without a father. Being both mother and father to them was not easy. My job was a challenge to say the least.

Mark stood up and went into the kitchen and as he walked away, I noticed how grown up he looked. His head almost hit the top of the doorframe. Although he was handsome and had a muscular build, his kindness toward others was one of his greatest qualities. Over the years, Mark became the father figure to Jeremy. Sometimes he acted bossy, and wanted everyone in the house to follow his rules. He took over soon after Sonny died. Mark grew up after the accident, and I did not intend for him to take on the added responsibility at such a young age.

Jeremy glanced up at me with his dreamy green eyes and his dark brown hair stuck up on the sides. His smile could brighten your day at any given time. His attitude could be cocky, at times, although, he had a tender side. It took time for him to trust someone enough to show it. My sons were complete opposites, and they each filled my heart with pride.

Mark joined us again, and sat down on the couch with a can of soda. "Can you give me a few dollars for the train until I get paid this week?" he asked. His tone was apprehensive, and he lowered his head while he waited for my answer. I knew he hated to seem like a burden to me. He had worked odd jobs since he was ten, and I felt like he grew up too fast.

"How much do you need?" I said. "You work hard in school. I know your classes keep you from extra hours at your job." I opened my purse.

"Thanks a lot, you're the best. Twenty dollars will do," he said.

Jeremy stared at the television, cuddled up on the sofa with a woolen blanket up to his neck.

"Move over. You look cozy." I squeezed in to sit beside him.

He squinted and gave me an annoyed expression.

"You look like a little boy who is about to be scolded," I said.

"Sorry, but I got in trouble today," Jeremy said. He put his head down. "I was late for school, and my teacher wants a note from you."

"When will you stop all this nonsense? I thought we discussed your time management in the morning. What happened?" I exhaled a forced breath. I placed my hand on his leg firmly and waited a moment. His attitude annoyed me, and I had work on a plan to change it. My face felt warm, and my pulse sped up. *Oh no, Pre-Menopause.*

"Gee, I said I was sorry. I overslept," he replied. "I'll try my best to be on time for the rest of the year. I promise." He gave me a bold grin.

Jeremy jumped up quickly and raced to the refrigerator. He placed the milk container on the table, rolled his eyes, and reached for a snack. He pulled out the chair, sat down at the kitchen table and dunked the cookies. I followed behind him.

We had the same conversation before. He says all the right words to make me happy. When he got up to get a napkin, his jeans fell below his waist. I gave them a tug to conceal his underclothes.

"Hey, come on, what are you doing?" His voice rose.

I rested my hand on the kitchen table and raised my voice. "I've had enough of your attitude! If you're late again, you're going away to school. I've given you enough chances, and I'm tired of repeating myself."

He cleared his throat before he gulped his milk.

Incomplete homework assignments and skipped classes had become a routine with Jeremy. He had been going to bed late, and he was not keeping up with his studies. Since he was a junior in high school, I worried he would eventually leave school and forfeit those essential years. I took him to a counselor, but he never opened up. The incident involving the school property, cost me hundreds in lawyers' fees, and I needed a different strategy since so far, his attitude did not change. I even detected the scent of marijuana on his clothes. The family doctor suggested we start him on an antidepressant if his behavior did not improve. The alcohol incident topped it off.

Jeremy finished his cookies and attempted to leave the room. I gave him a look to let him know he better put the milk and cookies away. I did not have to say a word. He immediately tidied up the kitchen, placed his glass in the dishwasher, and reluctantly gave me a hurried hug goodnight.

I went to bed early, and before I fell asleep, I thought about my day and my conversation with Nat. I looked forward to going back to the hospital. I had some days off from the restaurant, which came at the perfect time. Tony had planned a trip to Italy to visit his brother to plan a family reunion. I scheduled time to spend more time with Mother, too. My plan was to make a change in her living arrangements. I closed my eyes and drifted to sleep.

I had a date to visit Bonnie the next day for lunch. My heart was at peace with anticipation of our time together.

"Mom, are you up yet?" His voice sounded scratchy. Jeremy's knock on my door took me by surprise. I rolled over to peek at the clock. It was seven-thirty, and I did not plan to get up so early. I dragged myself out of bed and put on my robe and slippers.

Jeremy stood in my doorway with a mischievous grin on his face. He held his head down, and his hair stood up on top, like a Mohawk. His T-shirt hung almost down to his knees.

"What's wrong, did you miss the bus again?" I shrieked.

He gave me a half smile before he lowered his head. "I'm sorry if I woke you up, but I did miss the bus," he said. His shoulders slumped, and his voice remained low.

"Give me a minute, I'll drive you to school," I said.

I tried not to react to his tardiness in a negative way, this time. Jeremy's behavior was consistently defiant. I hoped his behavior would improve after his close call in the emergency room. This time, I tried a positive approach.

I knew my plan of sleeping in was destroyed. It was a usual occurrence in our house: Jeremy missing the bus, and my enabling, and I knew it was not good for him. I constantly went against what I wanted to do for me. I worried that the habits he had would follow him in the next chapter of his life. It was imperative that a young man got an education. Jeremy discussed, on many occasions, his desire to have a family of his own one day. I tried to set an example, but single parenting can be a challenge.

We drove to school with silence between us. Jeremy peered out the window with what seemed to be a lifeless glare. He handed me a typed letter from one of his teachers. She requested a phone conference.

I shook my head, and mumbled under my breath. I was angry that is father wasn't around to help. "When are you going to stop playing around?" I tried to calm down, and felt the start of a migraine.

Jeremy's rebellious attitude escalated each day. I hoped his irresponsibility wouldn't become a permanent part of his personality, and it would eventually pass. When I stopped in front of the school, he gave me a hurried goodbye. As I waved goodbye, I recited the "Hail Mary" in my head. After I got back on the road, and headed home, I daydreamed about my youngest son's future. I turned on the radio. An instrumental version of the song from the *Titanic* played, and I turned up the volume. An overwhelming sense of shame took over my mind. *Maybe I could have tried harder on my marriage*, I wondered. After all, I met Sonny when I was only nineteen.

Sonny was five years older and extremely ambitious. He worked at *The Sun News* for a year when the turmoil started. He wrote his own column with great pride. One weekend, he never returned home, and I panicked. I went to the mall with Bonnie on a Friday afternoon. I came home, and found his work clothes sprawled on the bed. The box on his dresser was open. His dress watch, and cufflinks were gone. That night I waited up until three am, with no sign of him. I even thought to call the police, but I chose not to. The next day, I called his sister Connie. She was his kid sister, and she usually stuck up for him. This time was different. Connie told me Sonny's plans to attend a wedding with his new girlfriend. I felt shocked and humiliated. He arrived home in the middle of the night, dressed in a three-piece suit. He must have purchased it behind my back. We argued all night, when he announced he wanted to leave me.

"I just can't live like this anymore," he yelled and pounded his fist on the table.

"What about the children?" I cried out.

He never answered; instead, he stormed out of the house. I called his mother and sobbed. She tried to console me, but Sonny never came back. He did attempt to see the kids, on occasion, unannounced. There were long stretches in between his visits. About a year later, the State Police found him unconscious behind the wheel of his Mustang. His father had quite a bit of influence in town, so I never really found out the cause of the accident. He handled the whole episode discreetly. I still could not believe thirteen years had passed already.

The drive home gave me time to plan my day, in my head. Since I was up early, I was able to get some work done on menu changes. Later in the day, I planned to visit Bonnie and Mom.

Bonnie lived in an old brownstone nearby. It was a suburban area close to New York City, called Woodbridge. It had good features, and Bonnie loved it. There was an award-winning school system, and it was near the train. The neighbors were not wealthy, just plain hard working people. Bennie's husband, Mike, had quite a few medical problems, and they struggled to maintain the mortgage. They worked extra jobs to be able to stay in the community. The homes held all the charm of the twenties with the attention to details in the architecture. There were five doors on each side of the corridor and on Sundays the scent of home-cooked meals filled the air. The moldings were custom crafted, with each room adorned with detailed high ceilings. The fireplace in the living area had a delicately carved mantel. When the building was in its prime, a door attendant greeted the dwellers.

While I stood outside, I looked up to the sky to gain inspiration. For a moment, I had a flashback of mother's lectures about the choices we make. Her comforting words remained with me; I could reach for them, whenever I felt the need. I entered the townhouse, and I saw Mother on the rattan chair outside on the veranda.

Luckily, Bonnie gave me a spare key, so I let myself inside. Since Mother acted strangely, I needed to be able to gain quick access to the house. The terrace was the perfect location for her to enjoy the view. Bonnie was fortunate to live in one of the few homes with this amenity. There was an enclosed space in the corner. The light from the afternoon sun lit up the entire area. The garden right below had beautiful topiary pieces, which she adored.

Mom peered into a large box on her lap.

"There's my girl!" she shouted. She reached out to me, and I bent down to kiss her on the cheek.

"What do you have there?" I asked. I peeked over her shoulder.

"I came across some mementos of the family, through the years," she said. "The years have passed by so quickly." She sorted through the keepsakes with her eyes full of tears. I put my arms around her, and gave her a squeeze. She had the softest skin and the brightest eyes. Her blue eyes sparkled when she looked at me. The extra pounds she gained over the years made her figure round, which helped her to keep a younger appearance. Her soft and curly white hair was neatly arranged with two antique gold barrettes on each side. I was amazed at the way she managed to keep her fingernails long and polished, when I had a hard time with mine. She took her hanky out of the pocket of her long full skirt. My mother had more dresses then any of us. She never needed much makeup, since she had a natural looking olive colored skin tone.

I laughed to myself, touched by her sentimental moment. "Come on inside, let's see where Bonnie is," I said. "We can look through the box together." I guided her to the sofa.

"Is that you, Madeline?" Bonnie stepped out of her office. "You look wonderful today."

Despite her welcoming smile, she appeared worn out with dark circles under her eyes. Her blouse stuck out of the sides of her jeans, and her hair looked stringy.

I took her by the hand and guided her toward the living room. The distinct odor of rum on her breath alerted me that she might have started drinking again. Bonnie was ten years sober, and I questioned if the responsibility of Mother's care might have caused her to relapse. It took a lot for me to bite my tongue and remain silent. I allowed her to manage her own recovery as difficult as it was for me not to keep my mouth shut.

Bonnie operated a home business. She started it when her son was born. This way she did not need to place him in daycare. It enabled her to earn a decent living, but recently due to Mike's illness, their finances dwindled. The arrangement of mother in the household helped them with the bills. Mike spent twenty years in the auto business before a layoff due to his repetitive use of sick time.

"Place your work aside. Let's looks at the souvenirs and photos with mother," I insisted.

We sat close to one another on her sectional while we sorted through the items. I turned the pages of the first album my parents put together, and thought about how well it held up over the years. Every clipping and snapshot was secured and preserved as if it were new. The three of us reminisced about the good times we had when our father was alive. Dad had been gone for fifteen years by that time. His loving nature held the family together. We had many happy memories. I felt safe and cared for when he was around. My father drew people around him with his kindness, and he had a genuine interest in others. He made everyone feel special.

Mother handed me a ticket to a musical that she attended with my father forty years ago. "We had dinner in the city after the performance. I wore my mink stole and best pearls that night," she said.

Her comment made me wonder how she could remember what she wore so many years ago with such vivid details.

Mother stood up. "I'll be back in a minute," she said.

"Are you and Mike all right? I mean, with Mom?"

I turned to face Bonnie, and lowered my voice, so not to upset mother. I did not realize how sharp she still was, since she was in her own world most of the time.

Bonnie had a troubled look in her eyes. She glanced down first, before she answered.

"You know I'm glad to take care of her, but she hasn't been sleeping well," she admitted. "I think I'm too old to care for her. I've haven't been sleeping, and by the time morning comes, I'm totally exhausted." She took a long, deep breath. "Mike will be out of town, two times a month, for a marketing class for our business," she said. She gave a sigh. "He's not used to such a busy schedule, with all the medication he takes. I have my hands full."

The skin on her face appeared dry and flaky with the fine lines more pronounced than ever. "The nights are the hardest. She searches through the house all night," Bonnie continued. "I hear weird sounds. Half of the time, I hide the matches. I'm afraid she'll set the house on fire. I can't figure out what's she's up to. I should stop complaining." She turned her head.

Mother returned, and went over to look out of the window. She searched through her pockets, and mumbled to herself.

"Are you all right?" I asked.

"I sure am." She gave a wink of her eye. Mother sat down on the couch.

"How are you, anyway? Did you start at the hospital?" Bonnie asked.

"I did, and it was pretty interesting. I attended a couple of lectures by this great counselor Nat, and I can't wait to go back."

"Sounds like there's more. What else is happening?" Her eyes took on a glare.

"What do you mean? You know how much I like to help people," I said. My face felt warm.

"Sure, I do. Anyway, is Nat cute?" She sat forward.

"Stop your insinuating. He is cute. Remember, we only work together."

"Is he single?"

"I believe so. It doesn't matter."

"Well, you can't fool me, even if you fool yourself." Bonnie arched a brow. "You know you're a tease, and guys take you seriously," she said with her mouth wide open.

My temperature rose from all the questioning. I moved closer to Mother. Bonnie must have realized her teasing got to me; she changed the subject.

"How are the boys and Desiree?" Bonnie asked. "Is Jeremy still misbehaving?"

"Desiree and I had dinner the other night," I returned. "As for Mark, he's on the honors list. I'm so proud of his determination. I can't figure out what to do about Jeremy," I said. "I thought that after the court case, he would have learned his lesson. He came home last weekend, got into another huge battle with Mark. He called the police when Jeremy punched a hole in the wall. To top it off, I just had the room painted."

"Oh, no," she said.

"Wait, it gets worse. I came home from lunch with the girls and found him on his bed, passed out from drinking too much. We spent the night in the emergency room."

"Why didn't you call me?"

"I didn't want to bother you. I would have, but he was discharged in a few hours." I *didn't want to remind you of your troubled times.*

"Maybe Mike can help. I'll try to convince him to have a serious talk with him" she suggested. Bonnie crossed her arms.

"Thanks, I could use all the help I can get."

I got up to look around the kitchen and I stuffed a cream puff in my mouth.

Bonnie and Mike had been married for almost thirty years. Their only child, Joseph, lived down the shore and worked in a marina near his house. Joey and I practically grew up together since we were only ten years apart. He married his high school girlfriend, and they had a baby girl named Dina. Even my nephew had a partner. This reminded me how lonely I was, especially when we get together and everyone was in pairs. I dreaded the day I would be the woman who had no companion to share her life with. My children had their own lives, and I did not want to become a burden. I dreaded the day when they would invite me over on weekends and holidays for dinner, because they felt sorry for me.

Mom yawned like a baby. She fell asleep, and I placed my hand to my mouth to alert Bonnie to keep her voice down. Bonnie picked up our teacups and motioned to follow her into the kitchen. She placed the drinks on the table and snuck back to get the cakes. She sat down at the table, and I sat across from her.

"I'm not able to do my work when she's awake. She tells me the same stories over and over. When she rummages through the house or lights candles, I get worried," Bonnie said. She exhaled. "I know her memories are precious to her, but I think she needs to keep busy in the afternoon. It's funny how she remembers all the details of her younger years. Her bizarre behavior is worse."

"Mother is driving me crazy," she said. Her voice cracked. "I really don't think I can take this much longer. I'm too old for this!"

"Calm down, Bonnie. What is it?" I asked.

"She's becoming too much for me," Bonnie said.

"What did she do now?" I feared her response.

"She woke up from the nap yesterday, and I found her at the stove. She told me she had to make dinner for her sister, Mary. Then she took out a pot while I went upstairs and put it on the stove, with grass from the back yard. She set the table for two and put an octagon shaped wooden box in the center of the table. She must be ill."

"I know it's been difficult for you. I'll make an effort to help more. Now that I'm out of school, I have more time," I said, trying to assure her. "I'll see if I can arrange to have mother come stay with us."

I sat back and felt confident with my decision. "I'll talk to the boys tonight."

"Good idea. I think she would be happier with you. I'm sorry, but I guess I'm over tired," Bonnie replied.

I took a sip of tea with my eyes fixed on her.

"I'll think of a plan. Don't worry."

"I hope so." She nodded. "The most challenging days are when she forgets where her purse is and dials the operator for assistance," she said.

"I know it's hard for you. I'll try to help more," I offered.

"Yeah, yeah, well, next time the cops knock on the door, I'll call you," she said in a bitchy tone.

I knew I had to arrange for Mother to move into my house, and I wanted desperately to spend more time with her, anyway.

"I'm sorry," Bonnie replied.

"Come here," I said. I pulled her close. We talked about our options, and eventually it seemed like she was calm enough for me to leave.

"Talk to you later. Thanks for the tea, and remember what I said." I hurried down the stairs, and knew I had to come up with a solution.

I arrived home in no time, and poured a cold drink of soda. After I picked up a magazine from the corner desk, I went outside on the patio to clear my mind. Bonnie had enough, and I realized it was my turn now. The boys and my schedules were pretty hectic, but with the help of the senior day care center, it might work. I had a good plan. It would take all of us to make it happen. I had a lot to do before it was time to prepare dinner. Nevertheless, I took advantage of the weather, and stayed outside longer than usual.

"Hey, is anyone here?"

Jeremy came home from school early. He pushed the screen door open, and stepped outside.

"Why are you home at this time?" I yelled.

He squirmed before he gave me an answer. "Well, umm, I had a study hall for the last period, so I left." Jeremy pushed his hands deep inside of his pockets.

"What do you mean, you left?" I screeched, annoyed by his arrogance.

"Come on Mom, lay off!" His eyes gazed down at his feet.

"Well, if that's the case, maybe you should open up your books and get busy." My entire body shook with frustration. I wanted him to have a good life, and I knew his behavior would surely lead him to destruction.

He stomped away and slammed the door behind him.

I counted to ten, and let it go. I would let him get away with it once, and I would make sure he studied an extra hour that evening. I ventured back outside, and tried to come up with an idea. The realization that my mother would have to move in was clear to me. There was a daybed in the basement and enough room in the corner of my bedroom for mother. I had only one bedroom downstairs. The other one was upstairs, adjacent from Mark and Jeremy's rooms. This would not accommodate mother at all. The carriage house might have been a more private place for her. I used the area to store the boy's bicycles and ski equipment. Finally, I decided Mother would be safest in the room with me.

The article I found in the Sunday paper about a medical day care center in the area seemed like the perfect solution. Their intention was to improve your loved ones' quality of life with structured and well-planned activities. The center gave the caregiver at home an opportunity to work or run errands. I felt optimistic they would have an opening, and decided to inquire further. My only wish was for my Mother to behave, and not get into trouble. I knew health care workers were used to people with dementia. *I hope she doesn't to try to put a spell on anyone.*

I made an appointment to visit the next day. The director gave me a brief overview, and it sounded like it would suit my needs. When I called and let Bonnie know my plans, she sounded ecstatic. For the rest of the afternoon I tidied up the house and washed the linens for mother's bed. I believed my idea was flawless.

Chapter Eight

Madeline

𝒜 message appeared on my cell phone. I stopped preparing the sleeping arrangements for Mother and returned the call. Miss Morris wanted to know if I could put in an hour or two to help out on the day shift. I replied without hesitation and told her I would be able to come in anytime.

After dinner that evening, the boys hung out in their rooms. It was the ideal time to introduce the idea of the move for Grandma. I hurried upstairs to Mark's room first and sat down on the edge of his bed.

"Jeremy, can you come into Mark's room, please? I have a decision I want to discuss with both of you," I announced.

He joined me, reluctantly, while he continued to play his handheld video game. He turned the chair to face me and sat down. I grinned and pushed the hair out of his eyes.

"I think it's time to have Grandma move in with us," I said, in a firm tone.

"Bonnie has had her for three years now, and she's tired. I have enough room in my bedroom for her, and you two will have to help while I'm at work."

Jeremy groaned and sounded annoyed.

"Sure, Mom, we can both help," Mark added in a positive tone.

He plopped on the bed, and put his arm around my shoulder. He shuffled his feet back and forth on the floor.

"I can watch Grandma while you are at work; she's easy to care for," Mark replied. He sounded eager. "I can talk to my job and put myself on when you're off."

Mark loved to spend time with her. Jeremy also had a special connection with Mom. He spent a lot of time at her house when he was younger.

Jeremy slid down in his seat. "Okay, you win. I'll try to help with Grandma when Mark's at school," Jeremy chimed in. He scratched his head.

I applauded and was pleased with their eagerness. It was a welcome surprise when Jeremy agreed so quickly. They were a team when he was younger. Mother had a lot of patience with him and never doubted his ability to succeed.

I gave a quick snap of my fingers. "Well, guys, that's settled. Grandma's coming to live with us," I said.

Jeremy yawned, and set his game aside. He reached Mark's channel changer, and turned on the television. "Mom, I think it will be awesome when Grandma moves in with us," he added. "She's the best. She lets me snack before dinner. I meant she used to let me when I was little."

I laughed, pleased with his comment. "It's all right, Jeremy. I'm glad you're happy to have Grandma with us."

Mark jumped up and moved over to the closet. "We had a class at school about music therapy for the elderly. I found an old radio with big headphones that Grandma could use," he said. "If we press the rewind button, she'll be able to hear her favorite songs repeatedly. I think it would be a way to keep her safe."

"That's a fantastic idea. I'm excited now. I think this will be good for everyone," I offered, happy with their enthusiasm.

Mark picked up an old radio out from under a pile in his closet. It had an area on the side where you could attach a headphone.

"Jeremy, turn off the television," I motioned for him to follow us. We moved into the living room. I dusted off the radio, and placed it on the round table next to the window.

Jeremy surprised me when he suddenly disappeared. He returned and struggled with a recliner. He stood in the doorway with a look of satisfaction on his face, and grunted, as he lifted the chair around the corner. It took some time, but he got it to fit through the narrow archway.

"Here you go; this chair will be more comfortable for Grandma," he said. "It even has a control that will help her stand up." He plugged it in, sat down, and played with it like a carnival ride.

The chair slipped my mind. Jeremy remembered that I placed it there and covered it with a heavy drop cloth. I kept it out back for safekeeping, because it really didn't match with my décor. The chair previously belonged to a neighbor. Her dad passed away, and I bought it from a yard sale. I thought at the time, maybe I would need it one day. Anyway, it was only ten dollars. I found a soft rose-colored throw in the cedar chest, and I draped it over the back. The cover blended with the other items in the room. It was just the touch needed to make it eye catching. I placed a large lace doily over the round table and grabbed the lamp from the desk. In less than an hour, we created a space ideal for Grandma in our living room. Surprisingly, the idea did not need much coaxing. The boys seemed happy to help.

I knew our lives could become difficult, so I did not allow myself to become overjoyed. There would be challenges, but we would give it our best effort.

Mark found a box of records out on the porch. He opened up the top part of the old stereo to reveal a turntable. I had a bunch of Frank Sinatra albums, which collected dust under the entertainment center. The three of us sat down cross-legged on the floor. We laughed and joked around while we listened to the tunes. There were also various hits from the fifties, sixties, and seventies. We played a few of them and giggled at the old melodies. I got up to make a bowl of popcorn and served iced teas along with it. My sons and I had a little celebration in honor of our new occupant.

Mark stood up, and reached for my hand. "Come on. Teach me to how to jitterbug. That dance looks real cool."

He twirled me around to face him. I was still young when that dance came out. I was lucky Bonnie taught me all the right steps. We would watch *American Bandstand* together on Saturday morning. I was a little rusty, but after a few tries I remembered all the routine.

Jeremy watched us dance, as he tapped one foot along with the music.

"Come on join us, I'll show you how," I said.

He stared at his feet. "No way, that's okay. I think I'll just watch." We enjoyed a festive celebration for Grandma's arrival.

Chapter Nine

Madeline

1 slept later than usual, because I knew once my mother came to live with us, I would be on a tight schedule. So, I took the opportunity to rest while I could. When I opened the curtains in my room, I noticed how exceptionally blue the sky looked. The positive energy remained with me, and I told myself it would be a splendid day. My daily routine flew by as I anticipated my return to the medical center. The weather changed suddenly, and I was not prepared for the sudden burst of showers.

I arrived at the hospital, and hurried in attempting to stay dry. I was annoyed at how I forgot to bring an umbrella. My coat was drenched by the time I entered the building. The lobby was crowded with employees and visitors. The greeters at the front desk welcomed me. It seemed as if they recognized me already. I entered the main foyer, and I glanced down at my watch. When I moved my jacket from around my head, I almost collided with someone. To my surprise, I came face-to-face with Nathaniel Griffin.

He pushed his hair away from his eyes. My mouth became dry as he got closer to me.

"Are you just on the schedule today?" he asked, in a friendly tone.

My heart fluttered. "Yes, I'm a little late," I admitted.

"Are you through for the day?" I held my breath and hoped he would be on the unit.

"No way, I'll be back in a few; I have a meeting at the facility across town. See you in a few," he added. He smiled.

I breathed a sigh of relief to hear that he would be back. The scent of his cologne lingered in the elevator. The doors closed in front of me, and I held onto the railing. I admired the way he seemed to be on a mission. The slacks he wore made his legs looked strong and muscular. The crisp white shirt fit his chest perfectly, and all of a sudden, I felt off-balance. My head spun, and I could hardly wait until I saw him again. I believed there was certain chemistry between two people when their connection is right. My need to know more about him became a mission.

The nurses continued their chatting as I entered the department. I stood in front of the desk and waited for someone to acknowledge me.

"How's everyone today?" I asked.

I didn't get much of a response, yet I was pleased to be there. They all seemed to be involved in a very important conversation. The two nurses at the desk never noticed me. They stayed close together with their legs crossed, and looked quite at ease while they speculated about Nat. Eileen and Laura continued the chitchat with their heads together, and kept their voices low. Lauren's raven black hair was secured into a ponytail with a tortoise shell barrette. During Eileen and Laura's conversation, Eileen's blue eyes sparkled with delight over the newest gossip. The two of them reminded me of high school gossip queens, no matter their good intentions. I overheard a conversation about Laura being engaged to a football player, and she let me know about the engagement when I complimented her diamond. I listened as they were arranging to introduce Nat to a nurse who worked in another unit.

They better not try to fix Nat up with anyone. It annoyed me to hear their cackling. I had my eye on him, and no one could stop me. Since I was a new volunteer, I was not sure how they would react if they knew how I felt about Nat. The staff was all supportive of me when I first arrived on the unit. They taught me the ropes in the hospital, and they even gave me an extra locker in the nurse's lounge. They finally realized I was standing in front of them.

"Are you working today?" Laura said.

"We didn't know you were on the schedule today." Eileen looked puzzled. "But we're glad to see you anyway." She managed a grin.

Nevertheless, they continued with their discussion about Nat.

"He just purchased an old house, and he's fixing it up. I have a friend at the garage he uses, and he gave me all the info. You know, he would flip if he knew how much we really know about him," Eileen boasted.

"It's a perfect time for him to meet the right girl now," Laura whispered. She lifted an eyebrow. "I wonder why he never married."

"I heard he had a girlfriend who stayed with him this past summer," Eileen added. "He once dated a girl from New York City. He would be furious, I'm sure, if he knew Hal from the station keeps us updated about his love life. Anyway, she left him for another man. He even let her keep the car he bought her." She moved in closer to Eileen. "I really think Sue is a perfect match for him. She told me she thinks he's cute and would love to date him."

They speculated about Nat, and I hated it. I felt honored he shared his stories with me, since he had been known to be secretive about his past. I wondered why he opened up to me. Although, he clammed up, when I asked about him about being an only child. It was as if I touched upon a taboo subject.

I knew the nurses had good intentions for Nat, but I felt uncomfortable with the subject, and I was not about to join in.

"He really is a great catch, and what a fantastic build," Laura said. She blushed. "I would date him if I wasn't already engaged." She waved her hand in front of her face. "He's really hot. Did you see the way he looked in those jeans at the picnic?"

While I listened to their discussion, I wondered if they mentioned this to Nat, and I was terrified of the answer. Eileen babbled on that he had not dated anyone for quite some time, and she thought he was fussy about the women he took out.

The chatter between them made me nervous. I was attracted to Nat in a way that I never felt before. He displayed a quick wit, and there seemed to be a fire inside of him. At the same time, he could be gentle and caring. His stories touched my heart. I felt as if I was the woman he waited for.

He actually seemed like his family's history was comparable to mine. The similarities I noticed were in the way he displayed sincerity when he reached out to those in need. I read a book that explained why we are attracted to people who remind us of our loved ones. The author uses situations from couples in therapy. Some people long for the comforting effect of sharing a life with a person who reminds them of their own family. Nat's intelligence and charm motivated me to be the best I could be.

My imagination took me away for a moment. I envisioned Nat's arrival and a chance to be alone with him in his office. When the door closes, he confesses his inner thoughts. He tells me he finds me amazing and wants to spend time together. I became lost in thought, and enjoyed the scenario I created in my mind.

Laura clapped her hands in front of my face.

"Madeline, are you there?" she shouted. "Hello, are you still with us?"

I tried to focus while she handed me a box filled with various pieces of clothing. "Can you bring to this lost and found?" she requested.

I shook my head and felt flustered. "Sure, no problem."

"On your way back, can you please pick up the patient in the emergency room?" she asked. "It seemed as if you were a thousand miles away," she said. "Are you sure you're okay?"

Her tone startled me, and I answered quickly. "I'm fine. I'll get the patient now."

"Would you answer the phone first? I'm about to pass out the medications," Laura requested. She motioned to the area behind the desk.

I reached over for the receiver. "Hello, Path to Life Unit, this is Madeline Young. How can I help you?"

"Hey, Madeline, it's Nat. I'm about to come back upstairs, and I wanted to know if anyone wants coffee? I'm down at the snack shop."

"Umm, hold on for a moment please. I'll check," I said, thrilled by the mere sound of his voice. I returned with the order for him.

"Would you like a coffee?" he asked.

I hesitated at first. "I would love one. Thanks," I said.

Nat's voice sounded smooth and sexy over the phone. I was delighted that I agreed to come in that day, and I hurried to run the errands.

I returned after a stop in the restroom to freshen up and spray a tiny bit of perfume on my wrist. When I arrived, Nat was at the desk with the coffees.

He stood in front of me, and he gave me a charming smile. "This one's for you."

I caught a glimpse of his hand around the cup. He handed it to me, and my eyes followed up to his face. All at once, I found it difficult to find the words to say. I stared into his eyes and took a breath. Never in my life did I experience such a desire to kiss a man, smack on the lips, and right in front of everyone. *Compose yourself, Madeline. You'll have your wish, in time.*

The nurses continued to joke around, and tease him. Eileen whispered to Laura before she handed him a card. It probably was the phone number of the nurse from three central. They reminded him about their previous attempt to play matchmakers.

"Nat, come on call her, she'd love to hear from you," Laura said. Her eyes shifted up to see the expression on his face. She rested her chin on her hands and gazed up at him like a schoolchild. He did not answer them.

I sat down behind the station, and moved the waste basket away from my chair.

Nat tread behind me and checked his schedule. His eyes darted toward the dip in my sweater. I could sense him look down at me. He stood so close I could practically feel his breath on my neck. Luckily, I wore my favorite off-white knit. I realized I chose it to look especially nice.

He glanced over to me and gave me a smile. I knew this pullover flattered my figure, and I hoped he would notice. We were close enough for me to experience an electrifying connection. I could listen to him speak forever and his presence next to me drove me crazy.

The nurses continued to discuss their plan to arrange a date with Nat and their friend Sue. Nat stood right next to me, and attempted to explain in a nice way how he was very busy, and might not have the chance to meet her.

He raised his arms up. "They don't realize I have a life outside of this unit," Nat offered in a serious tone. "I also work as a contractor, and I have a commitment down the shore on the days I'm not here."

"I think they do what we all do. They try to fix everyone up who's unattached," I said. I hoped my comment was not out of line.

"I would love to get out and socialize more. I will when I get a chance," he said.

I wished he included me in his plans to get out. Nat moved toward the desk, and rested his arms on top. I had a sense he had an interest in me, too. A woman can tell when a man finds her desirable. My intuition was usually right. I could feel his attraction.

"I recently bought a new car and would love to take a drive on the highway and floor it," Nat said. "I could sure use an afternoon to myself. I haven't put any mileage on the car since I got it, and it's about time I take it out, and see what it can do."

"That's great. I need to shop around for a good car, myself." I admitted.

"I found a deal at the South Street dealer, so I bought the sports addition Jaguar."

"I might trade my car in this year," I replied.

"Let me guess what you drive," Nat said. He raised two fingers to his chin.

He paid attention to me, and actually teased me.

"I bet you drive a foreign car," he said. He wore a playful smirk.

"How did you know?" I answered.

We continued to joke around like teenyboppers. The nurses looked at us out of the corners of their eyes. Nat gave me direct eye contact, and his undivided attention.

From what I gathered, Nat was not the type of man who asked many women out. I did not want to let this opportunity go, and I certainly did not want Sue to get a date with him. I hoped he would make a move soon. It was quite possible Nat would be afraid to ask me. He was polite and since they encouraged him to date a co-worker, he might just go along with them. Our meeting seemed like it happened for a reason. After all, the decision I made to volunteer, lead me to Nat.

That afternoon when I left, I thought about how alcoholism affects families. I approached my car, and gasped when I saw a flat tire.

"Oh, that's all I needed today!" I stood in one spot, with my eyes fixed on the vehicle. I kicked the wheel in frustration.

I did not have the slightest idea how to put on the spare. I spoke aloud, "Now, what am I to do?" I went back inside to see if someone knew a garage that was reputable in the area. I took the stairs, four flights and was exhausted when I finally reached the floor. I rested for a few seconds before I continued.

Nat stepped out of his office and stared into space. He buried one hand in his pocket. He appeared completely engrossed in his thoughts. Nat took a quick step back, and looked startled when he saw me. "I thought you left for the day," he said.

"I did leave, but I have a flat tire. I need a number of a garage in the area," I answered. I wiped the grime off of my shoe with a tissue. "I attempted to get the tire off myself, but I couldn't." I tried not to whine.

He gave me a look of confidence, as he straightened his shoulders. "Come on, I'll help you," he said. "Wait here a minute. I'll change my shirt and be right with you." He held his hand up to motion me to wait.

Nat exited his office in a white T-shirt. His physique was trim and fit. He looked absolutely dreamy in a short sleeve shirt.

"I'll have you on the road in a few minutes. Don't worry; I've been fixing tires since I was a kid. Follow me," he insisted. "I had a bunch of junk cars when I first got my license. I can practically put one together with my eyes closed."

I felt relieved to have his assistance.

"Thanks for your offer to help, Nat. I'm glad you were still here," I said and moved my hair away from my eye.

We hiked to the deck together. I tried to keep up with his fast pace. My struggle must have been obvious.

"I'm sorry. I'm used to a fast pace," he said, in a concerned tone.

I wore new shoes which were not broken in yet. "I'm fine," I said.

"Toss me the keys," Nat said, as he moved toward the trunk. "Do you have a spare?"

He changed the tire in no time. Nat stood up slowly.

"Sorry to interrupt your day," I said. I tried desperately to remain calm, although I was thrilled with his eagerness to help.

Nat looked directly into my eyes, as he wiped his forehead. "I'm almost finished for the day, and it was no trouble at all." He held my gaze and it made me feel much better.

I gave him a friendly hug, realizing that I may have been too forward. Nevertheless, I was grateful for his assistance. I placed my arms around him. He reached out to reciprocate, and it was all I needed to validate our attraction. Nat let me go slowly, and remained close. I saw a look in his eye that told me he wanted to say more.

I watched as he disappeared from my sight. All of a sudden, I felt like I was special. As I drove away, I wondered what to do next. My sixth sense told me Nat found me attractive and wanted to pursue a romantic involvement. My doubts remained about him ever asking me out. A strong sense, deep inside, told me I must be the one to reach out to him. It was rather bewildering; nevertheless, I wholeheartedly searched for the answers.

Chapter Ten

Nathaniel

*T*he gym helped whenever Nat felt tense. As he finished the third set of his weight routine, he felt a tap on the back.

"Hey, what's happening?" Bob Nagy was a trainer at the club. He gave Nat tips on his workout and seemed like the happy family man.

"How are you? What are you up to?" Nat said, surprised to see him.

"I had to switch my schedule, since I had to meet with my lawyer, yesterday. Later I'll need a quick massage," he said, as he rubbed his arm and flexed his biceps.

"I hope you're okay," Nat said.

"I'll survive. Third divorce," Bob admitted. He shrugged. "How about you, did you get engaged yet?" He snickered.

"No, not me," Nat answered without hesitation.

"Oh, I thought you had a serious girlfriend."

"I'm not seeing anyone."

"At least, I tried," he added. "Now I have to hold on to my wallet." He reached toward his back pocket and snickered. "Seriously, I thought you'd be snatched up by now."

"I don't think so," Nat said. He wished Bob would shut his mouth.

Nat cleared his throat. "Nope, I'm still single, and happy to do my own thing."

"You like girls, don't you?" Bob asked. He tried to hold a straight face.

Nat punched his arm. "You're a real jerk sometimes!"

"My ex-wives say the same about me."

"I'll be here next week, so give me a shout. I have a new routine to show you."

"Sure, I'll give you a holler."

Nat made his way into the locker room and showered. He hated the questions about his lack of a female companion. He had a good time with his friend at the gym and wanted to keep it there. Nat didn't feel like a blow by blow of his marriage problems, or his questions about why he was still single. It made Nat feel inadequate as a man, and like a freak of some kind. The last time they got together, Nat took Bob out on his boat. Bob complained the whole time, and Nat promised himself it would be the last time he took him fishing. Nat thought people should mind their own business. He knew if he spent an evening working out with Bob, he would have to defend his right to live the way he chose. Bob could not survive without a female in his life. Nat wanted to stand on his own, and not rely on anyone.

As he finished up at the gym, Madeline popped into his mind. He enjoyed their conversations and for a moment, he thought of her smile, and he remembered how she seemed so positive and upbeat. Volunteering at a drug and alcohol program took a lot of nerve and a special type of person. Nat had never met anyone like her before, and he found himself drawn to her. Her kind and loving personality, played with his emotions. He drove home and tried to plan his next lecture in his mind, but his thoughts returned to his conversation with Bob. Nat wanted to contact the therapist he went to for a few years, after he got his degree in counseling. Her office was in New York City, and he made a mental note to see if he still had her card.

When he got inside, he dropped his briefcase and gym stuff on the floor. He went into the kitchen to grab a soda, and took it onto the front porch. He lit a cigarette and took a puff, and watched the cars pass by. This was the life he wanted. No one greeted him at the door, no kids, no wife. He thought it would be better to live alone. *I live a good life.* His body ached for the softness of a woman like Madeline curled up beside him at night. He couldn't lead her on; he knew she wasn't the kind of girl to take for granted. A brief encounter would not suit her at all. After he smashed the butt of his cigarette in the ashtray, Nat went inside and picked up his guitar from the corner of the living room. He sat down on the couch and fiddled around with a tune he'd written. The notes came easy, and he surprised himself. He tuned his guitar and listened carefully, until the song sounded right. It turned out to be a melody unlike the ones he usually came up with. It sounded like a love song, and he played it a couple of times, until he got up to look for the sub shop menu.

Madeline

I phoned Bonnie to ask her if she wanted to join me at the coffee shop on Main Street. She let me know that Mike would be home early and could stay with Mom. I left the meeting satisfied with our progress. I picked Bonnie up on the way.

She hopped in the car and reached over to adjust the radio station. She turned the knob to the fifties channel and began to sing along with the music.

"I love your sweater. Is it new?" I asked. She wore a pastel green turtleneck which looked like cashmere.

"Oh, this old rag, I recently had it dry cleaned," she said. "I had it tucked away, and forgot about it. It's like finding an old friend. I like your outfit, too. Maybe I can borrow it someday." I laughed and knew Nat seemed to like it also.

The cafe had the best coffee and homemade muffins in town. It was our favorite place to sit and chat. We sat in a corner, and ordered two cups of mocha latte. Inside, there were huge booths with thick padded cushions. They had fixtures scattered around made the atmosphere resemble an old-fashioned soda fountain.

"I'm positive the medical day care center will be great for Mom," I said, as I took a sip of my coffee. "Miss Hadley, the director, assured me that structure and routine have been known to greatly improve the quality of life for their clientele."

"It's such a relief for Mike and I. We were at our wit's end. I'm glad you found a way to enhance her life," Bonnie replied.

"I think she needs something to keep her out of trouble. It will be good for her to be around people her age, and get involved in structured activities," I said.

"Maybe she will even stop her conversation with her imaginary friend when she makes new ones at the center," Bonnie returned. She sat forward. Tell me, how's the cute counselor? What's his name again?"

"His name is Nat," I said. I held back a grin.

"I knew you liked him; your eyes lit up when you said his name!" Bonnie exclaimed. She pointed her finger at me.

I cried out, "All right, I do like him!" I leaned forward. "I think I've found the man I'm meant to be with." I lowered my voice to a whisper. "We've had some great conversations, and he's really opened up to me. I think he feels the same way, but the staff at the hospital wants to fix him up with a nurse. What am I to do?" I sat back slowly, and placed my hands around my cup.

Her opinion was important to me, and I needed help to make the decision. As I took another sip of my coffee, I waited anxiously for her answer.

"Do you think he's really interested in you?" she asked.

"I can see it in the way he looks at me, and the way I feel when we're next to each other. I'm positive he's the one for me."

"What makes you think you have to make a move?" she inquired. "Maybe he'll ask you out."

I looked down, and still wondered. "I'm worried that he might just take the nurse out as a favor, and maybe he'll like her. The way they sounded, made it seem like he hasn't asked a woman out in a long time."

"Do you want to call him?" she asked.

My frustrations got stronger, and I could not sit still. "That's what I need to know, if I call him first, is it the right choice?" I crumbled the napkin in my hand, and squirmed around in my seat. "Maybe he'll think I'm desperate or a stalker. For the life of me, I can't get him out of my mind."

Bonnie touched my hand. "Maybe you should see what Mother thinks. Her predictions usually fall true."

"I know what you mean. I'll get her input. I really wish I could ask Dad, too," I admitted. I gave a defeated sigh. "I can't get this idea out of my mind. If I wait for him, his status could change, and oh, I don't know." I reached for my cup and took another sip, and practically emptied my entire beverage onto my lap. As I wiped the table, the answer became clearer to me. "I want to call him and ask him if he wants to get together."

Bonnie clapped her hands and gave a hearty laugh. "That's my little sister, you are the determined one. I trust that you will know when it's right. Go with your intuition, and I'll be here if you need me. You really have nothing to lose. You may just gain the love of your life." She sat back with a gleam in her eyes.

When I dropped Bonnie off at her place, I decided to stop inside to see Mother again. She sat in her rocker, gliding back and forth slowly. She held a long stick with a feather on the end of it, along with her white linen hanky. I wondered if she was up to her old tricks. She wore her navy dress, with deep side pockets, and she had two butterfly combs in her hair. She looked so content, lost in deep thought.

She opened her eyes wide, when she saw me and sat forward. "Madeline, is that you?"

I bent down next to her.

"What's wrong, honey?" she said.

"I'm fine. I wanted to ask you a question."

"What is it?" she asked. She looked into my eyes.

"What do you think Dad would have done if you asked him out, for a first date?"

She peered over the top of her glasses.

"Well, I think Nick would have loved for me to be so bold," she admitted and gave a robust chuckle. "I knew he liked me when he first came into the store. He practically spent all of his money for the week on candy. It was what fate had planned for us. It was supposed to be just the way it happened." She laughed. "Regardless who declared their desire first, we would have been together. We were preordained to be together. It was written in the stars. You'll make the right choice. Trust me, I'm sure of it."

I closed my eyes. Somehow, I knew that was what she would say. She reached over, and placed her hands on top of mine. Her touch was gentle, and it could still comfort me. I had my concerns that Nat would think I was easy, or aggressive, if I made the first move. I wanted the real me to shine through. I certainly did not want him to get the wrong idea.

Chapter Eleven

Madeline

When I arrived home, I began to search relentlessly for the charm bracelet my father gave me for high school graduation. It was on the bottom of an old ballerina jewelry box in the basement. I picked it up and held it close and wished I could ask his advice. He was old-fashioned and might say a woman should not ask a man for a date. A feeling of uncertainty, and doubt took control of me. All I wanted was to be able to ask him if calling Nat was the right move. The tears ran down my face and I never bothered to grab a tissue. It felt better to have a good cry. I needed to get the emotions out one way or another. I dreamt of someday being fortunate enough to have the same bond my parents shared as a couple. They both wanted me to find a worthy partner. Mom and Dad never let me know that their biggest fear was that Sonny would leave me.

I had a desire to find someone who was right for me. I walked to the window in a daze, and noticed that the mail arrived. The box was full, so I placed it on the table and went inside to make a sandwich. I carried my sandwich back to the table, and began to organize the mail. When I sorted through the envelopes, I tore the junk mail in half, and tossed it in the center of the table.

On the bottom of the pile was a larger brown package with European postage. At first, I wondered if anyone I knew that was on a trip. I opened it and found handwritten correspondence with a bunch of old letters tied together with a gold ribbon. I was amazed as I looked them over. When I started to read the note, I realized it was from my cousin Jen, who lived in England. Her mother, Lilly, was my father's older sister. She was fifty-five years old, and moved to England years ago, with her childhood sweetheart, Martin West. I read: "Madeline, I found some old boxes, and I thought you would enjoy these."

Inside I found the old love letters my father wrote to my mother. I had no idea how she got hold of them, and I was thrilled to have them.

I sat back, and at that moment, I knew I made the right decision. I hoped for a way to get my Dad's blessing in my decision. The box arrived at the right time. These odd happenings seemed to come to me on a regular basis. A sign would pop up out of nowhere, and I would know why or where I was headed. I was apt to believe that there was a force in my corner to look out for me. It reassured me to know I was not alone. Mother used to say it was my earth spirit. Something unknown to me, guided me through my life so far, and they never let me down. When I was younger I doubted the concept of a guidance from somewhere beyond. Now, it all made a little more sense. "They watch over us and guide us in times of need," Mother assured me.

She spoke such simple terms of love, straight from the heart. Was there any truth to them? It did lessen the blows from disappointments. The comfort of the realization of a guardian angel to look out for us, when we need it, washed away my doubts. I did not have all the answers. Maybe it was merely a coincidence, and Aunt Mary was a recurring dream. She may not have been my savior after all. The noise from the workers outside of my window broke my concentration that afternoon. I turned on the radio to block out the awful noise. My neighbor was in the process of a home improvement project. I would have loved to shout out to him to quiet down. My frustration got the best of me.

There were many changes in my life to be grateful for, and I realized I still had so much to learn. The decision to ask a man for a date could embarrass me, or alter and change my entire future. I waited until the next week to make the call to Nat.

The day was like any other. It was early autumn, the colors of fall began to appear, reds, yellows, and oranges, constantly changing. My morning ritual was to put on a pot of coffee, before taking a shower. On this day, I could not get this new concept out of my mind. It was unnerving to make a decision that would alter the course of my future. My vision was one-dimensional, and I felt like I was in a daze. The song on the radio supported me, and it added to my determination. The haunting melody from a disaster film sounded beautiful. All the events that led up to my decision fell together as if it was supposed to happen. A power unknown to me at the time pushed me forward. It pulled at my heart, with a steady grip. Somehow, the self-doubt I had in my earlier years, no longer held me back.

I repeated my opening sentence aloud and shook while I prepared to make the call. I gripped on tightly to the edge of the vanity, and tried to maintain my balance. The reflection in the mirror was my audience, as I rehearsed the words I would say. The scent of simmering potpourri filled the air in my house with the aromas of cinnamon and pumpkin spice. The rich earthy scents were strong, and I loved them. The phonebook was in the hallway closet, and I grabbed it, and hoped his phone number would be there. Nathaniel Griffin's number was right in front of me, in black and white. As I stared at the number, my thoughts sped. I paced back and forth, from one room to the next. My shoulders tightened. Would I remember the right words to say if he answered?

My emotions took over my body and soul, as I desperately searched for the answers. There was a pounding sensation in my head unrelieved by a couple of aspirins. My biggest fear was to find out he made a date with the nurse from the hospital. I imagined the man I wanted, in the arms of another woman. Would he take the suggestion of the girls on the unit, to date their friend from three central? Had they joined hand in hand, only to leave me with my heart broken? Could it be, I waited too long before I confessed my desires? I kicked off my slippers, and stepped around barefooted. I felt almost giddy.

The thought of rejection played over in the scenario in my mind. Would he respond with enthusiasm, or would he chuckle and forfeit the chance for romance? It seemed like hours passed, before I could pick up the receiver. I looked at the clock, and chewed my nails so short it was simply dreadful. I was thankful my sons were out for the day. If they caught me in this state, they would think I was crazy. My mind churned, while the furniture in my path began to topple. This idea of calling a man to suggest an interest, or ask him for a date was new to me. My heart skipped a beat when I fumbled to dial the phone. I was so anxious that I stubbed my toe on the coffee table. I never initiated a call to a man in my life!

The decision I made to make the first move and ask Nat out, was not what I had intended when we first met. The circumstances at the hospital left me no choice. The nurses tried to urge him to pursue a relationship with their friend, and I knew I had to move fast. My typical behavior would be to lose the opportunity to engage in a healthy relationship. The men in my past all needed a caregiver, not a partner. Nat did not appear to be the kind of man that eagerly pursed a woman. A mysterious aura followed him. At the time, I had no idea how complex he really was. I was determined not to let him get away.

In the past, you would become the target of neighborhood gossip if you made the first move. They would label you as a flirt or easy. A good girl from a Catholic school would never consider such a task. I knew morals had changed; doors were open for women in many areas. One of them was to be able to choose the partner of her desire, just as a man would select his ladylove. I found my decision to ask a man out on a date, quite intoxicating. There was only one way I would get the answers. That was to just do it! The phone rang, and it startled me. Bonnie called, and it sounded urgent.

"Mother is worse," Bonnie said. "I just can't ignore it anymore. I overheard Mother have a full conversation with someone; I heard a loud ring and it sounded like an eerie. Strangely enough, she was alone in the room. Today, I found her talking aloud in the kitchen. The other day I heard her on the veranda. It really bothers me."

"I hope she's not hallucinating," I said. "Don't tell me she's is not up to her old tricks."

"It's scary!" Bonnie added.

"Maybe we should take her to Dr. Martin for a checkup," I said, eager for a simple solution. "I read an article about a vitamin deficiency that could cause increased confusion." Bonnie ignored mother's magical abilities. She did seem worse since she got dementia. Mother's rituals and quirky behavior was second nature and lately concerned me. The odd happenings surrounding the Young family were not new. Although, Bonnie liked to make believe our family was the typical happy family. To the contrary, we weren't typical.

"I'll call and schedule an appointment for next week." Bonnie breathed a sigh of relief. "I wanted to get this out in the open," she said. "What is it?" I asked.

"I'm sure you could tell I had a drink the other day."

"Are you all right?" I asked.

"I don't know how I could be so stupid, after all these years," she said.

"I went to my therapist, and we had a great session." Her tone sounded confident. "I'll be fine. I need to get Mother a complete physical."

"I'm here if you need me," I said in an attempt to disguise my concerns about both Mother's behavior and Bonnie's relapse.

At the time, I did not realize the value Mother's tricks would hold for me. Instead, I shirked the whole topic off. When we were kids, Mother used to read tea leaves during her weekly card game. The thought of my mother still able to place a spell or conjure up a potion, made me shudder. My mother had practiced witchcraft since we were children and tried to get us involved. I wanted everyone to think my mother was a normal PTA mother, like everyone else's.

"I hope we can help her, before she goes off the deep end," she said before we hung up.

Chapter Twelve

Madeline

I paced back and forth in my house and rehearsed the words I would say if he answered. My hands shook as I reached for the phonebook. I knew it was now or never. Since the boys were still out, it seemed like ideal opportunity to make the call. Fortunately, Jeremy had a football game with his friends, and Mark went to the library.

The breeze made the sheer curtains in the living room move in a slow steady rhythm. The colors outside my window were beautiful. The leaves scattered across the lawn and created a soft bed of colors. I could smell my neighbor's barbeque pit, and I enjoyed the hickory scent. I spent the entire morning with the scenario in my mind, and I explored every angle. The Celine Dion song played again on the radio, and I became motivated.

As I flipped through the pages and located his name, I debated again, for an hour before I picked up the phone. The first time I dialed his number, I slammed down the phone right before it connected, and I changed my mind at least a dozen times. Nevertheless, I heard his inspirational words and imagined his smile. After the conversation I overheard the previous week about Nat and the nurse from three central, I almost gave up. I could imagine Nat and her on a date. After a few more times, their first kiss, and then anything was possible. Now I was serious. Finally I held my breath, and dialed the number, and took a nibble out of a Hershey bar. *Keep it up, and you'll need a whole new wardrobe.* It rang five or six times before I heard the voice on the other line.

I still could not believe I found the nerve. It sounded like he was out of breath.

"Hi, Nat, this is Madeline, Madeline Young, the volunteer at the hospital."

"How are you?" he said.

"I'm great, thanks. I called because I was wondering if you wanted to get together for a cup of coffee?" I closed my eyes, and quivered as I waited for him to speak.

"I'd love to," he replied in a high-pitched tone. I felt instant relief.

"I'm sorry if I surprised you, but I really enjoyed our time together on the unit. I thought it would be fun if we got together," I added.

"I'm glad you called. I'm flattered," he admitted.

I was thrilled with the sound of his reply. There was a certainty in his voice. His positive response reassured me as we spoke. What he said next was so wonderful, I could not believe my ears. My heart pounded in my chest, as I listened to his reply.

"You know, Madeline, it's funny, but I was upstairs in front of my paperwork right before you called, and your face flashed in front of my eyes. At that moment, the phone rang and it was you."

His explanation told me my premonition was right, he was interested in me. I paused and exhaled. My chest felt heavy.

"You saw my face in front of you!"

"It's true, I did," he said.

"Do you have any plans tomorrow?" he asked.

As I stared into the mirror, I fumbled with a pencil and paper on my lap and tried to stay attentive.

"I don't belief I have any plans," I answered. "What do you

have in mind?"

"How about a ride in the country? The foliage is great this time of year."

"Oh yeah, I remember you told me you'd like to take a ride in your new car. I'd love to do."

"Why don't you come over to my house? I just finished a fresh coat of paint on the kitchen cabinets, and I could use a woman's opinion."

"That sounds like a great idea," I said with enthusiasm. "What time would you like me to come over?"

"Eleven would be a good time. Is that okay for you? I think it's best to get an early start."

"I can be there at eleven. What's your address?"

He gave me directions to his house which was in a town next close to mine. I loved the area. It had some of the loveliest older homes, I'd even seen. I recently read that the owners restored many of the structures to their past elegance. I could not wait to see which one was his.

I remained in one position in a state of shock, and stared out the window in my room. It took a lot of guts to make that call. The cool air felt good against my skin. I reached for my address book and slowly turned the pages.

For an instant, I had a brief flashback of that night when I woke up to find the caller in my room, at dawn. At that moment, I heard a banging sound from the basement, but never bothered to investigate. I thought it was the typical sounds of any home.

"My house is pushed back from the street. It has a red door, and a long winding driveway," he said.

"I know the area. I'll be able to find it with no problem," I replied.

Nat sounded excited, too. He spoke quickly, "I can't wait to get that baby out on the highway. I'm glad you called. I admire your honesty." He paused a moment, and I wondered what could be wrong.

"Are you still there?" I asked.

"Of course, I am," he replied. "I have an idea. I was just about to go for a jog in the park. I saw you on Main Street one day, when I drove to the hardware store."

"You should have stopped," I told him.

"I didn't want to disturb you. Come on, I would love the company. It could a preview of our first date tomorrow." He chuckled, and I imagined his expression to be a happy one. It took only a minute for me to decide. A jog in the park sounded like a fantastic idea.

"I usually walk, I don't know if I could keep up with you. I'd probably straggle behind."

"That's nonsense. Have you been to Roosevelt Park?" he asked. "I can pick you up, or you can meet me, if that suits you better. I'll even buy lunch."

"Sure Nat, I'd love to meet you for an outing," I said. I hoped I didn't appear too forward. "I can be there in about an hour. Is that okay?"

"That's great," he said.

When I hung up the phone, I marched straight to my closet. My object was to find the right outfit to wear to the park, and the next day also. It was amazing how my wishes came true. My confidence, took control and I knew I could overcome my insecurities. Now, I was convinced that calling Nat was absolutely the right choice to make. I dashed around the living room and threw various outfits all over the furniture, in search of the best one. As soon as I decided what to wear, I dialed Bonne's number to tell her the news.

"Wait till I tell you what just happened," I said as I squeezed the receiver.

"Madeline, are you all right?" she shouted. Her voice rose to a shrill pitch.

"I've never been better. I called Nat and asked him if he wanted to get together. He told me he envisioned my face in front of him while he worked upstairs. He actually thought of me right before the phone rang. Do you believe it?"

"Oh, my goodness, that's fantastic!" Bonnie exclaimed. "That's why you seemed so strange earlier today. I knew you could do it. I guess you two were thrown together by a force of nature."

"Whatever it was I'm sure glad I went with my instinct. I have to run; I'm meeting him this afternoon at the park."

"I'm so happy for you, Madeline. Call me with all the details later."

Chapter Thirteen

Nathaniel

*N*at rushed upstairs to the third floor. He dashed over to the pile of old paintings. He threw the covers over them and tucked them into the corner just to be on the safe side. Nat knew he shouldn't have responded the way he did, but Madeline was a knockout, and he thought it couldn't hurt to be nice to a girl like her. She was his type, and he'd been alone for so long. He made himself a promise, not to hurt her, no matter what.

He ran downstairs, grabbed a glass of water, and swallowed a mouthful before he phoned his mother in Florida. Since he hadn't talked to her in a week, he took a minute to check on her. "How are you, Mother?" he asked.

"Good, son, but I still have those dizzy spells. The doctor gave me pills, and they help a bit."

Nat thought she sounded weak. "I hope you're eating." He worried about her recent weight loss. "I ran into Mr. Rosen the other day."

"Oh, my word!" she said. "I hope he didn't ask a lot of senseless questions about your father. You know how nosy he is."

"Everyone in town knew Dad drank too much," Nat added.

"No, they didn't. Your father was a respected man, and I forbid you to spread those rumors, and don't you forget it!" The sound of her high-pitched voice went through Nat like the sound of an alarm clock. He closed his eyes and tried not to respond with a rebuttal.

"I have to go. Call me if you need me," he said.

"Why do you do that?"

"What do you mean?"

"Every time I bring up the man who worked hard to put food on the table, you have to hang up. You have no respect for what your father did for you." Nat's head felt heavy and he thought his blood pressure would cause him to have a stroke. He could feel the heat on his face and the pounding of his heart.

"Are you still there?" she said.

"Yes, Mother, I'm here."

Nat sat still and wished he had never called her. He remembered one incident back in the old house when he forgot to take out the garbage. They had a playful mutt named Ginger. She would open the lid to the trash with her nose and spill out the contents onto the floor. In the morning, his father found the mess and locked Nat out of the house that night. He had to sleep in a sleeping bag in the basement. His mother snuck down after she heard a noise, but she did not tell him to come up to bed. She sided with her husband and let Nat remain punished for his mistake. Nat felt like his mother never stuck up for him and liked to play the martyr role. He heard a sound in the background on the other line.

"That's my timer. I have a pie in the oven. I'll talk to you another time."

Nat hung up the phone and wondered why he became angry whenever he spoke to her. He left the house and felt sorry for his mother. Their relationship failed no matter what he did. Nat tried to see her when he could, and each time he became more and more disconnected from her. As he sat in his car, and attempted to get the thoughts of his mother out of his mind, he kicked up the volume on his Sirius radio station as he listened to a sad melody. It had a distinct sound, and he felt a chill come over his body. He tapped his finger on the steering wheel. The horrible guilt he felt after the conversation with his mother lifted.

The bright glare through the windshield blocked his view, so he reached for his sunglasses. As he slipped them on, he thought about some of the reasons he still had resentment in his heart. Nevertheless, he tried to forgive her, when he learned about the cycle of addiction in his studies. He could not understand how he helped so many families in therapy and could not get close to his own mother. It became a sore topic for Nat. He hoped one day to learn about the woman who raised him. His effort to erase the painful memories one year when they took a vacation together. Somehow, Nat could not live up to her expectations, and she complained the entire time. He could not wait to get her off the plane and out of his sight. He tried to recall the comfort he felt when she helped him with his homework or baked him a cake for his birthday. The years did not bring them closer. It seemed as if the past would forever keep them apart.

Nat made a few stops, and he bought enough food for a party of ten. He knew he could use it for the rest of the week. When he finished at the store, he stopped at the car wash.

A wax with a hand dry and a complete vacuum for ten bucks sounded good to him. He watched as the huge brushes swirled around, and wondered if Madeline felt as excited as he did. Nat hadn't anticipated a woman like her would agree to join him, or want to meet him for a date. He never thought he'd be so fortunate. When he picked up the phone and she requested his company, he almost fell over. He hoped he wouldn't act like a jerk or seem weird to her. Then, he recalled her phone call and felt assured how much she already liked him. His doubts about dating Madeline subsided as the he anticipated the date. Nat began to enjoy what felt natural to him. The car wash ended, and

Nat went over to the counter to pay. As he spread his arms across the top, he looked inside the case. He selected an air freshener for his car, and hoped Madeline liked the scent of island breeze. A *nice smelling car can't hurt.* He wondered about some of her favorite hobbies. Never in his wildest dreams did he expect to have this happen to him. Women usually fell for the other guy; the one with more to offer or the fancy college boy with a corporate position. They looked down on the poor slob who counseled part-time and worked on houses for a living.

A surge of energy hit him as he approached the park. Madeline's smile came into his mind, and he had a strong desire to place his lips on hers. He decided to make an attempt to take it slow. Somehow, his strong attraction to her took control of him.

As he hopped out of the car, he took a breath of fresh air. The outdoors made him forget the tension his mother's call stirred up. He opened his bottled water and guzzled a mouthful. Nat rested his back up against his car, with his arms folded and watched the entrance. He put the negative conversation with his mother out of his mind. *She would not interfere with his life.* Nat relaxed as he waited for Madeline and felt like a kid again.

Madeline

When I jumped into the hot shower, I started to sing. Afterwards, I chose a new pair of sweats and placed my hair in a rubber band. It was easier then blow-drying my hair. I left few curls around my forehead and down my neck. A ponytail would allow it to stay smooth and not curl up into a ball of frizz. I put on a touch of mascara and a soft rose lipstick. Spending an afternoon in the park did not warrant a fashion statement. I still wanted to look my best. When I drove around the winding roads towards the entrance, my heart skipped a beat. After I indulged in too much candy earlier in the day, I had to pop an antacid in my mouth.

I checked my rear view mirror and noticed a car close to mine. The mirror fogged, as if we were in a storm, but the sun shone. I wiped it with a napkin I found in my console. I felt like a feather touched my shoulder, or an insect landed on me. A flash of light appeared in the seat next to me, and I jumped in my seat. *Maybe it's time to have to get my eyes checked.*

Nat stood in lot near the entrance. He beeped his horn, and signaled for me to pull over next to his car. His car was parked in a spot where the path led to the pond. There were all sorts of events in the park on Saturday afternoon. Small groups scattered in different areas involved in their activities. When I got out of my car, it seemed like I was in a dream.

Nat wore a huge smile as he stood next to his car, with a bottle of water in his hand. He looked strong and masculine dressed in casual clothes, and my attraction to him intensified.

"Hey, Madeline." He moved toward me with a quick stride.

Nat did not strike me as a man of great confidence with women. I knew he had some experience with the opposite sex, since the girls at hospital mentioned his last girlfriend.

"You really brought lunch?"

"I said I would. We have to eat."

He opened the box to display a complete picnic.

I laughed, and moved the items aside. "Looks like you really planned a feast."

"I hope it's to your liking. Since you're the chef, I thought I would give you a break," he said.

"My goodness, you did come prepared."

"Really, it was fun. I grabbed some great sandwiches from Deli Delight on Amboy Ave.," he said. "Have you even tried that place? Their selection is the best." Nat moved closer to me as we started toward the back of his car. He opened his trunk, still staring at me. He placed the cooler inside.

I snuck another peek before we got started.

"It's a perfect day to be outside," I said.

"Should we start over there?" He tossed the empty water

bottle in the front seat and pointed to a clearing.

I nodded in agreement.

His love for outdoor life fascinated me. The temperature was perfect. I only needed a light jacket. The pond appeared luminous, with a family of ducks who swam in a circle.

"Sure let's go," I answered. I felt comfortable in his company.

Nat showed me his considerate side, when he packed a lunch. I knew we hardly knew one another, but we formed a special kind of connection already.

Nat and I walked side by side, in a carefree fashion. I glanced at his legs and admired them, as he took wide steps. We started to pick up the speed. While we jogged, I kept up with him. I used all my energy, and I focused on my breathing.

"Are you tired?" Nat said, after about thirty-five minutes.

I did not want to admit, I was ready to stop.

"I am a little tired," I admitted.

"Let's cool down before we finish," he said.

"Good idea," I replied.

When I exercised on my own, I used a slower pace.

"It doesn't seem like you're even tired. I hope I didn't ruin it for you."

"Not at all, it's a welcome change to be here with someone." Nat switched to another path. We went back to the car.

"Let's get our lunch," Nat suggested.

"Sounds good to me," I said.

After Nat grabbed our lunch, we headed to find a place to eat.

The aroma of someone's barbeque filled the air.

"Let's follow the aroma," he said. Nat took a deep breath. "The fire reminds me of Maine and my favorite place to camp." He closed his eyes and pulled the sleeves on his jacket up. "There's a hidden grove on a highway that my buddies and I found when we drove up one weekend. It's the best place to pitch a tent and lay back and relax. Our camp would be the only one within miles," he said. "There's not much tourism in that part of Maine. You can build a fire, grab your guitar, and play all night if you felt like it." I listened to him reminisce, and wished I could have been there with him. We found a bench in a quiet area. Nat opened the cooler and took out the food.

"I'm sorry I didn't ask you what you liked so I bought one of each." Nat handed me an iced tea.

"Is this okay?"

"Yes, it's fine."

Nat watched as I sipped my drink.

I glanced around, and admired the setting. The park was clean and welcoming. The mature trees gave us enough shade to enjoy our lunch without squinting. It was bright and sunny that afternoon. I couldn't have asked for a better day. I remembered Nat's invitation to his house the following day, and I gained a sense of security that was new to me. Anyway, the Saturday afternoon get together was supposed to be our preview date. The next day was officially our first date, as he told me earlier. Maybe he thought I would change my mind. There was no way I would do that. I looked forward to another day together. I could be myself around Nat and no matter what I said or I did, he seemed to understand me.

Nat reached across the table for a napkin. "Does the menu meet your qualifications, Chef Madeline? I mean, would it pass your taste test?" he asked.

"Now, let me see, the texture is perfect, the mixture of seasoning is blended superbly. Yes, it is absolutely delicious. A grand luncheon for two I would say." I held the sandwich up and looked it over before I took the next bite.

I felt like I was on top of the world. At that moment, I knew what my mother meant. Her motto about the right time to find someone who would fit into your life suddenly made sense to me. She told me it would happen when I least expected it. I did not think it would take until I was in my forties. Nevertheless, it was finally clear to me. After lunch, we said our goodbye's and I felt happier than I had in a long time.

❦

I didn't sleep well, in anticipation of the next day. To allow myself plenty of time, I got up early to make an attempt look my best. I had to tell myself that it was not my imagination, and I really made the first move.

After I freshened up, I decided to take an early morning stroll by myself. It gave me a chance to clear my mind before I started the day. The streets were peaceful, as the wind swept across my face. I felt more confident than ever, and was satisfied with my decision. The neighbors kept their landscapes on the tree-lined streets manicured flawlessly. There were only a few cars on the roads. The day was glorious, and I felt as if the world was a fabulous place. I looked forward to my visit to Nat's house. A home could say so much about a person. I tried to remain calm, and I counted the moments until we met again.

Chapter Fourteen

Madeline

When I returned from my walk, I felt relaxed, and at peace with my decision to call Nat. I rubbed my hands together for warmth. They were cold from the chill in the air, but time outside in the early hours felt good. As I swung open the kitchen door, it surprised me to see Mark at the table. He usually slept in on Saturday.

"What are you doing up so early?" I said. "What do you have planned for today?"

He looked up from his bowl, with his eyes half-closed. "I have to go to the bookstore at the mall, and then I have to study for a final."

"How about you?" he asked.

"I have a date with a man I met at the hospital." I ventured over to the refrigerator and took out the container of half-and-half. I closed my eyes, and hoped my announcement went over well. "I left a chicken in the refrigerator with macaroni salad, and there's dessert in the freezer. That should hold you both over until I get home."

He frowned, and raised his voice. "Oh please, Mom! I hope he's not an idiot like that last guy you dated."

I grabbed a cup of coffee, and sat down next to him. His response upset me. "Don't jump to conclusions. I really think you'll like him."

"Yeah, sure," he said.

"His name is Nat Griffin, and he's a counselor at the hospital. He also operates a contracting business. Mark, he really is a nice person. I think Jeremy will like him. They have a lot in common. He lifts weights and owns a boat. You know how much Jeremy loves fishing."

Jeremy trotted up from the basement, where he lifted weights. "What's going on? Did I hear my name mentioned?"

"Do you want me to make you a special breakfast?" I asked.

"What's so special about today?" he asked as he gave me a suspicious glare.

Mark filled him in while he continued to munch on his cereal. "Mom has a date with a guy from the hospital. Don't be too hard on her. He sounds like a cool guy."

Jeremy admired his biceps in the mirror in the powder room. "He better treat you right, Mom, or else he has to answer to me!"

"Come on, boys, give me a break. I will bring him over when the time is right, and you can see for yourself what kind of man he is," I said. I hoped for a little cooperation. "I know you both care about me. You can trust me on this one. I'm positive you'll both really like him." I took a bite of a muffin and tried to remain optimistic.

"Okay, have fun today, you deserve it," Mark said.

"I guess I'll give him a chance. Have fun, but, I'll keep my eye on him," Jeremy declared, as he wiped his face with a towel.

I looked up and exhaled. "Thanks, guys."

With my nerves on edge, I pulled up in his driveway. An oversized wooden gate swung open.

Nat strutted from around the fence, and he wore a big grin.

His grey-blue eyes sparkled in the sunlight. He was dressed stylish in a sporty dark blue shirt, with a pair of tan chinos. Nat's skin was still tan from the summer months. The small lines around his eyes made him look like he had been around, but you could not tell his age by the way he carried himself. Nat held out his hand, to guide me out of the car.

What a sweet gesture.

"Did you have any trouble finding the place?" he asked with his eyes fixed on me.

I liked the way his words were soft and alluring. "No, not at all, your directions were simple to follow." I stood on the lawn, and took a quick look the property. I admired the way he restored the house. "Your place is beautiful."

The colors he chose captured all the style from the days when families had their homes painted in beautiful rich shades.

"Is it from the Victorian era?" I inquired.

Nat pointed to the top of the house. "No, see the lines of the roof? This is one of the first Colonial homes in this area. It was built in the early 1920's," he answered, as he led the way to the front door. "Come inside, I'll show you around."

The house had all the charm and character I loved about older homes. As we entered, I heard a pleasant sound. There was angelic music on the stereo, and as I continued through the foyer, the scent of musk candles filled the air.

"You have to excuse the mess. I'm still not totally unpacked." He followed behind me, while I looked around. Nat eagerly gave me a tour of his new home. He escorted me through each area downstairs first. He turned out to be a gracious host.

There were a few tools scattered around, but the place was divine. The house had a huge staircase with mahogany details. In the living area there was a large window box filled with colorful pillows. The hallway had gorgeous stained glass windows. There were beamed ceilings, with custom built in cabinets in the dining room. The family room had a huge picture window that gave you a view of the backyard. The main room was warm and tastefully decorated. A colorful area rug sat in the middle, complimented by a green sofa surrounded by accents in shades of blue. The best part of the room was a unique limestone, marble fireplace.

"Come with me upstairs. I want to show you my next big project," he said as his eyes lit up.

We climbed a steep staircase to the unfinished attic. The musty old smell reminded me of my grandmother's house.

"Here's where my master bedroom will be," he announced. Nat grinned like a boy who just got a puppy. We stood side by side in the huge attic. Nat moved closer to me, as he put his arm around my shoulder.

In the center, there was an antique rocker with a torn gold velvet seat. I made my way over to feel the fabric.

Nat's tone lowered to a whisper. He looked over his shoulder, as if someone might be in the room. He kept his tone soft. "This old chair was here when I moved in. It must be over one hundred years old. I sometimes think it moves by itself, especially at night. I can hear it creak up here, when the house is quiet," he revealed.

I inched closer. "Do you think the house is haunted?" I asked. My heart sped up as I listened to him speak.

"It may just be. Sometimes at night I can smell cigar smoke when I sit in the recliner to watch television." Nat came closer and whispered, "I found an old pipe and tobacco in the basement. It must have belonged to the original owners. It was inside an old icebox I found tucked away in a tiny room, set off to the side."

As I made my way across the attic, I tried to take light, easy steps. He was right; the floor beneath me did make creepy sounds.

"Isn't this room great? I can't wait to start the renovation," he said. He lifted his arms up.

I let my imagination go wild, and tried to read his mind. A fantasy took hold of me, and I imagined Nat as he thought how lovely Madeline looks today. I'm so glad I found this wonderful woman, and I really didn't expect to like her this much. Since I met her, I cannot get her out of my mind.

As I recovered from my moment of deep thought, I turned around. "Nat, I love your idea." I joined my hands together. "This room will be spectacular," I agreed.

Nat sounded eager to explain his plans to me. "Over here is where I will place the bed underneath the windows, and there is where I can make a walk-in closet." He pointed out each detail with absolute pleasure. Nat spoke so fast he barely took a breath between sentences. I felt like I was already involved in the plan for his bedroom.

When he moved toward the front of the house, he motioned with both arms. "I want to make an area for a settee and chair by the window." Nat turned to face a tiny alcove in the corner. "There's where I can put a stereo and maybe another fireplace in the center."

His ideas sounded fabulous. As I took a quick step, my thigh hit up against the edge of an end table. I turned to straighten it, and an odd shaped object caught my eye. Up against a back wall, there was a large pile, covered with a drop cloth. "What's over there?" I asked.

Nat turned in a hurry. "There a bunch of old paintings I want to get rid of. I plan to donate them to the shelter."

"I love old paintings. Can I see them?" I started toward them.

Nat's eyes opened. "You wouldn't like them," he replied in a louder tone.

His response took me by surprise, but I accepted his answer. I did not want to intrude on his privacy.

"Come on let's get started. I can't wait to get my car on the open road."

Nat lead the way downstairs. I stared at the back of his neck while we made our way toward the main level. I developed a strong physical attraction to him, and I anticipated what he had in store for the day. My legs felt heavy, and it seemed like I walked on air. There was a definite parallel between us, and I knew it was more than friendship.

"I thought it would be fun to take a ride to the Orchards in

Colts Neck."

"I planned to go there, but never did. I've heard it's really beautiful." I replied. I fastened my seatbelt.

I would have taken a ride anywhere as long as we were together. Once we were on the road, I pushed the seat back and stretched my legs out. The drive on the country roads was beautiful, with herds of horses and cows grazing in the fields. The trees had vibrant colored leaves. The sky was clear, and the sun was still bright. Nat seemed so upbeat and savvy. It was a perfect day for a ride in the country. I felt alive and happy.

"The scenery makes me want to take a trip to a National Park, or somewhere in New England," Nat said. The window was open on his side open, and his arm rested against it while he drove. He took a deep breath of the fresh rural air.

"I used to pack up for a weekend, and take a ride to the White Mountains in New Hampshire. My friends and I made it all the way up Mount Washington," he said.

"Sounds fun," I replied, eager to hear more.

"The summit is over 6,200 feet. On our most recent trip, I road my motorcycle all the way to the top," he disclosed.

"I don't think I would have been able to take a ride up that high." I admitted.

Nat wore a happy expression, and snuck a side glance at me from time to time, as he drove.

"The view from the summit is incredible. It's like being on top of the world," he said.

He griped on tight to the steering wheel, and he straightened his arms while he continued his stories. "I remember one trip I took with my friend Neil. We camped out in a tent, and it started to rain. I had to sleep with my hand outside in a puddle. I wanted to see if it would freeze. If it did, I knew we would have to hurry down the trail. It would have been too dangerous if ice formed."

Nat sounded so happy to recall his adventures.

"I went camping, and slept in a tent when I was in girl scouts, but I was terrified," I declared. "At night, we would sit around the fire telling scary stories. By the time we tried to go to sleep, we all gathered together with a huge flashlight in front of us. It was cold and dark, with bugs everywhere. I would jump up, with every little sound I heard outside the tent."

Nat placed his hand on my leg, and gently patted it.

"Don't worry, I'll take you with me, and you'll love it. I promise the bears are friendly," he teased.

"What do you mean, bears?"

"I won't let them hurt you," he assured me.

"You're funny," I said.

He looked at me out of the corner of his eye, and his voice lowered to a whisper. "We're almost there," he said.

I thought there might be a third or fourth date in the future. I put my head back on the headrest, and stared out the window. My mind wandered to a place where I was content and serene. My heart filled with emotions and longing. The man I dreamt about was next to me, and he was amazing.

Why did I really volunteer on the unit? Was I in the right place at the right time? Why did I walk into his lecture? Whatever the reason, I would continue the path I somehow fell into and let it all happen. My thoughts overflowed with what would happen next.

The store in front of the huge orchard tempted me with eye-catching displays. There were layers of fruit in abundance, lined up in front of the store. The separate bakery area in back had a glass case filled with delicious looking treats. A section where you could sit and have a beverage or a dessert caught my eye. Several picnic tables, some round, and the rest rectangle, were arranged in a corner area. Red and white-checkered table clothes added a country feel. We strolled through a small shop. Inside they sold hand designed items, candles, and homemade jams and jellies. I picked up a warm vanilla sugar candle, and raised it to sample the scent. When I handed it to Nat, he nodded and agreed on its strong appeal.

"Do you want to grab a coffee and try a piece of that apple pie in the showcase?" Nat asked, as he accompanied me toward the tables. He opened his mouth as if he wanted to sample a slice.

"You convinced me." The aromas of the fresh baked treats encircled my senses.

The temperature dropped as we approached the tables in the back. The one we chose faced an area that was filled with apple trees and pumpkin patches. I folded my arms in front of me.

"It looks like you're cold," he said as he took off his blazer. Nat placed his jacket around my shoulders.

"Thanks, that feels much better." I was impressed with his thoughtfulness.

"I'm still shocked over the fact that you're the mother of three grown children," he said. Nat picked up the tray with our treats. He continued to stare at me while I sat down at a table in the snack area.

"My mother's going to be moving in with us tomorrow. She's been at my sister's house for a few years, and she's a little forgetful, but still very dear to me."

"That's really nice," Nat said softly. "Sounds like you have your hands full, especially with your hours at the restaurant and your volunteer work."

It seemed like he understood me—unlike the men I dated in the past.

"The boys promised to pitch in and take turns with her day care schedule. My sons get along great with their grandma. They've been close with her all their lives." I hoped all the chatter about family would not frighten him away.

"I'm glad I made the decision to have my mother move in with us. She has her limitations with the dementia, but she has a good nature and so much courage. After she survived 'The Great Depression,' you gain strength of character, I suppose."

"I bet it will work out great for you, since you have help at home," Nat said. He placed his hands around his cup.

"She reminds me what's really important," I said. "I mean like family and friends, and the choice to help others. Family unity is her motto in life."

Nat sat across from me, and he watched my every move. He gently touched my hand across the table.

"That's really thoughtful of you to take care of your mother. I know it will be a sacrifice, but she took care of you and now you'll be her caregiver."

He cleared his throat.

"My mother thought about putting my father in a nursing home, when he became very ill. We really didn't want to do it. It turned out we didn't have to make that decision, because he died before we could arrange for it."

His eyes shifted to the ground.

I paused and took a breath. "That's a very difficult decision to make. I don't know what I would do, if I didn't have my family to support me." *This man is so considerate and attentive.* I hesitated to bring up the subject.

"Do you mind if I ask you a personal question?"

"Go ahead ask," he said. His cheeks changed to a ruby color.

"How did you manage to stay single?"

"I get that question all the time." Nat shifted around in his seat before he answered. "There was a time when I thought about marriage, but it didn't work out. It was lucky for me, because she had a ton of problems and was confused about life. I've been so busy with my business and the days I spend at the hospital, that I guess time just flew by."

He continued in a serious tone. His eyes held an intensity that deeply moved me.

"I'm kind of set in my ways and accustomed to living alone."

I was afraid that I hit on a sore topic, and thought I had better not pursue it any further. I quickly pushed his statement right out of my mind. I pretended I never heard it.

We finished our coffee and pie and got up to take a walk through the incredible orchard. The bright blue sky was amazingly clear. Birds chirped and flew through the trees. The beauty of our surroundings transported me into an enchanted place. We took small slow steps as we continued to share our thoughts.

"What happened to your husband?" Nat inquired.

"He became overwhelmed with the responsibilities of a wife and family," I said. "He left us when the kids were young, and he died suddenly a short time later. I never got the whole story from his family." I hoped I didn't bore him. "It was very sad; we were both very young. I'm glad that we spent that time together. I have my children now, and I can't imagine my life without them."

"I guess you went through a lot of drama with your ex," he said. Nat put his hands in his pockets. "It probably turned you off towards men, for a while."

I waited a moment and decided to be honest. "I dated a man named Jon for a few years when Jeremy was young. Desiree and Mark never really connected with Jon. Although Jeremy was crazy about him. They were very close, and he was sad when he disappeared," I said.

"It's a lot harder when you have a family. Some of my clients have trouble with their kids when they date. That's a whole different ball game."

"Unfortunately, since Jon left, Jeremy's had a hard time in school. I know he misses Jon, but he never admits it. He wouldn't open up to the therapist, and insisted he was fine."

"That's too bad. It must have been a difficult time for you."

"I've tried to be patient with him. I know a teenage boy has it tough enough. The older two did well in the sessions. Jeremy, I don't know."

I shifted my eyes away from his, while I delved into the touchy subject. My children meant the world to me, and I usually keep problems to myself.

"I had a lot of hard times when my Dad was drinking. I knew he was there for me," he said, in a serious tone. "Sure, there was a lot chaos in my house. It would have been hard if my Mother had to raise me alone. Are your kids close with your father?" he asked.

"They were close with him, but he passed away. Jeremy was

a little boy when he died."

"I'm sorry to hear that," he said. Nat's kindness was evident when he spoke. That was a quality I admired most in a man.

"Would you like to take a ride to a restaurant in town and have dinner?" Nat asked, as he stood close to me. "It's a nice ride. I know the chef will live up to your expectations, he's dynamite. The restaurant's name is The Scenic Inn, and the view from the dining room is the best. The menu is American cuisine, and the steaks are fantastic."

"It sounds perfect."

His shoulder brushed up against mine, as we moved toward the parking lot. I silently yearned to feel the touch of his body against mine. Never in my life had I experienced such a longing.

"Thanks for a great day." I placed my arm through his as we walked side by side.

He opened the car door for me. "Come on, I'm hungry. The pie was a tease," he said as he waited for me to get inside.

Nat's statement about living alone concerned me, and I tried to force it out of my mind. We had a great time together, and I was sure he had a physical attraction to me. It was obvious in the way he looked at me. Nat adjusted the radio in his car to a soft listening station. The music added a romantic touch for the ride to the restaurant. This time, a string version of *The Titanic* theme played and I felt as if I never wanted the night to end.

We sat next to a brick fireplace at a cozy table for two. The other patrons seemed to disappear while we focused on one another. A huge ceiling to floor window gave us a sunset view. Our date could not have been better. It was perfect. We ordered shrimp cocktails to start with a bottle of sparkling water. Nat suggested the New York strip steak. It came with mushroom gravy that made it melt in your mouth. The meal was basic, and it was scrumptious. We continued to discuss our views on the world as if we knew each other for years. There was a proverbial feel to our relationship. "I love the painting over there," I said. Above the fireplace, there was a painting of a Victorian woman on the beach. She stood at the water's edge, held one hand up to her hat, and she wore a long flowing white shirt. It made me want to escape to a time long gone.

"The colors are vibrant," Nat said.

"It makes the ocean look so real," I returned.

"Nat, do you have any brothers or sisters?" I asked, innocently.

"No, I don't," he replied, quickly, as he rolled up his napkin.

Nat confided in me about his mother's miscarriages after he was born and told me she regretted the fact that she could not have any more children. It puzzled me when he appeared upset and a flustered when he talked about his mother. He tried to dodge the topic of his family as if it were taboo. I was not sure what to make of it, but I sensed a conflict in the tone of his voice. I saw a side of him that was guarded. The topic of his childhood seemed to rattle Nat. The few memories he shared seemed like happy ones. I sensed that a part of it was also very painful. It obviously disturbed Nat to speak about his early days as a child. The frightened look in his eyes puzzled me. I was afraid he hid the truth about his family from me. Behind his carefree manner, there was a darker side, especially when he spoke of his parents. I left it alone, and waited for him to open up to me, if he ever felt the need.

The whole experience had a sense of kismet. The date turned out better than my wildest dreams. The relaxed way he gave me a tour of his home, started the day perfectly. Our walk through the orchard was romantic, and I loved it. To top it off, we had a great time at dinner. It all simply felt right, and I couldn't have been happier.

We left the restaurant and headed back to his house. We continued to enjoy the easy listening music on the radio. Nat parked the car and turned off the car radio. I thought we would say goodnight at the door. Nat and I had spent the last two days together, and gotten to know one another much better. Somehow, I felt like I already knew him, when we first met.

"Come inside for a while. It's still early," he said in an optimistic tone.

I gazed into his eyes, and could not resist the temptation. The look in his eye was one of desire.

"Sure, I can stay for a little while." As I accepted his invitation, I gave him a flirtatious smile. Nat made his way over to my side, and I quickly searched deep down in my purse for a mint. I popped it in my mouth while he opened the door. He led the way inside his house.

"Make yourself comfortable," Nat said. He walked over to the stereo. "What would you like to hear?"

I joined him next to the entertainment center. There were rows of all types of music neatly stacked. I bent down to look at the ones on the bottom. The same tune I'd heard everywhere, was the first one in the pile I picked up. *Does this song have any significance?* Then when I stood up, my leg touched his. An excitement mounted inside of me when our bodies touched. As I handed it to him, my pulse increased.

"This is one of my favorites," Nat said, in a soft seductive tone.

The day was about to end, and so far, it had been unbelievable. I felt at ease and relaxed in Nat's company. I sat down on the sofa and realized what might happen next. As I closed my eyes, I sunk into the plush velvety sofa. My mind drifted, while I listened to the melody. A warm sense of familiarity enabled me to enjoy the moment. Nat got up to dim the lights and placed a few candles on the mantle. The fireplace had gorgeous gold details around the marble, which added an extra hint of drama to the room. Nat returned and moved close to me. He looked into my eyes provocatively and gently placed his arms around me. Before I could react, he pulled me up against his chest. Our lips met in a kiss that sparked all the desires of a lifetime. It seemed to last forever as we embraced. I gave in to the temptation. While we remained in each other's arms, I felt his heart race. The warmth of his body heat tantalized my senses, and I felt the strength of his back muscles as he held me close. Nat placed my head on his shoulder, and kept his arms around me. The sound of our breathing meshed together as one. It seemed as if time stood stopped, yet an hour had passed.

He whispered to me softly. "Let's go to the second level balcony. I want you to see where I meditate. I think you'll love the view."

Nat took my hand, put out the candles, and slowly led me upstairs. He told me to close my eyes and guided me outside.

"Okay, open your eyes now." He gently moved my shoulders and faced me in the right direction.

In front of me was picturesque scenery, with trees as far as the eye could see. It was lovely and the stars sparkled in the sky above us. "It's amazing up here," I said. Vintage lampposts in the corners gave an ambience of romance. Trees with auburn tipped leaves mixed with tones of yellow and brown surrounded the area. Tiny lights sparkled in between the winding trails. The peaceful sound of a fountain trickled gracefully in the background. It was a magical garden.

"I come up here to relax and just breathe," he said.

"Oh, Nat, this is amazing."

He turned on the stereo upstairs. Before I could realize it, we were slow dancing. Nat gently placed his arms around me and held his cheek next to mine. We danced under the stars, as our bodies connected on every beat.

We finally managed to go back inside, where Nat tenderly laid me on his four-poster bed. We became lost in the natural instinct of our bodies that evening. I closed my eyes, and felt more sensual than I had in years.

Nat kissed me passionately, and ran his hands gently across my back and down to my thighs. He held his body against mine as if he knew this is where he belonged. When Nat ran his tongue across my chest with a swift motion, it caused a burning desire to feel him deep inside of me. He moved on top of me, and my emotions climbed to a peak. Nat was so gentle, as he made love to me, over and over again. We spent the night wrapped in each other's arms, our skin moist and hot. I had waited for what seemed like an eternity for a man like Nat.

As we lay next to one another in the early morning hours, I breathed a contented sigh. Nat tenderly stroked my hair with a tenderness that captured my heart. He caressed my back and I turned to face him. I stared into his eyes.

"I must have fallen asleep. What time is it?" I cleared my throat.

He kissed me gently on the forehead and glanced over to the alarm clock. He cradled my face in his hands.

"It's three a.m.," he said.

"I really don't want to leave, but I have to get home. I have so much to do to get ready for Mother tomorrow. Do you remember I told you, my Mother is moving in with us tomorrow?"

"Of course I do." Nat pulled me close to him. "I hate to see you drive home at this hour," he whispered in my ear. "Stay here tonight, and I promise to get you up in time. I'll even help you."

"I don't want to impose on your day off," I answered. I put my head on his shoulder.

He gently squeezed my arm. "I have no plans, and I'm glad to help, I insist."

Nat was so accommodating. Everything happened so fast. It all seemed too good to be true. I finally found a man who accepted me for who I was, and even agreed to help me move my mother into my house. I was exhausted, so I agreed to stay. Nat tightened his arms around me. He cuddled up against me, and we drifted back to sleep.

When I opened my eyes in the morning, Nat was already out of bed and downstairs. I could smell the freshly brewed coffee. There was an amazing surprise for me in the bathroom. A beautiful orange rose sat on the sink. Nat had cut a bud from the last few flowers in his yard and placed it in a tiny pill bottle that he used for a vase. A note sat underneath, and it read, "Just Because." As I closed the door, his thoughtfulness brought tears to my eyes. I began to realize what a treasure I found in Nat. He followed me to my house.

Chapter Fifteen

Madeline

"*I*'m glad you're up," I said. I felt a little sneaky. "I have someone I want you to meet. He's here to help us move Grandma in today," I announced.

Mark popped his head from around the sports section and looked surprised with his mouth open. He pushed his back up against the chair. The morning sun beamed in on the table, and made the whole room sparkle. I had a sense of pride for the design, since I picked it myself.

"How's it going?" Nat said. He made the first attempt to gain their friendship. I could tell he was worried that they would not accept his offer of amity. He glanced at his watch and swallowed hard. I studied their expressions and waited for a response. Nat rested his hand on the counter.

The long silent pause made me squirm. Mark finally got up and walked over to Nat. He offered Nat a friendly handshake. My sons were very protective of me, and I wanted to do this at a more appropriate time. Jeremy followed Mark's lead and shook Nat's hand, too. He cracked a leery smile.

"It's nice to meet you," he said, to my amazement.

"Glad to meet you, too," Nat responded. He gave me a wink

of his eye.

After he helped me put on a pot of coffee, Nat sat down at the kitchen table. I believed my sons thought I slept at home, and I tried to keep it that way. I left my bedroom door closed at night, with a small light in the corner. I kept my car in the garage, so I thought they might not have realized I was out. My intention was not to lie, but I felt some events were better unsaid. I didn't want to give them the wrong impression, since they were both skeptical of the men in my life. Inside my mind, I assured myself the evening was quite special. Yes, I knew I slept over. I was a responsible adult, and it just felt right.

"Can I offer you a morning sunshine muffin?" I asked. "They're really delicious, and they're good for you, too. Inside are grated carrots, whole wheat flour, walnuts, golden raisins, and brown sugar."

"Did you make them yourself?" Nat's eyes lit up.

"Yes, I did. They happen to be one of my favorites. Try one." I held the dish in front of him, confident of my original recipe.

I placed a couple of muffins on a plate and got out the variety of jam from the refrigerator. There were four different kinds, orange, strawberry, blackberry, and blueberry, which was my favorite.

He reached for the one in the center and dabbed it with blueberry jam. "This looks great," he said. He took a bite, and before I could sit down, the muffin was gone.

I laughed and placed my hand on my hip. "Would you like another one?"

"Sure, they're the best. I can't wait to try your other recipes," he said. He nodded his head.

Nat had a tiny spot of jam on his chin. I motioned to his face. I pulled off a paper towel from the rack and handed it to him. Nat wiped his face and devoured another muffin. I found this a perfect time to ask him for dinner.

"Do you have any plans tomorrow night?" I asked. "I'll prepare one of my new creations for dinner. It's the least I can do, to repay you for your help."

"I have to work down the shore again tomorrow. I'm about to finish up a job at a house on the water, but I can be here around six," he said without hesitation. "Is that all right with you?"

"That's a deal," I said. I was on cloud nine.

"Mark, will you be home tomorrow night?" I held my breath, and waited for his response. I wanted both of them to accept Nat.

Mark answered with his hands in his pockets. He seemed reluctant at first, but I suppose that's all I could expect. "I have a test next week, and I have a lot of cramming to do." He looked down and cleared his throat. "All right, I guess I can squeeze in an hour to have dinner." He shrugged his shoulders, and managed to show me an accepting grin.

I turned to face Jeremy. "What do you think? Can you can make it?" I waited, and hoped for a positive response.

It had been a long time since we had a man at the head of the table.

Jeremy sat back and rocked the back legs of the kitchen chair. "I'll try to be home."

I detected some resistance from him. That was typical behavior for my youngest son.

"I'll call to see if Desiree is available. I hope she can make it, too. That's settled. Now, let's get Grandma's stuff over here," I asserted.

I left the three of them alone for a few minutes while I changed. I was concerned if the boys sensed I did not sleep at home, and I didn't want them to resent Nat. While I slipped into my jeans, I dialed Anne. I wanted to tell her about my new love.

"Wait until you hear about last night," I said.

"What happened?" she asked.

"I'll fill you in on the details later, but for now, I'll tell you Nat agreed to help us with Grandma's move today."

"How on earth did you manage that?"

"We spent the night together, and it was unbelievable."

"I can't wait to hear about it."

"I have to hurry. He's outside my door."

"Can I tell Mara and Maggie the news?"

"Sure, go ahead," I said.

"I'm so happy for you," she said.

"Thanks, gotta go."

I returned from my room, and it surprised me to see them gathered around the television. They played around like old buddies. The expressions on Mark and Jeremy's faces brightened as they all interacted. The boys never even realized I entered the room. Nat's eyes followed me as I walked past the screen. He motioned for me to sit down next to him.

I placed my hands on my hips. "Come on," I insisted. "We have to get started. There's a lot of work ahead of us."

Nat fit right in with our family. I hoped he felt as happy as I did. Nat impressed me with his distinctive charm.

We planned to spend the entire afternoon on Grandma's move to our house. Bonnie had her stuff, lined up ready to go. Mother was fast asleep in her room when we arrived, and we did not disturb her.

"She got up early, and we let her go inside for a nap," Bonnie said.

Mike and Bonnie got along as if they were still young lovers. He had such a gentle way about him that you could not be mad at him if you tried. Mike cooked dinner almost every night, and even did the laundry. It amazed me how he never complained and supported Bonnie in whatever she did. If you had a problem, he would counsel you, and make you feel like he really cared.

"I know Mike and Nat can handle the bigger items, and we'll take the clothes," I said.

"Let's do it," Mike said.

After the first trip, Nat and I set up her daybed in the corner of my room. I separated the area with a violet screen decorated with gorgeous hand-painted magnolias. I knew it would be perfect for the theme I wanted. The owner of the shop I purchased it from informed me how a wealthy woman from Monmouth County donated it only days ago. The last trip was to pick up Grandma, and a few large items.

Mother was up from her nap when we got back. She sat in the recliner, and her eyes lit up when she saw us.

She sat forward, and held her arms out. "There's my girl."

"I want to introduce you to my friend Nat. He's here to lend a hand today," I said as I reached for his hand.

Mother looked up at him and smiled. She motioned for him to come closer to her.

"I'm happy to meet you, Nat," she said. "Is that short for Nathan or Nathaniel? He's so handsome, and his voice sounds sincere."

I put my arm around her shoulders and gave her a squeeze. Words come from within and despite her forgetfulness, she still had a keen sense for what was right. She didn't remember dates, and appointments anymore, but she still knew who we all were and vividly remembered her younger years. She could tell us details that we'd long forgotten. Her good judgment guided me through many moments in my life, and her integrity made me proud.

Mother continued to chat with Nat, and slipped her arm through his. It was odd to watch the two of them interact. She usually resisted a new person at first. She typically waited until after a few meetings before she opened up, and offered her friendship. Their instant alliance took me by complete surprise.

"What's going on?" I exclaimed.

I could not believe my own eyes. They continued to exchange views, right there in front of me. Mother never opened up so quickly to a total stranger. She was usually reserved with someone she did not know, and I never thought I would witness this revelation. Bonnie would have to see it to believe it. I ran into the kitchen and took her by the hand to witness for herself. The change in character shocked us both. Bonnie put her hand over her mouth.

"Mother has her arm inside of Nat's. I tell you, he must have a quality no one has ever shown her before!" Bonnie exclaimed. "She didn't really start talking much to Mike until after we were married." She watched the two of them as they continued their conversation. Bonnie crossed her arms and rested one hand on her chin.

We put our heads together in bewilderment and whispered to one another. Whatever the connection between the two of them was, it left me speechless. I eventually tapped Nat gently on the shoulder.

"Excuse me. Remember why we're here today, please."

Nat gave a grin, stood up, and took my hand. "Sure, babe, I know we have work to do. I had a nice chat with Katy."

Nat moved in close to me and gave me a quick peck on the forehead.

We moved the rest without delay. Nat helped us on a very important day. I hand wrapped the breakables. I was peacefully satisfied, knowing I was doing the right thing. We worked all afternoon to get it done.

Mother had a beautiful, old-fashioned tiffany lamp that had vibrant blues, golds, and reds on the shade, and a vintage end table with hand painted tiles with roses, on the top. I admired the pieces she received from Grandma's house. Nat dragged a huge barrel to the center of the room. Scrawled across the top were the words, "photos". It took Nat and my brother in-law Mike to carry it downstairs. Mother saved all the albums from the family's history, and cherished each one. The photos all held a special significance to her. She protected the frames with bubble wrap, before placing them inside. One of the best photographers of that era took her favorite one in a studio.

Mother and her sister, Mary, were the only ones who smiled for the camera. Her parents posed with the aunts and uncles, along with their children. The photographer arranged the seating with the younger members in the front.

"Young man, please be especially careful with this one," she said. Mother motioned to the massive crate filled with pages from the past. Her voice rose as she directed the family in the care of her most precious belongings. She held a sentimental value on her prized photos.

When we were finally through, the first one she wanted to unpack was the crate of snapshots. I washed my hands then opened a soda, while I helped her unwrap the items. We placed the smaller ones next to her bed on the dresser.

Mother gloated as she dusted each one individually. She placed the frames meticulously on the Irish linen cloth that was on top of the chest of drawers. Her favorite portrait was the black and white one.

I noticed a nail I missed when we spackled the walls. It seemed like the perfect spot, so I hung the portrait of her family above her mirror. It was quite unknown to both of us at the time, the impact the mystical photo would hold for us, and how it would affect our future.

After we settled Mother in, Nat and I sat down to grab a quick snack. Mother fell asleep in the bedroom chair along with her favorite doll. It was hilarious to see her cuddled up with a pair of oversized headphones on her head.

Mark and Jeremy put in a hard day's work, so I rewarded them with money for a pizza, and the movies. They both looked exhausted. I knew they needed to have some fun. Mark and Jeremy had worked all day and deserved time off. Nat and I were happy to have some time alone. I opened up the refrigerator and took out the cheese and pepperoni, along with wheat crackers from the basket on top of the counter. We gobbled them up in a few minutes. We were so busy, we never had lunch.

I nestled close to Nat, and felt warm and appreciated.

"Did you notice how impressed my mother was with you?" I

placed my hand on his thigh. "Mother has a lovable nature and has gone out of her way to open her home and heart too many families in her lifetime," I said. "But, she's a bit shy at first. She usually warms up after a while. I think it's from her upbringing. Her parents instructed her to remain quiet. A proper young lady does not share her thoughts with a stranger. It usually takes time before people earn her trust."

Nat turned his head to the side, and squinted. He yawned as he munched on the snacks. "Well, I guess she really liked me because she went on and on," he said. "I must admit I felt like I met her before." He stood up. "She is certainly a character. I really like her," he admitted.

We carried our plates to the living room, and sat down again on the loveseat.

Mother remained fast asleep in the bedroom. Nat put his arm around me, and gave me a light nuzzle.

"Babe, do you want to order out for dinner tonight?"

"Yeah, that sounds great," I answered, pleased with his offer.

We decided to order Asian takeout. Nat chased me around the kitchen, as I searched for the menus. When our order arrived, Nat and I took it into the family room. The soft glow from the television, gave us just enough light to gaze into one another's eyes. By eleven, we were ready to get a peaceful night's sleep. We said our goodnights at the door. The end to a long and busy day was finally upon me. It was long, but certainly one to remember.

I felt completely refreshed and full of energy the next morning. I could not wait to prepare for my dinner party. Desiree agreed to come early, and stop at the bakery to pick up fresh baked bread. I decided to make pork tenderloin stuffed with pears and cranberries, an apple cake with a dollop of vanilla ice cream, and a caramel drizzle on top.

Mom slept while I showered and dressed. I set out her

clothes for the day, alongside her bed. The senior center planned a special outing to an art exhibit that day. The director of the center assured me that structure, and routine was beneficial for the elderly.

"Did you have a good night's sleep?" I asked when I noticed her eyes were open.

Mother poked her head out from under the quilt, and she looked like a little girl. Her hair was messy and her expression curious. She pulled the covers up to her chest.

"Where's Mary? She was lying next to me."

"Hurry, Mother. Today's your big day." I turned my back and held my breath. *Here we go again.*

"What is it?"

"You have a trip planned today. The bus driver will be here at nine sharp, and he'll drop you off later in the afternoon. You'll meet plenty of new friends at the day care center. They even have a piano that you can play." I tucked in the corners of the sheet on my bed, while I continued the explanation of her new routine.

"I better get ready. I don't want to be late," she said. She quickly sat up and moved to the side of the bed.

"Will you be home later when I get back?" she asked wide-eyed. She seemed a nervous as she fumbled with her slippers. Mom grasped onto the top of her night jacket. There was a faraway look in her eyes.

"Yes, I'll be home. I invited everyone over for a dinner party tonight, and I'll be here when you get back," I said.

Mom gave me a big smile. "Is it a birthday party?" she asked.

"Not this time, but I invited Nat. Do you remember the man who helped us yesterday?

She waved her hand in front of me. "I remember Nathaniel. Wasn't he the handsome fellow I met yesterday?" Her eyes began to sparkle as soon as she mentioned his name. "What a nice young man, and he really likes you, Madeline. You can't fool me," she said.

She held on tightly to her locket, and gave me a smug grin. I took her by the hand, and led her toward the bathroom.

"I can hardly wait to meet my new friends." She slipped her arm through mine. She stopped to look at the photo of Dad on the dresser. She picked up the frame and gave it a light kiss.

There were times I felt like I had become the mother, and she was my child. I knew she was forgetful at times, but when I least expected it she gives the best advice. Maybe it's intuition, because as I helped her with her shoes, I touched my chest.

"What's wrong? Are you ill? Sit down for a minute and rest. There's no hurry," she said in a concerned tone." She stepped next to me, and placed her hands on my shoulders. "I'll make you a tonic. I have all the fixings in my bag." She pointed to a bag at the foot of her bed.

I looked up at her and gave a sigh. She spoke the concerned words of a mother and for a moment, she was still there for me.

The bond between mother and child is the strongest union I've ever seen. I learned through my own children that there is no greater love than that of a mother. She will stand by your side, and never give up on you. She views you as the most unique being on earth. A mother's love shows in all she does for you. Even then, her love was evident in her voice whenever she spoke. I was still her youngest child and she would continue to guide me until she took her last breath. Her words continue to linger in my mind, "You'll find love when you least expect it."

"All right, Mom, I'll take a moment and have breakfast with you."

We sat down together, at the kitchen table. We chatted while we ate. I felt blessed to be able to share her knowledge and enjoy the whimsical charm she managed to exude. It warmed my heart to hear the stories of her life. It was pleasurable to hear her tales as she spoke of her life as a young woman. She was able to enjoy a life filled with simply pleasures. Mom had forgotten how to worry or obsess. Mother would become lost in the beauty of a bird's song, or when she ate an ice cream cone down to the last drop. She already taught me how to stay in the moment and enjoy small wonders.

While we waited by the front door, my mind wandered to the night I spent with Nat. The bus arrived on time, and I escorted Mother to her seat. The vehicle had soft, cushioned seats. The pastel colors on the inside went perfectly with the bright blue exterior. I admired Mother's cheerful demeanor, and as the bus pulled away, for an instant, I thought to myself, I *think I'm in love.*

My concerns about Nat's ability to share his life with me became stronger, and I couldn't quite explain why. I had a feeling that I may have attempted another rescue of a man that was unavailable to give his heart. My track record of bad relationships made an impact on my life, and I knew it halted my emotional growth and stifled my creativity. *This time would be different.* In the past, I wasted so many days, years, and hours, as I waited for someone to change. I had a list of qualities the man I spend my life with should possess. My parents urged me to believe in myself and put myself first, but I had to learn for myself.

I'd been resistant to their messages in the past. Instead, I held onto the decision to the belief in the power to change another. The men I chose were flawed. I thought I could enhance their lives. It would upset me when I failed. My instincts told me Nat would be different.

Chapter Sixteen

Nathaniel

*T*he day started out hectic, when the customer wanted them to change the paint colors, and Nat didn't think he would make it to Madeline's house on time. The middle aged couple bought a vacation home in Ortley Beach, and the wife could not make up her mind. Nat wished he'd get a place in the area one day, so he would be able to take his boat out more often.

Luckily, he was able to get two extra workers from the union hall to make the deadline. He looked forward to another night with Madeline. He worried about meeting her daughter, but knew if she was as warm as Madeline, there would be no problem. Nat usually did not take women home with him, or sleep with them so early in the relationship. This time, he could not help himself. The strong attraction to her weakened his self-control, and he did not regret it. There was a deeper connection with this woman, and he knew she was not someone to take for granted. He realized she had been through enough with the men in her past. After their walk through the orchard, he had learned a lot about Madeline. Nat never thought he would open up to a stranger, or be able to understand the emotions he experienced. It did scare him, and he tried to push his negative thoughts out of his mind. He lit a cigarette, and took a puff, as he put the blueprints in the glove compartment of his truck. After Nat wiped his forehead with a hanky, he walked inside to see the progress.

"Boss, I think we're done," Geraldo said. He folded the drop cloths and gathered the tools. Nat checked over the place and nodded.

"Great job," he said. "Come on, let's get out of here."

The workers piled into the box truck with Geraldo at the wheel, and Nat in his pickup.

When he stopped for a pack of cigarettes at a small deli, he passed a quaint little gift shop. He stood in front of the window, and he wondered why the painting in the display looked so familiar. Then he remembered. It was a replica of the painting at the Scenic Inn. Madeline raved over it, the night he took her there for dinner. Nat opened the screen door and stepped inside. There were assorted items on shelves with lace doilies. A shelf with colorful teacups sat in the corner, and a dresser with the drawers half-open held fancy linens. Nat would have never browsed through such a feminine store if he hadn't spotted the painting. An elderly woman with white hair, and a friendly smile approached him.

"Isn't she marvelous?" she asked. She ran her slender hand over the frame. There's a magical quality about the Victorian era, and the sea."

He gave a quick nod. "I'll take it."

"Is it a gift? I can wrap it for you," she offered.

"If it's no problem, I'd like it wrapped."

The woman used shiny gold paper and topped it with a glittery bow. After she gave him his change, she carried it around the counter. "I hope she likes it," she said.

"Oh, she will. Thank you, and have a nice day."

He hopped into the truck and headed home. Nat could not

wait to give it to Madeline. When he arrived in town, he started to get jittery. Not only would he be at a dinner party with the woman he made love to, but her family would be there to check him out. He loosened his collar and opened the refrigerator. After he took a cold drink of iced tea, he went upstairs to shower and dress. Nat did not want to be late.

Madeline

It took all day to prepare for my dinner party, and I prayed my family would welcome Nat. I arranged the accent pieces until the house was just perfect. I added beautiful bouquets of colorful mums, in various crystal vases, along with daisies that I purchased at the farmers market. I placed the burgundy ones on the dining room table, and the yellow and white in the living room.

The boys arrived home early, and I handed them two large bags of garbage to carry outside. Later, Mark waited for Grandma's bus, and Jeremy made an attempt to open his math book. The doorbell sounded, and I hurried to answer it.

"I left my key at home. Am I too early?" Desiree balanced her purse, and two bakery bags, filled with dinner rolls.

"You're right on time, and I could use your help. I'm glad it's you, and not Nat. I don't want him to see me yet. I was just about to change out of my sweat pants," I said. Desiree always wanted me to meet a good man. I knew it was not easy to grow up without a father.

"I can hardly wait to meet him," she said. Desiree hurried into the kitchen. "The dinner smells great. What's for dessert?" She peeked in the oven, and poked around in the refrigerator.

"I made a new recipe. It's an apple cake with walnuts, and cinnamon. There are six granny smith apples inside," I said. I hoped it would be delicious.

"Nat will probably ask you to marry him after he tastes the

way you cook," she offered. She gave me a nudge. Desiree's mood was jovial. I could not resist, and I giggled along with her. I knew she worried about me and did not want me to grow older alone.

"Let's have fun tonight, and see what happens. I don't want to scare him away," I said, in a serious tone.

"I know what you mean, but I can tell you're already crazy about him, and it's about time you found someone special." She grabbed my hand. Her eyes held a sparkle while her voice rose with enthusiasm.

I pinched her gently on the arm, and handed her the china. "Help me set the table, while I finish dinner," I said.

The night held a special meaning for me. It held all the mystery of a new love, and I was happy for the opportunity to have all the people I cared about together to share it with me. I closed my eyes and wished for a wonderful night.

My closet looked like a hurricane hit it, as I tore it apart, in search of an outfit I fit into. Way in the back, I had a few larger sizes stuffed in-between. Luckily, I saved them. I made a note to either buy larger sizes, or end my obsession with chocolate. When I finished my make-up and hair, I sat down on the edge of my bed for a moment, before I went out to check the roast. Bonnie and Mike arrived while I dressed, and helped Desiree set the table.

My handsome new love arrived on time. He had a large wrapped item in his hand. His fitted navy blue sports jacket made him look distinguished. It was matched with a pale blue shirt, and charcoal pants. I welcomed him inside, and I placed my arm through his.

"You look exquisite tonight," Nat said. He lightly brushed his lips on my cheek.

"Thanks, you look very nice, too." I could not take my eyes off of him.

"Nat, I want you to meet my daughter, Desiree."

She sashayed over to him, and it made me happy when she gave him a welcoming hug.

"It's very nice to meet you. Mom has told me a lot about you," she said. Her eyes let me know she approved.

He grinned and set the box on the side table, next to the couch. I wondered what was inside the mysterious package, but I thought it was better if I waited for him to offer an explanation, since it was probably a gift for me, I assumed. I think once the shock of everyone at once wore off, he began to loosen up.

"It is great to finally meet you," he offered, with a smile.

Nat and Desiree moved toward the couch, and immediately struck up a conversation. The two of them continued to chat, while I put the final additions on the meal. Before long, Mark and Jeremy joined in the discussion.

"How many days do you work at the hospital?" Desiree asked. She sat forward.

"I work on the unit two nights a week, and whenever they need me I'm on call," Nat said. He seemed eager to answer. "I run a building company, full-time. I juggle the two jobs pretty well. I'm used to it." Nat sat back, and crossed his legs.

I had faith in Desiree to set him at ease. "Sounds like you're a pretty busy guy," she said. Desiree was comfortable meeting new people. She kept her tone calm and confident.

"I've held two jobs ever since I was a kid. I traveled a lot, and I needed money. I would work in every state I landed in, at the time," he said.

"You must have a lot of good times while you visited other places." Desiree said. "I love to travel," she admitted. "I especially enjoy the scenic routes. Did Mom tell you I recently spent a week in Wyoming?"

"Yes, she did." Nat's eyes opened as if the topic really held his interest.

"I tell you, I've never seen such a beautiful land."

"Did you visit Yellowstone Park?" Nat asked. He reached for a cracker.

"I stayed in a cabin outside the park," she replied, while she tucked her hair behind her ear. "I enjoyed it so much, I actually wanted to pack up and move there."

It felt good to see how the two of hit it off.

"There are a lot of great places in the United States," Nat said. "I'd be great to take off, and travel the countryside in a motor home. It'd be neat to escape from the daily hassles."

"I know a couple who retired, sold their house, bought a camper, and traveled from state to state," Desiree said.

Nat raised his hands up." That's the way to go."

"I think it takes guts to make a spontaneous decision like that one," she admitted.

"You bet, it does take nerve, but sometimes you just have to take a risk. If you wait too long, before you know it you're old and you missed your chance for happiness," Nat said.

As they discussed their philosophy on life, Mother relaxed in the chair, and listened to her music. She sang so loud, I could hardly hear the conversation. The look of joy on her face was obvious. It was wonderful to see a grandmother's face when she is surrounded by her loved ones.

I finally announced, "Dinner's ready."

They all popped up, like a bunch of school kids at the end of the day.

"I suppose everyone's hungry," I said, relieved, since I made extra. We took our places, with Nat at the head of the table. Desiree sat next to Nat while I moved to the other side. Nat said grace with his eloquent way with words.

We enjoyed a lovely evening, and then went into the living room for dessert. Nat sat back on the couch. I sat down next to him; relieved the night seemed to go smoothly.

"Madeline, the meal was fantastic. You amaze me," he said. He rested his hand on my leg.

"I'm glad you enjoyed it," I answered.

"Come on, I'll help you serve the cake." Desiree stood up quickly. We paraded into the kitchen together.

She turned to me and whispered in my ear. "He's a nice guy. I really like him, and he's handsome, too."

"I'm glad you like him."

I gathered the cake, and ice cream. "Do you think we're too

much for him to handle? I mean the family, and Grandma. He's been alone now for so many years." I shrugged my shoulders, and took a deep breath.

"He'd have to be crazy to give up an opportunity for a relationship with you. Men his age are on their second marriage by now," she said. "I think you're perfect for each other."

"Just be smart, Mom. Let him wonder how you feel, don't give it away," she said. "Try not to be too eager. Most men pursue the girl that's a challenge for them. I think it has a lot to do with testosterone, and their masculinity,"

I grabbed a napkin and wiped the whipped cream off of her lip.

Desiree took another sample of the topping I made for the dessert.

"You have the wisdom of a much older woman. I'll try to remember, but it's not easy. Come on, let's have some of this yummy cake," I said, as I carried my work of art inside.

After I placed the cake on the coffee table, Nat handed me the box wrapped in shiny gold paper.

"This is just a little thank you gift for dinner," Nat said. "Go ahead open it."

Nat was so thoughtful to bring me a present. I removed the paper, and was surprised to find a large framed painting exactly like the one I admired at the Scenic Inn, where we had dinner. I raved over it, and told him I couldn't wait to find the perfect place for it. My eyes filled with tears. I reached for his hand and squeezed it.

"Nat, I love it. Where did you find it?"

"I saw it in the window of a small gift shop, down the Shore," he said. "I passed by after I finished work tonight. I knew how much you loved it, and I couldn't resist."

"Thank you so much, I can't believe you remembered."

The look in his eyes told me he was happy I liked it.

"Oh, you would be surprised at my memory," he said.

Bonnie joined in, "That is absolutely gorgeous. Why is it you never remember what I like?" she said, with a wink of her eye, as she turned to face Mike.

He gulped hard and seemed to take her comment serious. "All right, I'll try to take note next time, honey," he said. He turned red, and looked embarrassed.

Nat moved toward Mike, nudged him, and they chuckled like men in a locker room.

I had an urge to tell Nat how wonderful I thought he was. Instead, I simply gave him a hug and a little kiss on the cheek.

"You must have a hammer and nails. I can help you hang it up before I leave," he said.

"We'll do it later." I said.

"This cake is the best so far," Desiree said. She took another piece.

"Thank you. I think I have to agree." I ran my finger along the edge of the plate, to scoop up the crumbs.

Desiree got up and went into the bedroom. She reappeared with a large plastic case. "I need help to find a baby picture for the bulletin board at work. The team leader came up with an idea to create a collage of photos of the staff when they were children. We plan to write captions underneath each one. It's for fun, and our entertainment. I want the photo from first grade with my Barbie convertible."

"It may take us all night to find it," I said. I had no idea where it could be.

Nat got up, and moved over to the table where Desiree was sitting. He pulled his chair next to hers, and flipped through the albums. He took his time, as he looked at each picture. It was apparent he really wanted to get a look at my past.

It surprised me at how easy he blended in with the whole family. I tried to place any negative thoughts out of my mind, especially the one that it was all too good to be true.

Mark and Jeremy joined us in at the table. Grandma even noticed all the excitement. "Come over here, Grandma, sit next to me." Jeremy moved over, and they looked at the pictures.

"Look at this one." She pointed to an older photo. "Here you are when you were born," Mom said.

She held up the photo of Jeremy at his christening. The picture practically touched her nose as she singled him out.

"See Jeremy, you were such an adorable child, my dear. You still are," she said. Mother had a look of admiration on her face.

He shook his head; his face took on the color of fire. Jeremy did not like to be the center of attention, but Mom got a kick out of it. She enjoyed getting a reaction from him.

She laughed and gave him a squeeze. I showed her some of the larger pictures. Mother studied each one with a serious expression. I wasn't sure if she actually remembered any of them. It amazed me when she pointed out aunts and uncles, rather easily.

"Maybe you can inform us on some of the family secrets," I said.

"Look there's Nick's mother and daughter-in-law," she announced.

She handed it to me and examined it closely; I found she was right.

"How do you remember people from so long ago?" I laughed.

"Nick and I lived with her and Juliet for a short time. I recall the night when the men worked late one night, and I made a large pot of tomato sauce. I opened a box of spaghetti to find there were bugs in it," she said. She put her hands to her lips. "It was too late to go to the store. We knew the men would be hungry when they got home. Juliet told me to serve it anyway, that the men would never know. I scooped the bugs out of the box."

Mother moved her shoulders up and down. "They never knew the difference. It was hilarious; the two of us laughed to ourselves all through dinner. We didn't eat very much that night, and went to bed hungry." She sat back, and waited for our reactions. We all laughed along with her; after all, it was a funny story.

"Those were the good old days," she said.

Nat laughed the loudest, and bent over in his seat.

"Grandma, I bet you were a lot of fun when you were young

woman," he commented.

"Oh yes, I was, young man. I used to go out on Saturday night to the dances, and stay out late. One night, I even put spell on a retired dentist, and the next day, he proposed to his long-time girlfriend," she admitted.

I nudged her, afraid Nat would think we were all nuts.

She sat up straight, and cleared her throat. "It was all in fun, no harm done. I had hard times, and good times, but that's life. I never went to bed mad at Nick. If we had an argument, we kissed and made up, before bed. Life is too short to hold a grudge. We had a marvelous relationship, which grew stronger year after year. I wish he could be here with us."

Her eyes filled up with tears.

"Sometimes I can't remember where he is," she said, with a sniffle.

I put my finger up, to let Nat know not to react.

"Mom, it'll be all right," I said. "You're doing wonderful."

I kept my voice low, and took Nat to the side. "Occasionally at night, she becomes more forgetful," I said. "It's better to go along with her."

"One night around midnight, she stood at the back door. She held a lantern from the garage in her hand. 'Your father should be home soon,' she said. A tear fell down her cheek. 'I made a wish on a star,' she said."

"In the morning, she managed to find her way back to reality. The expression used by the medical field for this was Sundowners. The events in their life get cloudy when night falls. In the morning, she can describe each moment from the past with wistful sentiment. Sometimes, she forgets what she had for breakfast, but so did I."

Nat nodded and motioned to me that he understood.

"Come with me, I'll help you get ready for bed," I said.

"Thank you so much, honey," she said.

"Excuse me a moment, Nat."

"Desiree, can you entertain Nat while I help Grandma?"

"Sure, Mom, go ahead, we're fine." Mark took Grandma by

the hand.

"Goodnight everyone thanks for a wonderful evening," she said.

Mark was so kind to her. She put her face next to his arm.

"Thank you, my dear," she said in a soft tone.

We tucked Mom in for the night and went back to the living room. Nat yawned, and sat back on the couch. Jeremy flicked through a sports magazine.

"What are your plans for next weekend?" Bonnie asked.

Nat looked at me and remained silent. My heart sped up. I know she wanted to invite us on a double date. I didn't know how Nat would react. Nat sat back. He shifted to one side and appeared a little uncomfortable.

"I'm at the restaurant for lunch that day, and my evening is free," I said. I waited for Nat's reply.

"I don't know. I have a big job, and I may have to work late," he said. He looked away. A bead of perspiration appeared on his forehead, and his hands trembled. He seemed a little distant, and left soon after. He really did not appear interested in her invitation. Bonnie gave me a suspicious glare, when he fumbled with her invite. Nat instantly transformed by the suggestion of a family night out.

"I have an early appointment, guess I better be on my way," he announced.

"Thank you for a great night. I'll see you soon. It was a pleasure meeting all of you. I think it's time I leave, and let you all get some rest."

"I'll wrap up some dessert for you to take with you," I said. I wished the night were just beginning. I thought his reply to go out with my sister and her husband was a bit cold. Although, I let myself rationalize his answer.

"Sure, that sounds great," Nat said. We strolled into the kitchen together.

He put his back up against the counter and grabbed me around the waist. He buried his face into my neck, and stayed there for a few minutes. I pulled back to see his face.

"We had a great time. I'm glad you could join us," I said. "You look tired. Come on, I'll show you outside."

I tried to remember Desiree's advice, and tried not to cling. "Drive safe." I told him.

I bent down, and he kissed me goodnight on the cheek.

"I'll call you," he said before he rolled up the window.

Nat drove away, while I remained by the door.

I drifted back inside, and wondered what he meant by "I'll call you". Did he mean tomorrow, when he gets home or in a few days? I gathered I would have to wait and see.

Mark waited for me in the kitchen. Jeremy sprawled out on the floor in the living room

I kicked off my shoes and sat down next to Mark at the table. He sat forward and frowned, with his hands on his knees.

"Mom, I think Nat's a great guy, and I'm happy for you, but I wonder why he's still single at his age," he offered, with suspicion in his tone. "I sure hope he doesn't let you down. I'll have to keep an eye on him." His words were firm, yet I knew he cared.

Jeremy jumped in from the other room. "Yeah Mom, he better not hurt you or else he will have to answer to me." He sounded skeptical, as he hit his fist against his hand.

"That's enough," I said. "I appreciate your concern, but I can take care of myself. Try not to be so hard on Nat."

"I still think it's strange that he's never been married," Mark said. He squinted with a suspicious glare. "If you get along, and he respects you, we can give him a chance. Jeremy is that all right with you?"

Jeremy grunted as he got up and joined us in the kitchen. "All right, I'll go along, and I'll try to give him a chance to prove himself. We did have a neat time tonight, and he told some real cool stories about his adventures. He might even be able to take us on his boat fishing someday," he said, with optimism.

"See guys, you do like him." I felt like I could finally relax.

"I realize you both have my best interest in mind." I gave them each a hug and kiss on the cheek. They were still my boys, and they seemed proud to be able to give their input on my choice of men.

"I'm going to bed, too," Mark said.

Jeremy went into his room, and closed the door.

I could not believe how fast the years had gone. I once fought their battles now; things were reversed.

Bonnie and Mike stayed later, to help clean up. Desiree came up from the basement.

"I put the linens in the basket. Is that okay?" she asked.

"Sure, I'll get them in the morning." I walked her to the front door.

"Call you tomorrow," Desiree said.

I went back into the kitchen. Bonnie and Mike had their coats on, and waited for me.

"I really like him, but I felt a little put off when he shirked off my invitation," Bonnie admitted. She shook her head.

"I don't know why he acted that way," I answered. "I'm sorry."

"Don't be, it's not your fault," she said.

"Well, maybe he has a good reason," I added.

Bonnie raised her shoulders. "Maybe he does. The dinner was delicious, Sis. Talk to you tomorrow."

"Thanks, it was fun."

"I'm sure he would have jumped at the offer, if he was available," Mike said, before he closed the front door.

I waved, and I thought, *sure.*

The night light flickered brightly in the corner of my bedroom. Grandma lay sound asleep, cuddled up with her little doll. She was a woman that raised two children, took in laundry, and cleaned houses to earn extra money. She lived through the hard times, working day and night to make ends meet. The whole time she never complained. She was a wonderful caring woman. If it rained after school, she would wait outside with an umbrella. She never let me down, even when she performed her silly tricks. She made countless sacrifices for her children.

It was my turn to be there for her. No matter what happened

in my life, I decided to put her needs first. As I got into bed, I said a little prayer to hear from Nat soon. He was so attentive that evening. The painting he gave me came straight from his heart. I closed my eyes, and the night drifted away.

Chapter Seventeen

Madeline

I had the urge to dial his number countless times throughout the day. All I could do was watch the clock, and imagine reasons why the phone didn't ring. I was still on vacation, so I had extra time to think. I spoke with Bonnie earlier that day, and we went over the details of the party together. She gave me her undivided attention as usual. After our conversation, I felt a little better.

Although we had a wonderful time, and Nat seemed to get along with everyone, I still had a sense there was a problem with his family. He showed me a side of him that was kind and thoughtful. I simply could not put my finger on it. I wondered why Nat got flustered every time he mentioned his childhood. He sounded disconnected from his mother. He told me he didn't see her very often. When I asked if he wanted to bring her over to meet my mother, he quickly changed the subject. I thought he was out of character, when he declined the opportunity to go out with my sister and her husband. His excuse was he had to work, but he never made the slightest attempt to reschedule.

The days were shorter, and before I realized it, the bus from daycare was in front of the house. As I assisted Mom inside, the phone rang. I sat her down in the nearest chair, and I rushed to answer it.

"Go on get it, it's probably that nice young man!" Mother shouted.

"Hello, it's me, Nat. What are you doing later?"

I was relieved to hear his voice.

"I'd like to see you tonight. Are you busy?" he asked. "I could come over this evening, if it's all right with you."

"I don't have any plans," I replied. "Sure, I'd love to have company. What time can you stop by?"

"I can be over around eight. Will it be too late?"

"No, that's perfect. It'll give me time to put Mom to bed."

"Would you like me to bring dinner?" he asked.

"I already prepared it, but you could pick up a dessert. I've been in the mood for sweets, all day," I added.

He agreed to stop at the Italian deli shop, and we left it at that. I was pleased with the idea of a quiet night together. He must have longed to see me, as I for him.

After I cleaned up the kitchen, Mother listened to her music. Her shoulders moved up and down to the beat, and she tapped her foot. She seemed happy and content in her new home.

She suddenly threw her headphones on the floor. They landed next to the magazine rack. I picked them up, and plugged them back into the stereo.

"Are you all right, why are you upset?" I asked, concerned for her safety.

She took a moment to answer. "The song was sad; it reminded me of Nick and Mary, and I miss them both. I haven't seen Mary today, and I'm worried about her," she said.

The comment about Aunt Mary concerned me. The fact that she still thought she saw my late father, terrified me. I could not imagine how she could see her sister, either. It made me wonder if my encounters with her were also a fiction of my imagination, too. The night was the hardest for mother.

I bend down to face her. "Don't worry, it will be all right. I understand," I said. It was better to go along with her.

She wiped her eyes and seemed calmer.

I made her an ice cream cone, and she quickly forgot her sorrow. It only took a moment to bring her back to a harmonious state of mind.

"Thank you, honey, this is delicious," she said. Mother finished her ice cream, and it left her with a vanilla moustache. I laughed, when I saw it.

My mother and father met when she was sixteen. They spend their life dedicated to one another, and I hoped to be as fortunate. I could never imagine how it felt to lose your partner after so many years together.

"Don't worry about me, I know I am forgetful at times, but I know exactly what's on around me, and I can tell when there is a problem," she offered. "You'll enjoy a long splendid life with that young man. Never fall short of your dreams. Take chances, it's your life."

I found her advice helpful as usual, but this time it seemed different. I put my mother to bed that night with a feeling she had a little secret.

cÀɔ

My heart melted as soon as I saw him. "Come inside," I said

Nat looked tired. His eyes were reddened, yet he remembered the pastry. I put the bag in the kitchen, and we sat down on the couch. The boys were in their rooms, so the house was quiet.

"You look beautiful tonight," Nat said.

I struck a pose. "Do you like it?" I spun around to model my new blouse. I didn't let on I had gained three more pounds.

Flattered by all the attention, I put my head down. I never had so many compliments in my life. Somehow this time, I believed him.

"How was work?" I asked.

We sat on the sofa.

"I finally finished a big job that was a nightmare." He sat back, and rested his head. "I'm glad to be out of there," he admitted. "The owner was a fanatic and nit-picked over every angle."

"I bet it turned out perfect," I said.

He looked good in his faded blue jeans and a tight knit shirt.

I wanted to do throw my arms around him, and never let go, but I tried not to show my eagerness. I sat back, and put my head on his shoulder. We cuddled in front of the television. My legs quivered when he caressed my shoulder. The warmth of his body drove me crazy.

He turned his face slowly, and we meshed into one. His lips gently touched mine. We knew we were not alone in the house so we kept our embraces short.

"Let's have our snacks in here." I said. I brewed some fresh tea leaves and served it along with the pastry.

"Does Grandma like the new day care center?" he asked.

"I think she does," I replied. "She got upset earlier this evening. She started to cry over Dad again. I know it's hard for her. It must be awful to lose your partner after so many years together."

"At least they had the time together. Some people don't even get that. They spend their whole life alone," he speculated. Nat got up and changed the subject. "Let me hang that painting in your bedroom."

"I think it would be perfect in the dining room, anyway I don't want to wake Mother," I said.

We found the right spot for my beach scene above the buffet. It looked perfect, like it belonged there. In between our conversation, and reruns of a few funny sit-coms, he would steal a kiss from time to time. Before we knew it, the night was over and it was two a.m.

Nat's scent remained on me when I retired to bed. I remembered my son's words, "Why was he still single?" I quickly pushed them out of my mind, as I stared at the ceiling. The stillness of the night fell, and I wondered.

The next day came with feelings of self-doubt and insecurities. I shoved the little hints on Nat's reservations about a serious relationship aside. I knew I wanted one. Nevertheless, I denied the clues, and rationalized the situation.

Mother woke up happy. She sat at the bistro table with her hands folded, sweet as a child. I placed a plate of eggs and toast in front of her.

"You make such delicious food, and you keep this place clean and fresh," she said in a gracious tone.

"I made the breakfast for you," I said. I gently touched her hand.

She looked at me, and chuckled. "You take such good care of me. When you were a little girl, I knew you were special. I'm delighted you found that nice young fellow. I told you the right one would show up, just for you. I was positive you would find him. I think he's in love with you, honey."

She puckered her lips as if she were a proud peacock. It was as if she knew a wonderful event would take place, and she gloated over it.

Mom grasped onto her locket; she held it tightly in her hands. Her supportive words came at the right time. I stood on the sidewalk, amazed at the way life had its mystery. I lingered outside for quite some time, and waved until the bus was out of sight.

Chapter Eighteen

Madeline

The winter menu for the restaurant needed a new approach. Tony left me the keys. In return, I agreed to keep an eye on the crew who worked on the repairs. There was plenty of time to work on my creations, and I loved to spend time alone in my domain. It was a great opportunity to work without interruption. A plan for a unique type of cookbook, sat in the corner of my mind. The outline was done, and I simply had to make the final decision to take the initiative to get started. The next step was to work on the market strategy. A book with a special blurb about each recipe was what I wanted to do, and I had a few secret recipes tucked aside for the right time. The restaurant was famous and had a good reputation, and I was sure this would be to my advantage.

The time flew by as I diced vegetables and chopped herbs. The vibration from my cell phone caught me off guard and I fumbled to check it. The call was from the hospital, and I quickly called back the number. Miss Morris wanted to know if I had a few hours in the morning. I agreed willingly. It would be the first time back, since Nat and I started dating.

It was my initial thought to keep my relationship with Nat a secret. It worried me to have the gossip interfere with Nat's work. I found this a good reason to give him a buzz. I walked over to the window, and out to the water.

Nathaniel

"Hi, it's Madeline," she said. "Got a minute?"

"Sure, I was just about to call you," Nat said.

Nat felt good to know Madeline thought of him, too.

"I thought I'd let you know, I'm at the hospital tomorrow. I wanted to know if you were on," she said.

"Yup, I happen to have an early lecture," he answered.

Nat knew Madeline would feel uneasy if the staff at the medical center found out that they were a couple. He heard the fright in her tone of voice.

"What's wrong?" Are you uneasy about us?" Nat asked.

"Well, I worry that it will cause you unneeded attention," Madeline admitted. She lowered her voice. "I'd rather keep our private lives between us."

"I could care less!" Nat replied. "You know how people love stuff like this. In the first place, I'm proud of what we share. We can still be a couple and remain professional on the job."

"I don't want you to be upset," Madeline said.

"Not a problem. I'll make sure no one gets out of line," he insisted. "They know better than to mess around with me. By the way, there are a number of couples, on other units. Marcy and Bob, from the fourth floor are dating, and the lab has two couples who are dating. There are also quite a few married couples."

"I feel much better now. Thanks so much," she said. "I'm probably wrong, anyway."

"I understand. Don't worry, babe." Nat had his own concerns, too.

Chapter Nineteen

Madeline

When I arrived on the floor, I was still uncertain about the response the nurses would have if they saw us together on the job. As soon as I bent over to get a sheet from the linen cart, I found Nat next to me.

The unit seemed so different since my first day. Nat's eyes followed my every move, and his admiration showed.

"It's good to see you, babe. Are you any better?" he asked. He tried to kiss me. I pulled back a little, and hoped no one saw us.

"Well, maybe I feel a little better," I said in a soft tone.

It felt like ages ago since we first met. I could feel my heart flutter as I folded the towels. The cart was big enough to shield us from the front desk. It took up a part of the corridor, and it blocked the view from the nurses' station. The staff carried out their assignments. Call bells rang and in between tending to the client's needs, they were engrossed in their charts and answering the phone. We stood behind the grey plastic covering which flapped off to the side.

"It's all good, trust me," he whispered.

Somehow, his presence put me in a calmer, more reassured mood. His words convinced me the day would be all right. When

I listened to his lecture, I felt so proud of him, as he displayed true professionalism. There were so many facts about addiction introduced to me. It helped me to understand how my grandfather's drinking was a disease. He had good and bad qualities. It was not up to me to change him. All I could do was take care of myself. I memorized the steps of the program, and found them extremely helpful. Nat led as if he knew the answers to the universe.

We left together later in the afternoon. The nurses huddled with their heads together as I envisioned. As Nat and I passed the desk, they grew silent. One of the nurses peeked over the top of the counter to catch a glimpse. *Oh well, I guess it's human nature.* As we headed toward the exit, Nat suggested we take a ride to the beach. He must have remembered how much I loved the Jersey shore.

"I think it'll be fun," he said. We can go down by the water's edge, and later play some games on the boardwalk. Maybe I'll beat you at basketball."

"I don't know. I'm pretty good at shooting hoops." I reached for his hand and squeezed it pleased that we would spend the day together. "I'm still technically on vacation," I said. I stood on my toes and gave him a quick brush on the lips.

"Will the boys watch your mom?" he asked.

"I don't see why not, as long as I get in touch with them to get her off of the bus."

I loved the way he remembered what I liked and disliked. It made me feel like he really paid attention when I spoke. Nat held his head high while we moved through the lobby. It was official we were a couple; he even said so.

"You see, I told you it would be all right," Nat insisted.

I took a moment to call Mark at school. He would be home in time for Mom, and he agreed to stay with her until I got home. We rode with the windows open, and the music blaring. I felt totally liberated, and free. We stopped at my house, I grabbed what I needed, and we were on our way.

The whole area had the feel of summer. You would never

know summer was over; since the weather was still warm. We were not the only ones who wanted to take advantage of a beautiful day in early October. There were quite a few people with the same idea.

We had to drive around a couple of times in search of a parking spot close to the water. I brought folding chairs with an umbrella. I was convinced I looked like a movie star, with my big straw hat, and my designer sunglasses. I struggled with my bags, as I hiked.

Nat reached for my hand, and wrapped his fingers through mine.

"Let me take those," he said.

We began a leisurely stroll toward the sand. We passed a hotel that was a replica of a fifties model. It looked retro with its hot pink paint, and it had a goofy swan parked out front. I peeked inside, and saw a shiny silver jukebox, and a soda fountain. There was a gigantic pool on the side, with white chairs, and umbrellas that had mint green and pink stripes.

"That place looks like it would be a blast. Maybe we can book a room for the weekend, next summer," Nat said. He pointed to the bird.

"Sure, that sounds like fun," I answered, glad that he placed our relationship in the future. I brought more than I needed, and I even packed a bag with sandwiches and soft drinks. Nat held onto the beach chairs, as we headed toward the water's edge.

The gulls flew low, and the sound of the ocean roared. I found the atmosphere mesmerizing. We sat together in front of the water, and sipped our drinks. The sand was white and immaculate. Nat and I became lost in the tranquility. We actually sat for quite a while before we spoke a word. We exchanged glances from time to time. Couples moved together next to the shoreline. An elderly pair, strolled hand and hand. They made their way, slowly out toward the ocean, and you could sense their devotion by their body language. There was simplicity about the way they moved together.

Nat gawked at them, and never said a word. His eyes

saddened. He dug his feet into the sand with a quick jerky motion. I wondered why he appeared so indifferent.

Two boys, about eight or ten years old played in front of us. They threw a Frisbee around, and it accidentally smashed into Nat's leg. He tossed it back to them, in a playful manner. They splashed water from their buckets on his feet.

"They're only teasing you," I said.

I stood up, and took Nat's hand.

"Let's take a walk. Come on, let's get closer to the edge," I said. I wanted to savor the last bit of nice weather.

His hand slipped free of mine, while I ran ahead. I snuck a look over my shoulder. With a quick twist of my head, I caught him when he wiped his eyes. I kicked up the sand with my bare feet.

"Wait for me," he shouted out, as he secured our area.

Nat began a slow pace toward me, and eventually picked up speed. He finally met up with me, and held me around the waist. We jogged along the water for about a quarter of a mile. It was nice to spend time together in the afternoon. We slowed down, both of us with our feet in the water, as Nat slipped his arms around me. He lifted me up off the wet sand, and held me in the air. The waves hit our legs, as we continued to gaze into each other's eyes. Nat gently lowered me, with my body pressed up against his. He moved my hair away from my face. Our lips met as soon as my feet reached the sand. I could feel his heart pound.

"I love you, babe," he said, in a sweet whisper. At that instant, I truly believed him.

"I love you too, Nat," I spoke softly, my mouth next to his ear.

Nat and I rushed to our spot on the sand. We sat down on the beach chairs.

Nat squinted to the sun. "Let me adjust this umbrella." He stood up and fixed the umbrella.

"Is that better?"

"Thanks, Nat. It's perfect," I said, thrilled by all the attention.

Kathleen Ann Gallagher

As I closed my eyes, I inhaled the scent of the salt water. All around us were couples, young and old. The beauty of the ocean breeze brought you to a place where all the wonders of life were right in front of you. The peaceful sound of the waves allowed me to drift off to sleep for a nap. There was no need for words between us. The setting spoke for itself, and the sun gave me added pleasure. I could not remember when I had a more joyous time at the shore. The smooth sand tickled my skin. The beach was like home to me. I felt as if I were born to visit nature's fantastic playground. It never occurred to me, in my wildest dreams, that one day I would be in this setting completely at peace with my life. We decided to begin the drive home before the rush hour. It would take at least an hour, but I didn't care. When you're in love, time is not a factor.

181

Chapter Twenty

Madeline

*N*at kept his eyes on the road, and was unusually quiet on the ride home. It seemed as if I must have said something to upset him. Maybe it was all too much for him, too fast. His total change in behavior surprised me. He would usually sneak a look at me, smile, or tell me a story. Back at the beach, he told me he loved me for the first time. I hoped his confession was not the problem. Panic took hold of me, and I did not want to believe I may have made a bad choice in men, once again. I still had faith in him. Mark, and Jeremy had a suspicion there could be a problem, especially when they found out Nat was never married. I, on the other hand, pushed that out of my mind. I wondered if he suddenly became concerned about us on the job together, or, if my family life overwhelmed him. Maybe it was just too much of a challenge for a bachelor, I surmised. I took a long deep breath and closed my eyes for the rest of the way home.

We arrived at my door after we sat in heavy traffic due to an accident on the Parkway. I suffered in silence over the sudden change in Nat's mood.

The porch light allowed me to see the outline of someone by the window. When we got closer, I realized it was Grandma. She stood behind the curtains with a tissue clenched in her hands, her eyes riddled with fright.

"Mother, what happened? Are you all right?" I shouted.

I must have startled her. She shook and held her mouth wide open, and took a step back, before she spoke.

"Sure, I'm fine," she said. "I'm worried about you, Madeline. I was afraid you were in an accident."

Nat stood close to me, and all at once, he looked away.

"Don't worry, I'm home safe and sound," I assured her.

"Are you hungry?" she asked.

"No, we had dinner."

Mark came out of his room. "How was the beach?"

"It was fantastic, but I'm worried about Grandma. How'd she do tonight? I'm sorry I left her for the entire day. Maybe I should have stayed home with her," I said.

Mark placed his hand on my shoulder. "Don't worry, she had a great night. I made her spaghetti, and she listened to Frank Sinatra. She even had her ice cream cone already. Grandma's tired from her busy day," he said, with assurance.

"What else happened? It seems like there was a problem. Grandma's eyes are watery," I said.

"I took care of it," he bolstered.

"Took care of what?" I persisted.

"The cops," he admitted.

"What on earth happened? Is Jeremy okay?" My mouth dropped open.

"Yeah, Jeremy's fine. He's in his room and we didn't have a fight this time."

"Grandma called the cops to report a lost handbag," he said. "The bag was under her bed."

"I guess the dementia is worse," I said. "Did the police make a report?"

"Yeah, they said this happens all the time with people Grandma's age. The officer said if she continues the behavior to take her to the doctor." Mark laughed.

"It's not funny," I said.

"I know, Mom. She cracks me up. I'm sorry." Mark said.

It was a serious issue to me. I realized if mother's short-term memory deteriorated, we would have to keep a closer watch on her. We might have to consider a change in our routine, to accommodate an around the clock babysitter. Sometimes we left her alone, to run to the store.

We had her examined last week for the second time. "The doctor told us she checked out fine," I said.

"Here, she brought this home for you," Mark said. He handed me a small wrapped package. "I think she'll be all right." Mark sounded confident. "Don't overreact."

I opened it without hesitation. Inside was a beautiful trinket box with tiny seashells layered on top. Mother placed a personal note on the bottom. It read, *"To my daughter Madeline, Enjoy the wonder of life."* A layer of sand surrounded the outside of the box.

"Mother this is beautiful. Thank you. What a good choice," I said. She sat down in her chair.

"I made it at my class today. I'm glad you like it," she said. She displayed a proud grin.

"Well, I think I overreacted, she seems perfectly fine." I took a breath, and relaxed my shoulders.

Nat and Mark sat in front of the television.

Jeremy appeared and rubbed his eyes. "I must have fallen asleep." He plopped on the couch next to them. It was important to me to see him get along with his brother. When I moved closer to Jeremy, I got a whiff of smoke. Nat winked at me and signaled for me not to embarrass him. Mother rocked in the recliner and her eyes closed before long.

"Well, I guess it's time to put Grandma to bed."

"Do you remember me?" Nat asked.

"Of course I do, you're Nat. I know a nice man when I meet one."

"My Madeline is a good girl. I hope you know that," she insisted. She shook her finger at him.

"Ah-ha, I sure do," he replied.

"Come on Nat, join Madeline in my room. I want to tell you both a story," she said in a firm tone. She kept her eyes on us.

The sound of her voiced startled me. There was a different tone in her voice. It was as if she had a plan. The night seemed strange. It was as if the sundowners had suddenly disappeared.

Nat and I accompanied Mother to her bed, and tucked her in. I folded the blanket down, and adjusted her pillow. She cradled her doll in her arms. I sat down next to her, on the edge of the bed. Nat pulled over the small chair I kept in the corner.

"We're ready for the story, Grandma," Nat said. He folded his arms and waited.

Mom gathered the top of her nightgown, and began to reminisce about the day she met my father.

She was only sixteen-years-old, but my dad was much older. Dad walked in to her parent's candy store, immediately intrigued by her beauty, he eagerly pursued her.

"I wore my white lace dress with a beautiful satin bow in my hair. My father was at the counter." She raised her hand and ran it gently across her head. "He told me I had the most beautiful curly hair he ever saw. My dad warned me not to date an older man, but I didn't listen to him."

She shook her hand back and forth. Her voice lowered to a whisper.

On their fortieth anniversary, we surprised them with a party. They entered the Elks' dining room hand and hand. Mother cried when she saw her family and friends. Father serenaded her while she gazed into his eyes. Their love grew stronger with each year of their marriage. When they held each other on the dance floor, the room fell silent. It was beautiful to see a couple still so much in love. I was concerned she might get upset and start to ask where he was. For some reason this time, she seemed to know he was gone. She accepted it with such grace.

"We had such a wonderful marriage. I still miss him so," Mother said.

Her eyes held a glassy appearance. I soon realized Mother's

eyes were filled with tears of joy.

My emotions climbed with passion, as I listened to her recall her past. Mother found pleasure in her memories, while she revisited each moment.

Nat and I quietly snuck out of the room when we noticed her eyes were heavy. Mother fell sound asleep with the most satisfied look on her face.

There were various pictures of my parents on their wedding day next to her bed. Nat glanced over to them as we left her bedside. He stopped and examined each one intently. It seemed like his mind was a thousand miles away. On the wall above the wedding photo, was the family portrait. It was an old black and white that was taken in a studio. Mom kept it in a beautiful antique frame. The picture was from the thirties, when she was fifteen-years-old. She wore a white lace dress, the same one she had on the day she met my dad. Her twin sister, Mary, posed next to her. They both had their hands on their laps, and they looked quite stylish. They were dressed exactly alike. Next to the portrait, was a rose-colored frame with a lock of Aunt Mary's hair, intertwined with a lock of Mother's hair. It rested on a lace handkerchief. I think it was supposed to signify unity. It was a tradition in her family, but, it frightened me.

Nat remained silent for quite a while, as he stared at the family. Suddenly he began to sway back and forth. He opened his legs in an attempt to steady himself. I was shocked to see the color suddenly draw from his face. His face became so pale I thought he would pass out. His skin took on a moist, almost chalky appearance.

"Are you all right?" I shouted, afraid he would hit the floor at any second.

He shook his head and reached inside his jacket for a hard candy. He put the Lifesaver into his mouth, and I saw his mouth tremble. Nat kept his hands deep in his pockets as he moved away from the dresser. He lowered his head. His expression became sullen, and he never uttered a word.

Nat left the door cracked open, as he staggered slowly

toward the couch. He remained silent, as he stared at the television screen.

He sat on the sofa, and when I sat next to him, he moved to the far end. It surprised me to see him acting so differently. It took a while for the color to return to his face.

"Nat, are you certain you're not ill?" I said, concerned that he needed medical attention. It took a few minutes for him to answer.

"I'm all right, give me a minute. I was just a little lightheaded. Don't worry."

I had a sensation of impending doom in the pit of my stomach. We watched a game show, but we sat apart, and never touched each other. After the program, he got up, and headed toward the door.

"I have to get up early. I better get home," Nat said in an emotionless tone. His shoulders slumped, and he dragged his feet.

"Wait for me, I'll walk with you," I insisted.

We embraced, and kissed as usual. Nat placed his arms around my waist and pulled me close to him. It seemed like he never wanted to let go. I heard him sigh as he released me. His caress felt sincere, yet there was obviously a problem.

Jeremy joined me outside, as Nat drove away.

"What's wrong, did you have an argument?" He frowned.

"No, we're fine. Why do you ask?"

"I don't know, you seem upset tonight. Are you sure you and Nat didn't have a fight?"

"Come inside, I'll make you a snack, and then we can talk," I replied. I realized he could sense my tension.

"Great, I'm hungry," he said. He gave me a skeptical glare.

I quickly prepared a ham, onion, and cheese omelet. Fortunately, I had the makings in a Tupperware container, ready to go in the refrigerator.

Jeremy sat down at the table and unfolded his napkin.

"How are you doing in school?" I asked. "I haven't gotten any calls from the principal lately." I tried to take the focus off of me.

Jeremy took on a look of confidence. He sat straight up in the chair.

"I have to take school seriously if I want a good life," he said. His expression told me he meant business.

"That's good, because Mr. Rounds, the truant officer, informed me we were headed to court, if you continued to cut school. I really don't want that to happen," I said.

"If he finds out you came home drunk, he'll pursue it further, I'm sure of it," I told him.

"I promise not to goof off anymore. I swear," he said. "Anyway I want my body to be in shape, so no more booze," he added.

"Fantastic! Sounds like you mean business." I rested against the counter, and crossed my arms. "I'm amazed. What happened, that made you finally realize this?"

"I don't know, Mom, but when Nat and I spoke after dinner the other night, I started to think about my life. He told me stories about his decisions when he was my age," he said. "I have choices, you know." He paused. "I can go to college, if I work hard."

Jeremy got up, and opened the cabinet. He took out the potato chips. He started towards his bedroom. "Goodnight, I have to get up early," he said. He smiled.

I stared at him for a moment, happy for his new and improved attitude.

My hope was for Jeremy to open up, and talk to Nat. Nat and I shared our dreams with one another. My senses picked up the clues that somewhere inside of Nat, there was a longing for family. I wasn't sure if he was prepared to change his life. He may have become apprehensive and felt he was pushed to settle down.

All I knew was a strange occurrence took place that night after Nat looked at Mom's photos. For the life of me, I could not understand what could have been so dreadful about the family portrait. It was definite, I had fallen in love with Nat, and I thought he felt the same way about me. His confession of love caught me by surprise. That night, I went to bed with a wish, that one day, I would join hand and hand with the man I loved.

My mother adjusted to the daycare center in no time at all. The bus driver, Mel, was warm and friendly. She really liked him, and this made it easier during her commute. It was nice to see her gaze up at him, and give him a girlish grin when he buckled her seatbelt. I think she enjoyed all the attention. It wasn't long before our new schedule seemed easy. We actually forgot what it was like at our house without Grandma.

Nat and I formed a strong bond. I never brought up the topic of his speedy exit, after Grandma's nighttime remembrance. In the following months, we spent numerous evenings at the movies, and spent many intimate nights at his house, too. The only times I did not prepare a home cooked meal, and invite Nat over was when I worked nights at the restaurant.

The entire family enjoyed Nat's company, nevertheless, Jeremy and Nat had the most in common. They took a hiking trip one weekend, in late October. The two of them arrived home after ten with their clothes soaked from when they were stuck in a storm. Nat was prepared, he brought the rain gear, but they left it in the car.

After a few months of steady dating, I was still convinced Nat and I would join as one. I thought he felt the same, especially after he started the work on the master bedroom suite. He had the blueprints drawn up, and he purchased all the supplies. His crew worked meticulously to add all of the precise final changes. Nat amazed me with his eye for perfection. In just four short weeks, the room was completed. The skylights were my favorite feature; they were four grand dazzling windows to the sky. Nat invited me over, bringing me upstairs for the reveal. I could not believe how gorgeous the room turned out. It was more than I imagined.

"What do you think?" he asked. "Do you like it?" He waited,

his chest rose quickly with anticipation.

The only items he needed were the spread for the bed and window treatments. He asked me if I would shop for them, and I was delighted. Nat plopped on the new bed with his hands behind his head.

"What color do you think would be the best for the accessories?" he asked.

I got on the bed next to him and sat up to browse through the magazines.

"I think I have an idea for a great color scheme. I found the perfect set in a Vintage Victorian line. It's rich in color, made out of the finest fabrics."

Nat scanned the pages briefly. "Whatever you like would be all right with me."

"I'm sure you can bring it all together. I need you to add the feminine touch to the room," he added.

Nat gave me a signal with a nod of his head and a seductive look in his eyes.

"I know you'll just love it," I said. I threw my arms around him.

I believed that meant I might be by his side someday. I was so excited when we discussed the colors and fabrics.

Nat wanted to stay in bed for a while, and he tempted me with his passionate embrace.

"Stop it, not now; I have so much to do. Let me get started, please." I gently pushed his hands away.

"All right, you win. But I'll wait for you. Try to hurry back," he said. Nat held me around the waist.

He handed me the blank check, and I was off to the store. I was glad Nat let me decorate his bedroom. I thought it would be our own private sanctuary one day. I returned with the purchases in a couple of hours.

I chose a gorgeous set which had a velvety feel and lace details.

Nat seemed pleased with my choices. He had a big smile on his face. "These are fantastic," he said. He held the curtains against the window. Nat picked up his tool chest, and gathered the supplies he needed to put up the window treatments.

We even dressed the bed together after Nat hung the curtains. It quickly took on the feel of a room designed for a couple. The bed had a lavish appearance with the ensemble I choose. I found a vintage inspired gold duvet, with specks of pale yellow flowers and the borders were fringes and roses. It reminded me of the rooms that might have been in the beautiful Victorian homes I admired. That night was an exceptional celebration for us. We enjoyed a romantic evening. Nat played his guitar for me, later we retired to our retreat hand and hand. He nuzzled next to me on the satiny new sheets.

"I love the soft feel of the comforter," I said, running my hand across it.

He put his lips on mine, and he wrapped his legs around me. I felt the love he had for me in his touch. When I opened my eyes, his gaze met mine. I had a sense of satisfaction, I had never experienced before.

"I'm so glad you like the room. If you weren't in my life, I would have never been motivated to complete it."

He showered me with kisses and sweet words of love all evening, and I felt as if Nat would ask for my hand in marriage by the holidays. All I wanted was for Nat to be the one to decide. After all, I was the one who asked him out in the first place. The least I could do for my own self-esteem was to let him propose.

Chapter Twenty-One

Nathaniel

"*I*f only I could win the lottery and give up this business," Nat said as he straightened up the back of one of his work trucks. The sky became dark grey, and the temperature dropped drastically.

"See you tomorrow, boss," Marty said.

Nat jumped inside his vehicle and switched the channel on the radio to the weather channel. The weather predicted storms for the rest of the afternoon. *There goes another wasted day.*

"Boss, you need a vacation." Marty stood on the driver's side of Nat's truck. "Is there a problem with you and the girlfriend?" Marty had a wife and five kids. When they ate lunch, he would brag about how great his marriage was. It became stronger after they attended a couple's seminar. Nat understood how crucial it was to work on communication, and it would help any relationship.

"I'm worn out, that's all," Nat said. He did not want to get into it. *I'll tell her how I feel. She'll understand, or maybe she'll dump me.* Nat knew he had to get it over with. He did not want to lead her on. No matter how he tried he could not function. For the last two weeks, Nat had not been able to get more than three hours of sleep on any given night. He felt like such a hypocrite. It made him feel like a fool to promote positive changes, when he could not share his life with the woman he loved.

Nat pulled away from the job site and raced down the parkway. It was a miracle he didn't get stopped by a trooper. The crew took off behind in Geraldo's pick-up.

The guys motioned to him to slow down, and made a sign with their hands that he was crazy. Nat arrived home in thirty minutes, showered, and went over what he planned to say to Madeline. He smoked half a pack of cigarettes, and debated whether he should pick up the phone.

Nat decided it might be better to go for a jog to change his mood. He ran to the basement and rummaged through the pile of laundry he needed to put away. After Nat grabbed his sweatshirt from the stack of clothes, he headed out, and drove to the park. There was a great runner's path in the next town. Nat wanted to avoid anyone he knew. The guilt he felt over their discussion hit him hard. Nat realized Madeline deserved so much more then he could offer her. It was nearly impossible to give up what they shared. Nat thought he should tell her the truth about how he had been feeling. Lately, he felt the urge to push away and take time to think about his life. He enjoyed the soft feel of her hand as she reached for his, or the way her voice sounded excited to hear from him whenever he would call. A strange sense of obligation made Nat uneasy, and he hopped out of the car and took off in a jog. An hour later, he wiped the back of his neck with a towel he kept in his back seat. On the drive home he kept the radio off. The music would only remind Nat of Madeline. As soon as he entered his house, he flopped on the couch. This time there was no desire to turn on the television or stereo. Instead, he picked up the throw pillow and put his face up against it. The scent of Madeline's perfume remained behind, and he closed his eyes. It gave him an urge to want to hold her, but first he would have to tell her how he felt. The need to stand alone did not leave him, and he knew what he had to do. Nat went upstairs to his bedroom, pulled back the covers, and remembered how happy Madeline was when she helped him decorate the room. As he ran his hand across the silky material of the sheets, he thought about how she felt lying next to him. *Maybe I'll feel different in the morning*, he thought before he retired to bed.

Madeline

The call came after I finished the laundry. Somehow I managed to foresee the end to my saga. I felt an awful event would take place that day.

"What's up?" he asked. Nat sounded dismal.

"Are you okay?" I held my breath and waited.

The tone in his voice was one of uncertainty. It was obvious he had a major issue on his mind.

"I'm okay, I guess. We need to have a talk," he said. His tone was serious. "It's going to rain, so I have to put the job off until it clears. Can I see you?" he asked.

"Sure, I guess if you insist," I responded. "I had planned to go to an anniversary sale at the mall, but I don't have to go," I answered. Nat's sudden urgency disturbed me.

"I have tons paperwork to do this afternoon, and I wanted to know if I could come by later?"

I felt my heart sink. Suddenly my entire body felt heavy.

"All right, Nat, call before you come," I answered. I could sense his negativity.

"I'll see you later," he said.

When I put down the phone, I fought back the tears. I ran into my bedroom and closed the door. My ears started to ring, and I feared heartbreak. Nat's attitude changed when he saw Mother and Mary in their family photo. Then he started to work on his bedroom. It was easy to place all my insecure premonitions out of my mind, when he introduced me to his decorating idea. We had a wonderful time together when we fixed up the master suite. It had been almost two months since our day on the beach.

I was not ready to face the inevitable, and I hoped he was sad about another matter. All sorts of crazy thoughts went through my mind. The grey clouds mimicked the way I felt inside on that dismal afternoon. I dreamt up all the worse case scenarios. A call to Bonnie for advice popped into my head, so I picked up the phone. I gripped tight to the table. *Please be home, Sis, I needed to talk.* There was no answer. I slammed down the phone, disappointed to have to leave a message.

The tears started to flow as I sat down in the kitchen. As I stared into my coffee cup, I cried. I should have known a woman's instinct is right on target. The knowledge I gained from the meetings at the hospital allowed me to calm down. It took a lot out of me to hold my head up high. The day felt like time stood still, and before I knew it, evening arrived.

My mother got home on time. I prepared dinner, and she studied my every move. She knew when I had a problem.

"What's wrong?" Her frail hand gently rested on my knee.

I moved close to her, and she gave me a hug. I tried to hold back my tears, afraid to upset her.

"I'm worried about Nat and me," I admitted. I took a deep breath. "He wants to talk today, and by his tone I can tell it could be serious."

"You must not worry. He loves you. I'm positive he does. He's just scared of commitment," she said. "The older a man gets the harder it is to change, and he's used to his time alone."

Her glasses slid down her nose. I adjusted them as she continued. She looked so philosophical, as she lectured me on the affairs of the heart.

"You have to take care of yourself. Don't lose sight of your ideas, my dear and let him think you don't care," she insisted. "I'll get out my book, and muster up a spell. Mary and I were sure he would be the one for you."

"What!" I shouted.

"Never mind." She patted the top of my head. "Now simmer

down. It will all come together." Mother sat back and crossed her legs.

Her words circled my heart with hope.

"You need to be mysterious. Listen to your mother." She pointed her finger at me. "I have been around long enough to know how men are." She handed me a tissue. "Dry your tears, he'll come around. He won't let you slip away. If he waits too long you'll move on, and he'll regret it. But, he'll be back, I promise you!"

She made an attempt to share her years of experience with me. I knew she sometimes got the details mixed up. Her long term memory still remained intact. It amazed me how Mother still made me feel better.

"I hope you're right. I really do love him."

She held me for what seemed like an eternity and rocked me as she cradled me in her arms. Strangely, it did manage to make me feel much better.

Nat arrived around six, and I was afraid to hear what he had to say. I shook with anticipation as I welcomed him inside.

"Are we alone?" he asked. He avoided eye contact.

"No, but we can talk in here."

We marched into my room, and I closed the door behind us. Nat sat in the chair while I sat on the bed.

I tapped my foot and fumbled with the clip in my hair. I felt self-conscious.

"Madeline, I'm concerned about my feelings," he stammered. "I really care for you. There's a problem with me. Sometimes I feel like I want to shout out loud: I want to be alone!"

He turned away. "I've been in turmoil with this. I can't figure out what to do. I don't want to leave you. Oh, I don't know if I can do this. You're so sweet, and wonderful. I never intended to hurt you."

Nat broke into tears, and I realized it wasn't a joke. I glanced out the window, and the sky was dark.

It would be better if we continued this conversation in private.

Mark had been in his room, buried in school work since early afternoon. I knocked on his door, with tears in my eyes. "I'm sorry to bother you. I need you to keep an eye on Grandma. Nat and I will be back in about an hour. Is it okay?"

"What the hell happened? Why are you upset?" he said. "Is it Nat? What'd he say to you? I told you he would hurt you." He curled his fist on one hand. "Where is he?"

"Don't get carried away." I said. It took a lot for Mark to lose his temper. When he did lose it, he would really flip out. "I'm fine. We'll be right back."

"You didn't answer my question," he said.

"What question?"

"What are you upset about?"

"We had a little dispute, but we're fine." My tone must have convinced him.

"I hope so. It makes me furious to see you hurt by another man," he admitted. "Sorry, I yelled. See you in a few." Mark smiled.

I wanted my sons to like Nat, and I certainly didn't want to get them involved in a conflict. Nat and I hurried outside, and hopped in his car. Since we were both upset, I suggested we go to the park, or another isolated area where we could talk. Nat followed my advice, and we went to the nearest park. When we got there, he turned off the ignition and slumped down in his seat.

It started to rain in a steady downpour. I could not see out of the windshield. We both sobbed uncontrollably. Nat held me in his arms as if he never wanted to let me go. It was torture to see him in such pain. I silently prayed to wake up and find this was just a terrible nightmare. My whole world shifted downward. My dreams were shattered. I turned toward him and raised my voice. "Can you honestly say you don't want to see me anymore?"

Nat looked at me intensely with a cold stare. "I need time to think," he said. His voice had become hoarse. He paused to clear his throat before he went on.

I remained silent.

"Maybe I should speak with the Monsignor at church. He might be able to help me sort through my issues," Nat said. He kept his eyes fixed on the dashboard.

"If you really care for me, we can make it work," I insisted. "It doesn't have to be so hard. If I'm not the one for you, then it's over. Just tell me, and it will be the end of it!" The tone in my own voice made me frightened. "What is it?"

"I told you; I feel like I want to be alone. I do love you, Madeline. There's a strange fear deep inside of me," he said. "I've been by myself for such a long time now. I don't know if I can, I mean, you're so sweet," he stammered.

"Well, just bring me home and do whatever you want." I did not want to hear another word. "Maybe you need to grow up," I insisted. "What the hell is your problem? Why did you agree to meet my whole family?"

My worst nightmare was in front of me, and I had no idea why. I was shocked to hear his words. The little clues he gave me when we met, were there, but I never thought they were this bad. If he had different goals, and I was not included, then, that was his problem. Why was he so afraid? Did he experience a trauma in his life? Did an event from his past force him into a solitary existence?

I glanced in the car mirror. My eyes were red and puffy. I tried to erase the signs of a dispute. I wiped my face with a tissue I had in my handbag. We drove back to my house. There was no further discussion. Nat accompanied me to the porch. He hung his head down as we approached the door, as if he was so ashamed of himself. We embraced in the foyer, and I felt sick to my stomach. When Nat stepped outside, the lights suddenly went out. The house took on an uneasy silence. We had lost all power.

Nat's eyes widened. His mouth opened, his jaw dropped. "That must be a sign," he said. "Maybe I'm not supposed to leave just yet." He rushed toward me and pulled me close. He threw his arms around me. I felt like I was in an altered state of consciousness. Our lips touched, and Nat whimpered like a child.

"Can you come home with me tonight?" he asked. "I think we need to talk a little more. God, I feel so terrible."

I was in a desperate state, so I agreed, and told Mark I would be home in a few hours.

When we arrived at his house, it all felt different. We sat down together in the living room, and he attempted to explain once again. Although, his efforts failed, I could not quite understand, no matter how hard I tried. Nat gave me mixed messages, and it confused me. We attempted to comfort each other with tender kisses. Instead, I felt used, not loved. I went home at midnight, alone with my thoughts, and cried all the way home.

"What about the room we decorated together. What on earth was that all about?" I spoke aloud. For the life of me, I could not understand why he would involve me in such a project to turn around and take it all back. It seemed like such a devious act. It was impossible to figure out what made him regress. Why was Nat so frightened to share his domain with someone else? I was shocked and humiliated at the same time. *What would a bachelor do with a room filled with roses and lace?*

Before I went to bed, I said these glorious words: *Thank you for these gifts: my health, my house, my kids, my career, my boss, my mom, and most of all my strength.* I tossed and turned all night and felt so distant from Nat, and I believed my dreams of a partner were lost forever.

I drifted through the morning in a state of shock. I wanted desperately to get out of the sad mood that took hold of me. I waited until the house was empty, and I had a good cry. Finally, I pulled myself together after a long talk with Bonnie on the phone. She stood by me, no matter what. She reassured me that Nat loved me, and needed time to sort out his fears.

"Just leave him alone, and he'll realize what he wants," she assured me. "You should keep yourself busy, and don't be at his beck and call."

A fire built inside me that drove me to push harder. I went straight to work on the cookbook I had planned to do. When I dusted off the top of my desk, I found my outline. I opened the drawer, where I kept the recipes I had accumulated over the past few years. Inside a folder, I kept the recipes I selected: all tested to perfection.

It was necessary to take care of myself at any cost. I had grown up over the last twenty years. The idealistic young girl was still inside of me. Yet she was wiser and more confident.

The information I needed for my project took all day. I made calls to associates in the business, just to give them a heads up on my ideas. After I developed a group of supportive connections, I knew I was ready. At last, the work was in progress. My goal kept me focused and I planned to work hard until it was completed.

My mind would wander to the feel of Nat's lips on mine or the sound of his voice. I remembered the thoughtfulness he showed when he gave me the painting. Nevertheless, he did not want to commit to our relationship.

I knew we didn't actually break up, but I still felt different. I recognized that Nat had serious reservations. I knew I had to strive forward, no matter how I felt inside. The connection we formed was real. I felt it, and I knew it.

My heart yearned for Nat to realize how strong our bond had become. The love we shared could not be duplicated with anyone else. It seemed as if it was our fate. We had so much in common, and I did not want to face the awful mistake of my choice to date an unavailable man once again. I knew that only he could change his mind, if he wanted to. For whatever reason, Nat could not seem to settle down. My inner strength grew from the lessons I learned throughout my life. The concept of honoring my own needs became clearer to me. I began to take care of myself from the theories in the rehab center. At times, the wisdom of the program would follow me. It seemed to protect me, and it kept me strong whenever I remembered the slogans. Their motto, "Believe in faith and providence," did help ease me through the days. The support of my devoted friends and family allowed me to remain focused.

Chapter Twenty-Two

Nathaniel

Nat pulled in to the garage downtown to fill up his tank, and spotted Jeremy as he walked out of the snack shop next to the station. He got out of his car to open his gas tank. Jeremy cracked open a Red Bull and took a gulp. Nat reached into his car and beeped the horn, and Jeremy stopped. Nat advanced toward him.

"Didn't you see me?" Nat asked. He knew the kid wanted to avoid him.

Jeremy wore a leery grin, as he made his way across the store's lot.

Nat put his hand out, and he shook Jeremy's hand with a firm yet friendly grip. Jeremy lifted the hood from his sweatshirt around his head, and crossed his arms. Nat could barely see his eyes.

"Are you hiding from someone?" Nat asked.

"Why do you say that?"

"Oh, no reason, it's just that your sweatshirt is big enough for a giant," Nat said.

"Yeah, I know. That's how I like it."

"Well, excuse me."

Jeremy laughed and moved the hood from his eyes. "There, is that better?"

"Yes, thanks. How've you been?"

"Okay, I guess." Jeremy turned away, and Nat detected a tone of sadness in his voice. "What's wrong, buddy? Hop in, I'll give you a ride, and we can talk."

Jeremy shook his head. "Sure, thanks."

"So, what happened, now?"

Jeremy put his head down. "I'm in trouble again, and Mom said I might have to go away to school."

"She's had it, I guess. The old 'I'll send you away to school' line has been used for many young boys."

"What do you mean?"

"That's what all parents say to scare their kids when they're in trouble," Nat said.

Jeremy's eyes opened wide. "Did your parents say it to you?"

"Sure, they did."

"Tell me, why are you in trouble? It's not cool to stay back. It's cool to go on to college and accomplish a goal." Nat hoped Jeremy understood and did not hold a grudge against him.

Jeremy hesitated before he answered Nat's question.

"I don't know why I hate school. I want to change, but it's not easy. I used to like it when I was younger, and I did great in art class and in math, too," Jeremy admitted.

Nat felt a strong desire to help Jeremy. He knew how it felt to be a young man with no male role model. Jeremy seemed like a lost soul. Nat had his father, who was drunk most of the time, and he could relate to the troubled youth. He knew he wanted to help Madeline and her son, even if Madeline became sick of his inability to commit, he could still be part of her life. It would be the ideal way for him to remain close to her, and display his love. If Nat could not live with Madeline, he could at least, find a way to help her. Nat did not want to appear selfish in any way. He wanted to do right by Madeline.

"Why don't you come over tonight? You could bring your books," he suggested. "I can show you how to study better. Don't forget I went back to school, and it wasn't that long ago."

Jeremy didn't ask about his relationship with his mother. Nat did not ask about Madeline, or bring up the fight they had either. He wondered if Jeremy knew about their discussion. He hoped Jeremy would not hold it against him if he did.

Jeremy agreed. "I guess I can come over." His tone of voice was hesitant, and he looked away. "Maybe you can let me try out your motorcycle."

"Yeah, sure. You can ride it in the driveway." Nat gave a hearty laugh.

Nat dropped Jeremy off at the corner. He wanted to give this kid a chance at a good life, and he knew how hard it was without a supportive father. They kept their meeting quiet.

Nat knew that if he helped Jeremy, it would benefit not only him, but it would make Madeline's life easier. He knew he had his work cut out for him.

Madeline

The winter season settled upon us. Nat and I continued to spend time together. There was still the doubt and fear of commitment to come between us. I sorted through one hundred or so recipes for my book, which I had scattered in front of me on the dining room table. My reading glasses hung around my neck on a long chain. I held my head down, and focused on my cookbook as I listened to the greatest hits of Journey on the stereo.

The loud knock on my door startled me. I wasn't expecting anyone. I peeked out of the window and chuckled when I saw Nat. He stood in the corner, as he shivered. He wore his wool hat, a big scarf, and gloves. It was bitter cold outside. There was a winter storm alert for the entire area. I opened the entrance, to find Nat with a grocery bag filled to the top.

"I brought dinner. I hope you don't mind," he said.

My emotions took over as I welcomed him inside.

"I hope it's okay," he said. "Do you have plans?"

"It's all right, come inside. You look frozen," I said.

I helped him with his coat, and hung it in the closet.

"I probably should have called first," Nat said.

"Where's Grandma?" he asked as he placed the bag on the kitchen counter.

"She's in the bedroom. I think she fell asleep. I closed her door, so I would not disturb her." Somehow, Nat managed to win my heart. I was still bothered by his inability to commit.

"I think it's time for a fire," I proposed.

It seemed like a good time to light the hearth with a crackling log. The room took on a warm glow within minutes. We went into the living room, and sat next to one another on the sofa. I snuggled next to him. "I didn't prepare dinner yet, and I'm famished. I've worked on my book all day. I was so involved, I never even thought about food," I said. "Mother had a late lunch, and she might just sleep the night. Mark is away with friends on a ski weekend in Vermont, so it's just you and me."

"What about Jeremy?" he asked.

"He came home, in a good mood for a change, and cleaned his room," I said. "Now he's at a movie with his friends. He begged me to let him sleep over Billy's house. I agreed since I spoke to his mother."

"I'm glad," he said. He gave a boyish grin. "We hooked up at the garage the other day. I invited him to study at my house."

"I can't believe it," I said.

"He's a good kid. Maybe he needs a little guidance." Nat nodded.

"You don't have to, Nat."

"I want to," he added. "I missed you today. I thought about you all day."

"I missed you, too."

If you could get over your commitment phobia, we could get on with our lives, instead of playing games. We were not teenagers, and I believed he still acted like one. Nevertheless, every time I was ready to give Nat an ultimatum, he would allure me, and I was at his mercy once again.

I closed the shades, and snuck a quick peak at the sky. The wind picked up, and the flurries had begun. I arranged our plates on the coffee table, and went over to adjust the thermostat. I had a suspicion my mother played with it. The temperature dropped quickly, so I grabbed my sweater, before I peeked in on Mother.

"She's fast asleep. Just as I thought," I said. Secretly I was happy we were alone.

We positioned ourselves on the floor in front of the fire. I could not resign myself to the thought of our relationship being over. For the life of me, I could not understand why he had such a hard time with commitment. The whole family adored him, and it was the perfect time in our lives to join as a family. My beliefs may have been different then his. It felt so unnatural to live apart, especially when two people were truly in love.

I continued to hear my mother's stories of undying love between her and my father. It was not easy for her to forfeit her parents respect and marry a much older man. They were set in their ways and wanted her to take over the family business. They owned a small grocery store, and she worked at the counter even as a young girl. She fled the life she knew at home to be with the man she loved. Mom never regretted her decision; she raised us with her loving nature. Over the years, her parents finally accepted my dad. Her father may have had moments of fury, especially when he drank. Nevertheless, she stood strong in her belief, and did not let his commands control her life. Although, they gave her a hard time for years, she stuck by Dad's side.

I tried to figure out Nat's dilemma, but I decided to let my mind rest that night and step back, and try to enjoy the night.

We dined on the floor, with our legs crossed, in front of the coffee table. Nat let me in on the latest news with his jobs. I loved to hear his stories. The details of his chaotic schedule held my interest. He stared into my eyes through most of the meal.

I enjoyed his company, and I had an ardent desire to feel his gentle touch on my skin. Nat reached for my hand. "Come on, let's get comfy in front of the fire," he said.

I got up to lock the French doors to the family room. I wanted to give us privacy just in case mother woke up. When I returned, I reached for the crocheted blanket from the back of the chair. We moved close together enveloped in each other's arms, as the fire illuminated the room. The look in his eyes was one of desire. Our bodies joined under the covers. Nat held me in his arms and softly caressed my back and neck. His sweet tender lips gently touched mine, and his tongue wildly searched my mouth. His passionate touch lifted me to a level of pleasure I only dreamed possible. Hours passed, finally the fire burned out with Nat and I side by side. The only light was from the glimmer of the streetlights through the window. I rested my head on his chest, and gently ran my hand across his thigh. He looked so content while I felt warm and protected. Nat snuggled up to me, and we peacefully drifted off to sleep. The night felt glorious with the resonance of the wind soft and easy.

We awoke to find the snow left only a dusting. The white layer over the lawn glistened with an icy coating.

Nat jumped up and hurried to dress.

"I have to leave now," he said.

He had a serious expression on his face, and his tone sounded cold. It was only six a.m., but I dare not question him. The boys were not expected home until later in the evening, so I didn't think the possibility of their entrance concerned him.

Silently, I longed for him to stay. My disappointment must have showed in my face.

"What's the matter?" he asked.

I brushed a piece of lint off of his shoulder. "I'm tired. I'll see you out." I stood at the front door in my robe, and watched as he drove away. When his car was out of sight, I closed the door and went to my bed.

Mom lay fast asleep as I placed my hand over the empty spot next to me. I closed my eyes and wished Nat and I could be man and wife. I wanted him to fill that space so badly. He was off to his world, and I was alone with my dreams, and beliefs, unmet once again. There had been no conversation or change since Nat informed me of his fears. We stifled the subject as if it were a deep dark secret. He was an intelligent man with knowledge of women's needs. A sense of resentment took control of my emotions. His ambivalence gnawed at me, and I suppose I resented my own.

Chapter Twenty-Three

Madeline

Later in the day, I got a surprise phone call from Anne. We usually did not get together until our lunch date. Since it was not time for our get together, I was concerned there might be an emergency.

"Anne, it's nice to hear from you," I said.

"Madeline, girlfriend, I have great news."

Her sentence had such a positive tone. I wondered what could have possibly made her this enthusiastic.

We chatted for a few minutes before she told me the good news. "Amanda and Matt got engaged last week. He took her for a carriage ride in the city and popped the question while they rode through the park."

My head spun while my brow tightened. Her oldest daughter was engaged. Amanda was dating a young man she met away at school. He had finished his studies and worked as a stockbroker.

"Congratulations! How wonderful," I said and felt sick at the same time. The room got warmer, and began to close in on me, as she went on with the story. It was terrible of me to wallow in self-pity at her expense. When she announced her news, I was happy for her and glad her daughter met a nice young man, but inside it made me more aware of my ridiculous position. We would share our concerns about the futures of our daughters. Amanda and Desiree were the same age. Here, my best friend's young daughter had an engagement announcement, and I was in a relationship with a man who still didn't know what he wanted.

"I'm so disappointed I couldn't make it to Clare's wedding. I could not believe how sick I was. The flu knocked me out this time," Anne said.

"How are things with you and Nat?" she asked.

"Great," I replied.

"Did you bring him to the reception?"

"No, he had previous plans," I said.

"I bet she was a beautiful bride. Post some pictures when you get a chance, please. Did you have a nice time?"

"Don't ask," I said.

"How bad was it?"

"I sat next to a weirdo who tried to hit on me all night. But Clare looked beautiful, and I'm happy for her." It would have been better if Nat had been with me. I felt like an outcast, alone. "The food was great, and so was the band. It's funny. I caught the bouquet," I laughed.

I was too ashamed to tell her my story of lost love. To share this information with a trusted friend would only make me feel like a fool. I knew what should be done. I was in denial and resisted the obvious.

❦

As I pushed the cart in the market later in the day, I noticed the people in the store. It was a busy afternoon, and there were mostly young mothers with their children. One by one, I carefully selected the items on my list. I strolled along the produce aisle, and saw a woman farther down. She wore a navy blue tweed suit. As she examined the fruit her beautiful diamond engagement ring caught my eye. A handsome man rushed towards her, and gave her a kiss on the cheek.

"Sorry, I'm late. Let me take the cart for you," he said. He took hold of the handle and they walked away. They stood close to one another.

At that moment, I felt cheated and used. My eyes opened up to the realization that stood in front of me. Nat wanted to have the best of both worlds. This must have been all I needed to push me over the edge. I had waited long enough. I think the combination of events earlier in the day were too much for me to accept. My skin began to crawl.

I decided to talk to him immediately. My needs came first. A sense of peace slowly came over me. It entered my body like a bright light. All of a sudden, all the sorrow left me. It was about time I did what was right for me. There would be no more time spent on a man who could not give me what I wanted. I deserved more, and I was determined to fight for what was right. I would not make any more excuses for Nat's fears. Nat was a grown man. If he was uncertain of his love for me, it was his loss. I dialed his number with a quick steady hand. *It's now or never*.

"Can you meet me at the coffee shop? I must see you. I promise it won't take long," I said in a firm tone.

"Is there a problem, babe?" he asked.

"Can you meet me?" I spoke louder.

"Sure," he said. "I can be there in an hour."

"That's good." I slammed the phone. I was more determined than ever.

❧

Nat arrived on time. He slid into the seat with a puzzled look on his face.

"What's wrong?" He raised his brow.

"I have a question to ask you. Do you love me?"

"Of course, I do," he answered.

"Well, it's time we discuss where this relationship is headed. Since the day we discussed your fears, you haven't mentioned how you feel now. Have you given it more thought?" I asked. I realized my voice traveled across the room, but I didn't care.

He seemed shocked by my remarks. His eyes opened wide, and he fumbled with his keys.

"Madeline, I still don't know what I want," he said. "I love you, and I don't want to hurt you, but I still want to live alone."

"So, you have no thought of a commitment," I said. "I don't want a part-time relationship. It just doesn't feel right. I deserve a man that loves me enough to want to spend his life with me."

"Now, wait a minute," he said in an arrogant tone.

"You wait a minute. I'm done."

"You're not serious," he said. He reached for my arm.

"I'm uncomfortable with your answer and don't understand. Furthermore, I don't want to continue to waste my time any longer."

"That's what you think, we're wasting our time," he raised his voice.

"We're in our forties, hello!" I returned. "I think by now a man should know what he wants in life. Don't you agree? You're a great guy Nat, but I have to move on."

He remained silent as I pushed back the table and stood up. There was no more he could say. He had said it all before.

As I forced back my tears, I swiftly rushed out of the shop. When I got into my car, I turned off my cell phone, and threw it on the seat next to me. My decision to stand up for what I believed in took priority now. The tears began to fill my eyes, but I held my head up and took a deep breath. I started the car and drove home.

I told my family that it just didn't work out with Nat. They continued to offer their undying support. Mark and Jeremy told me that the flags went up for them, when they heard he had never married. Bonnie stood by, and supported my decision. Mom told me not to cry, that he loved me and would be back.

She assured me, *He does love you. Don't worry.*

Mom would not accept it, when I told her we were finished.

Nat will to find his way back to you, she insisted, over and over. *I promise you, so dry your eyes.*

I could not figure out why her words sounded so confident. There was fervor in her words which frightened me. All I knew is that I had to move on despite Nat's indifference.

Mom's behavior had been more eccentric, and I was sure her intention was to make me feel better. Deep inside, I had a nagging feeling she knew more about Nat. Her outlandish and unpredictable actions scared me. One night, I found her out on the back steps in the middle of the night. I even counted her pills, to make sure she didn't take an extra one by accident. For the entire week after our break-up, she did the evening dishes, and helped fold the laundry. She reverted to a role as the caregiver while I sulked.

During this difficult period in my life, I received emotional support from my entire family. Everyone encouraged me to pursue my dreams. When I told Jeremy, he kicked his desk. Mark and Desiree were convinced he'd be back. My boss called Nat a jerk and said he would be alone for the rest of his life. Tony insisted he was foolish to give up a woman as wonderful as I was. He was convinced that Nat would never find a partner as trustworthy as I was, even if he searched forever. I knew Tony was partial, since he adored me. I could validate his feelings.

Chapter Twenty-Four

Madeline

*I*t wasn't easy to do, but I went back to my life as Madeline Young: chef, mother, and now, aspired author. The days were easier with my job at the restaurant and the project of my cookbook to keep me busy. I dreaded the night and hated when the darkness surrounded me. I tossed and turned in bed each night. I craved Nat's embrace, but, most of all I missed his stories. When I closed my eyes, I could hear the sound of his laughter. My heart yearned for what we once shared. I got through the days with the reality of his inability to share his life. There were times I doubted my decision, but I kept it to myself.

Secretly I feared I would never experience the happiness I had with Nat with any other man. Our time together was a period in my life, I would never forget.

The following weekend after our breakup, I made plans to go Christmas shopping with Bonnie. While I waited for her to pick me up, I heard a thump outside my front door. I rushed to open it, tripped on the area rug, and landed on my butt. I laughed at first, and then struggled to stand up. Luckily, I was not injured.

Outside on the step was a box. The delivery man must have placed it there. I could not remember when I placed the order. I hurried to rip it open. When I broke up with Nat, I ordered a jacket, a gorgeous new pair of boots, and a designer bag. I quickly put on the coat and slipped into the boots, and stood in front of the hallway mirror.

At last, I was able to place my needs at the top of the list. I received this precious gift from my time at the rehab center. The items did make me feel better. The value of self-love, with the ability to honor my beliefs foremost was difficult for in the past. The life lessons I learned made me strong, but it didn't shield me from the inevitable. It would take time, and I knew there were days when I was able to accept my decision with confidence. My emotions were all over the place. The worst moments of all were when I suddenly burst into tears. Sometimes I would cry if I saw a sad movie or heard a love song. I knew this was the natural grieving process.

Nat did not try to reach me. There were no messages on my machine at home, and no texts or messages on my cell phone. I gathered Nat respected my decision. I felt pity for him in a way, and I still believed he really did love me. For whatever the reason commitment was too much for him to deal with. Maybe I really did not want to uncover the answers. I knew the truth would hurt. I imagined it would not have made a difference in the fact that Nat still wanted to live alone.

Bonnie let herself in while I admired my new purchases. "Are you ready?" she asked.

"I love it. How much was it, and can I borrow I?" she asked. I held up my new bag, for her to examine it.

"I forgot all about it, but I'm glad it came today," I said as I escorted her outside. We got in her car and buckled up.

Bonnie drove to our favorite shopping outlet in Jackson. It had over seventy shops, and a trip there could take all day. The trees were bare by now, and the air had the brittle chill of winter. Icicles hung on the tips of the branches, and I could not believe how fast autumn flew by. It was unusually cold for December.

After we purchased more than we could carry, Bonnie and I stopped in a quiet place for lunch. We ordered grilled chicken salads since we knew how we would add a few pounds over the holidays. I loved the bright, festive feel of the dining area. We sat next to a wall of original paintings on sale to the public. They were done in bright blues and pinks, and had a feel of the tropics. I looked at the one next to me, and tried to make out the price.

"Do you think Nat will call for Christmas?" Bonnie asked.

I smirked. "I don't think so. I can't figure him out. He has a problem."

"What do you mean?" Bonnie asked.

I lowered my voice since the waitress was nearby. "He has acted strange on a number of occasions. I saw a large object in his attic, and he kept it covered like it was top secret," I said.

"I wonder why," she said.

"I wish I'd met his mother. Unfortunately, the cold weather was too much for her. Nat sent her to Florida every year to stay with her younger sister. The cold winters have become too much for her. He put her on the plane right before we became serious," I said.

"Did you see any photos of her?" she asked.

"A couple when she was much younger. I spoke to Mrs. Griffin once on the telephone. She sounded like a kind woman," I added.

"I wonder what big mystery surrounds the Griffin family," Bonnie said. She sounded almost frightened.

"Nat showed me a few frames once when we stayed up late on a Saturday night. I wondered why he gave me only a select group of pictures. He kept an album in a locked chest," I divulged. I reached for a sugar packet.

"Go on," she said.

"I got a glimpse of him one night, when he added a magazine

to the locked box. I could see the books and photos piled up to the top. He had another small book which he kept next to his bed. He would not let me see it. One day I asked him about it, and he quickly changed the subject. I thought Nat might have hidden some of the pictures of his old girlfriends. Maybe I could have understood more about his fears, if I would have met his mother."

"Yeah, maybe," she returned. She had a faraway look in her eyes. We paid the cashier and started on our way back.

Nat did not resemble his mother; he looked just like his father. He kept a pad on his desk with some of his father's drawings. Mr. Griffin was an artist when he was a young man. He sold a few paintings to an art dealer in New York. Nat told me that if his father would have stopped drinking, he could have had a fabulous career. Nat's relationship with his father may have been the underlying problem.

There may have been additional information in his secret pile of photos.

The holidays were difficult for me. Bonnie and I drove to Holmdel to a find the perfect Christmas tree. We searched the lot for an hour before we found the right one. We chose a balsam fir from Vermont. The salesman tied it to the car. We had decorated the tree on Christmas Eve at my house since I moved in. My home became the new meeting place for the festivities. The whole family gathered for the holiday tradition. Mom and Dad started the tree event when we were kids.

It really was my favorite celebration of all. This year we chose an old-fashioned theme for the tree. I still hung the stockings on the mantle, for fun. Jeremy hadn't come home yet, but Desiree and Mark sat next to the tree and eyed the envelopes. Instead of goodies, I put a little bonus in an envelope taped to the stocking. I put red and gold one's, tied with a sparkly tie twist. I found this year's new ornaments in an old-world shop on Main Street. They were all handmade, and were exact replicas of the ones used in the holidays past.

"This one is my favorite," Desiree said. She put the angel on top. It had a lacy white gown with a pink silk ribbon. The face looked almost human, and the eyes were crystal.

Mark stood up and put his face next to the branches. "I told you a real tree beats any old artificial one," he said.

There was a magical feel with the scent of a fresh tree in the living room, on a blistery cold day.

While we listened to the old Bing Crosby albums, we put the final touches on the tree. The garland consisted of a white beaded string with just a flicker of gold around the edges.

Mom sang "Jingle Bells" so loud I thought my head would burst. She knew all the words to her favorite songs. It would not be Christmas without mother singing the carols. We all joined in on the chorus, and she sang the lead.

I tried to be joyful, but it was still difficult for me. Fortunately, after we finished the tree, we were able to enjoy a great meal. The traditional holiday menu included a seafood variety. I dabbled with a few variations, but still stuck to the favorites. They all loved the buttery lobster bake with crusted salmon. It became my specialty.

"You really topped yourself this time. The salmon is yummy," Desiree said.

"Dinner tastes great." Mark added. He looked up as he reached for more.

The one person who missed the day of the tree ceremony was Jeremy. He did not arrive in time for dinner. I made sure to tell him what time to be home. We all gathered in front of the hearth, and enjoyed the fire. I served dessert when the front door flew open. I quickly turned my head and caught a glimpse of Jeremy. He stood in the foyer, with a guilty look on his face. His boots left a trail of dirt behind.

"Am I too late, Mom?" he asked.

"What do you think, Jeremy?" I answered, disappointed in his tardiness.

"I stopped to pick these up for you." He was out of breath, and he flashed a huge grin. His sweatshirt hung down past his thighs, and his coat was two sizes too big.

Jeremy handed me four lovely poinsettias. They were the biggest plants I had ever seen. They each had fancy gold paper wrapped around the bottom with velvet bows attached. Two were white and the others red. I turned my head to the side, and frowned. I was surprised, since I knew Jeremy had a limited flow of money.

"My friend works at a flower shop, and he gave me his discount," he replied.

They were beautiful and were just the final addition I needed for the house. The happy tone in his voice made me forget that I was angry with him for his lateness.

"I left your plate on the stove for you. Bring it in here and join us," I said.

Desiree squirmed and placed both hands on the seat of her chair. When Jeremy left the room, Desiree whispered. "Mom, he's been so different lately, I mean more responsible. I know he was late today. But, yesterday he asked me if I needed anything from the store," she said. "He ran to the drugstore, and picked up Christmas paper for me. Haven't you noticed how polite he's been?"

I crossed my arms, and put my hand on my chin. "Now that you mention it, honey, I agree, he has been different. I noticed he's been reading at night, and I found a couple of college brochures on his desk."

"I know what you mean. He hasn't been as quick to snap and cop an attitude like he usually does," Mark added. "I hope he's not on drugs. But, how is he getting better grades if that's the case? I saw a test with an A on it last week."

"It's about time he grew up and became a responsible young man," I said.

"I told you all he would straighten out," Mother added. "He's my grandson, and he'll grow to be a fine young man." She shook a finger in the air. "Uncle Joe was the same way when he was a youngster. Dad would whip him every Friday night when he came home late. Look at him now, he's a successful businessman." She threw her arms up as she continued her speech. "Now listen to me, Jeremy is fine, and he does the best he can. I don't want to hear any more negative remarks about him."

She defended him no matter what he did.

"Don't get upset. We just want to figure out what caused the drastic change in his behavior," I said. I tried to calm her down, so I kept my tone soft. "He's been out late on the weekends, and he doesn't tell me where he's been. I've even tried to reach him at some of his friends' houses. He's impossible to get in touch with. I would appreciate a little consideration on his whereabouts in case of an emergency."

"Don't worry. Maybe he has a new friend who is a positive role model. That could account for his change in behavior," Mark said. "You know, I met a kid when I was his age who was a big shot around school. He was a flashy dresser, yet a great motivator, and I wanted to be more like him. Jeremy may have got involved with the preps at school."

"Well, whatever it is I'm sure pleased with his growth. I pray it continues," I added. I straightened the bows on the plants.

Desiree stood up, and jolted to the window and smiled when she opened the curtains. "Look, it's snowing. It's what I wanted for Christmas. I hope it sticks." She applauded the event as if it was a miraculous happening.

Mark stood up and opened the door to see for himself.

"Wow, let's check it out. Come outside, Desiree."

They both hurried to put on their jackets and flew down the steps. All I saw was a flash, before my eyes. They raced each other to get the first handful of snow.

I watched the two of them jump around and enjoyed the wintery mix. This year the holiday felt different. It was a season to remember, despite my break up with Nat. The family was together; everyone was healthy. I had a sense we should grasp onto each moment. Mom was getting up in years. I knew she would not be around forever.

The chill from the front door was a little too much for mother. She shivered as she pulled the ends of her shawl together and pulled it up to her neck.

"Mark, Desiree, come on inside it's freezing out there," I said. I held the outside door and motioned to come inside. The snow covered their jackets with a sparkly glow.

"The flakes are gigantic. It's really coming down out there, and I think it's starting to accumulate," I predicted. "The roads are already blanketed by a layer of ice. That's settled, everyone is sleeping over." I closed the door, and made sure it was secure with the double lock in place.

I would not take no for an answer. Bonnie and Mike would sleep in the library on the pullout couch. Desiree would take the small bedroom upstairs. The sleepover gave us an opportunity to wake up on Christmas all together. I began to think about the breakfast menu. My plan was to make a breakfast pizza and a cream cheese-filled French toast. The kids loved my special brunch treats, especially when I let them sleep late. All the items I needed for a homemade marmalade were readily available in the refrigerator. It was fun to prepare a special family breakfast. Although, I thought I felt happy, I must have had a distressed tone in my voice. We all moved in by the fire. I arranged the seats to face the hearth.

"Are you all right, Madeline?" Bonnie asked.

"Why do you ask?" I shrugged my shoulders.

"You may have a smile on your face, but there's a sad look in your eyes tonight."

"I appreciate your concern. Tonight has turned out to be a wonderful night," I said. "It's great to have you all here with me." Inside I still hurt, but I tried to conceal my inner thoughts with a big grin.

I knew she could read my mind and tell I was still upset over Nat. Bonnie crinkled her nose. "I still cannot understand what happened with Nat; he seemed so into you," she said. "The way he looked at you on that night you had him over to meet the family was a dead giveaway of the way he adored you. I thought for sure he would have come to his senses by now. I think there's more to his story than we imagined." She crossed her arms. "Yes, I'm sure of it. An awful experience must have made him change his mind."

Jeremy poked his head from around the corner and tried to listen to our conversation.

"Excuse me, Jeremy. What are you up to?" I asked.

"I didn't even hear a word of your discussion." He looked away quickly, and I sensed he was uncomfortable.

"We're wondering about how Nat's doing," I said.

He seemed upset when I mentioned Nat's name. Jeremy spoke in a louder tone than usual. "Oh, come on, forget it. I'm sure he's great," he snapped.

I stood up, stunned by his outburst. "How would you know that?" I asked.

"I don't know. I just think he's a grown man, and can take care of himself. Whatever he's up to is his business. Oh, I don't know what I mean." He gave a quick sigh and turned his back to me. Jeremy suddenly became fidgety. His hands trembled. He put his hands in his pockets, and held his head down. He trotted over to the tree. He looked over the ornaments, and attempted a grin.

I saved all of the special little ornaments they made in school. The rest of the night, we enjoyed the Christmas carols. I must have played the songs from every old artist that night. It was wonderful to reminisce about the special moments over the years. Mom recited her famous stories about when she was a little girl. Her eyes still held the glimmer of wonder behind the creases and tiny lines. She ended the evening with her tale of her Christmas when she was a child, and still slept in a crib.

We gathered around with Mother in the center.

"My mom and dad snuggled under the covers," she said. "I stuck my hand inside the stocking that hung on my crib. I was at least four or five years old. In those days, we slept in a large crib in our parent's room. My parents couldn't afford much more for me to sleep in back then. I was so excited to find out what Santa left me. When I stuck my hand inside the stocking, I pulled out an awful chicken foot," she said.

Mom's face displayed the pure expression of a sweet child of five. She recited an event that stayed in her memory for over seventy-five years. She continued with the story while we all gave her our undivided attention.

"Way on the bottom was a lump of coal. I could feel my heart break as I realized I must have been a bad girl that year," she admitted. "My parents continued to hide under the covers. They giggled the whole time I cried."

"Ah, that's terrible," I said.

"They played an awful trick on me," she proclaimed. Her tone was serious. "Finally, Mom took me in her arms and gave me the gifts from under the bed. They surprised me with a coloring book, crayons, nuts, and candies." Her eyes opened wide.

She laughed along with us, and she started to look a bit sleepy. The night came to a perfect end. I felt a renewed appreciation for the holidays.

"Goodnight everyone. Have a Merry Christmas," she said, as she waved.

Mark and Desiree helped tuck Grandma in that night. It was a memorable evening.

There was an extraordinary feel to that night. It remains in my heart, and I will forever treasure the night we all slept under one roof and awaited the day Christ was born. We spent New Year's Eve in front of the television and made a list of promises for the year to come. One of the priorities on the top of my list was to complete my cookbook. January flew by as did the dreaded Valentine's Day.

Chapter Twenty-Five

Madeline

Despite the cold weather, Grandma was able to attend the day care center regularly. She only had a few mishaps. I expected as much. When the director told me she brought a dead frog back from an outing at the aquarium, I held back the laughter. I told her she must have thought it was her pet. She had a blast at the center, and her sleep habits improved immensely. I, on the other hand, wasn't as well. I experienced sudden mood swings. It was so unlike me when I argued with Bonnie over a sweater. She called to ask me why I never returned it. We typically got along no matter what, but that time I lost my temper. I jumped in my car, and drove to her house. I knocked on her door, and pounded harder than usual.

"What's your problem?" she asked.

"You have a lot of nerve when you accused me of losing your stupid sweater. I didn't keep it, here it was in my trunk," I said. I threw it at her.

I couldn't believe how terrible I treated my sister. I immediately became ashamed of myself. I reached for her hand. "I don't know why I'm so cranky," I admitted. "I've gained another five pounds, and my hair is brittle and dry." I held out my hand.

Bonnie waited a moment, before she burst into a robust laugh. I giggled along with her, as we apologized to one another.

Desiree came over for dinner more often, which was a special treat. The boys were great with Grandma and helped me so much. I got through the difficult time with the support of my family. The winter months were slow at the restaurant. I kept busy on my cookbook a few hours a day. This time of year was dark and miserable in New Jersey. I desperately needed a break.

I dialed Bonnie on a Sunday I requested off. I simply needed rest and relaxation. "Do you feel as tired of the cold as I do?" I asked. "I think it's time to take a long weekend getaway."

Bonnie and I agreed to a well-deserved weekend trip to an island getaway. She had wanted me to take a break for weeks. I decided to pack a bag, and the two of us were off.

Mark promised to care for Grandma while I was gone. Since he was in between classes, he could stay with Mother. It was a perfect time for me to get away. Mother told her stories repeatedly, but he would listen, as if it was the first time. I knew when he was a little boy that he would become a compassionate young man. My children were all very special; each one had a quality unlike anyone else.

"Don't worry, Mom. I'll be all right. I'll keep an eye on Jeremy, too," Mark assured me while we got into the car. He locked the door and turned to give me a smile.

"Please don't fight," I asked. "I don't want anyone injured."

Last time I left them alone, Mark socked Jeremy in the eye when he couldn't take his attitude anymore.

"I promise you I won't let him get to me, you'll see. I mean it," he insisted. "Anyway, if I want to get my nursing license, I can't afford any trouble. It's not worth it."

"Good for you," I offered.

Mark tried to take care of me. I knew it was supposed to be

the other way around. Jeremy was still doing better in school. He really made a complete turnaround in his behavior. His grades had improved consistently. I felt confident to leave them for the weekend. I decided it was time for me to have a good time. Sometimes you need to change your routine.

I stepped off the plane, and immediately felt the warm climate. I looked forward to the sunny beaches. I could not wait to jump into the pool. The water enticed me, as soon as I caught a glimpse. Our rooms were luxurious, each with a gorgeous spa like bathroom. We had a two-room suite that overlooked the water. The view was remarkable and had wall to ceiling windows.

Bonnie and I treated ourselves to a massage that afternoon and spent the rest of the day by the water. We planned to see a show that night. I felt like my old self again and was glad we decided on the long needed escape. I don't know what I would have done without Bonnie's support. At sunset, it was different. I still tossed and turned, with nightmares that tore me apart. When I fell asleep the night before our trip, I could have sworn I closed my window. At two a.m. I felt a strong gush of wind, and I woke up. I noticed the window open, so I got up to close it. As soon as I fell back to sleep, my nightmare continued with a childlike figure in a wildflower field. She ran through the grass in her bare feet. The muffled cries of babies filled my head. My night gown felt damp and I thought I must have had a fever. I was afraid the strange visions would never stop. *Maybe I needed to talk to someone professional about the visions of Aunt Mary and the nightmares.* She didn't try to hurt me, and I did feel comfort from her visits, so I put it all in the back of my mind. I did believe in spirits, especially unsettled ones. My mother pulled a lot of stunts with her Ouija board, and it left no harm done. But, this time I did not share all my visits with her. I thought it would only upset her. It was time to put my worries aside and enjoy the island.

ॐ

I gained renewed energy after a walk along the water the following morning. Later Bonnie and I played cards on the balcony, with all visions of work or a schedule the furthest thought from our minds.

The early evening atmosphere sizzled with energy. The sky was a beautiful shade of electric blue. The cool breeze was just enough to relieve you from the heat of the daytime sun. Everywhere in site, there were so many happy faces along with the sound of laughter.

I agreed to go to a dinner celebration, later that night. The party had an island theme that people of all ages could attend. We enjoyed the music on the beach with a beautiful fire in the background. Out of the crowd stepped a tall handsome man, who asked me to dance.

"Go on Madeline, it'll be fun." Bonnie encouraged me.

Reluctantly, I agreed.

We danced to the same song I heard at Nat's house after our first date. It became our song, and as I listened to the music, I remembered the way he told me he saw my face in front of him, right before I called. My mind drifted to our first date, and the fun we had on his deck under the stars, and I enjoyed each moment. The music stopped, and I slowly walked away and never looked at my dance partner.

"Bonnie, please understand I'm just tired. I want to go back to the room," I said. I hoped she wouldn't mind.

"It's still early, and the music is fantastic. I think I'll stay a bit longer," Bonnie replied. Her skin took on rosy glow from the sun. The long sundress she wore made her look like a goddess. I nodded. "Have fun. I'll see you in the morning," I said. I made my way toward the elevator.

My heart was somewhere else. So, I retired upstairs and opened the drapes on the huge floor to ceiling window in my room. I stared at the view, which was gorgeous, and I could see the entire area all lit up in front of me. The whole place was filled with energy. The atmosphere was out of this world, but somehow the night changed my mood. I sat alone with my thoughts, which were miles away with Nat. *If only it could have been different between us.* There were times when I wanted to pick up the phone, and proclaim my love for him. Luckily, I stopped myself, just in time. I knew that if I called him, it wouldn't change his mind. If he made a decision, he would have reached out to me. I finally decided to get into bed.

About four-thirty I rolled over to find a shadowy image in the far corner. At first, I felt a wave of cool air, and a bright light encircled the top of my bed, and then stillness took over the room. The soft chant was familiar. She moved toward me, and I did not fear her. I could not make out her features, but I knew who she was. She usually appeared when I was at my worst.

"What do you want?" I asked. Her appearance startled me more, since I was away from home. A circular formation appeared above my bed, and it caused me to squint. I raised my hands to my forehead, to cover my eyes from the bright ray of light. My head pounded, my pulse raced. The smoky message appeared.

"What do you want?" I asked again.

She was gone in a flash.

The letters, in smoke, dangled once again. This time it took great effort to make them out. *A time for forgiveness. SG.* The strange initials remained until they faded into dust.

I blessed myself before I checked under the bed. She hadn't paid me a visit in such a long time. I did sense her presence on many occasions over the years.

The room became cold, as I shivered and wondered if the air conditioner was set too low. I got up to adjust the thermostat, and then went into the bathroom to splash water on my face. When I returned to bed, I reached for the remote, and turned on the television. I stared at the screen, and felt the need to divert my attention. *Some Like It Hot* with Marilyn Monroe and Jack Lemmon was on, and I watched it. Somehow, I could not shake the awkward sense of reality which took me out of my comfort zone. It took an hour or so before I could relax. I adjusted the bedside radio to face me, and turned on my side. Surprisingly, I woke peacefully at nine a.m., and vaguely recalled the mysterious appearance. But I still wasn't sure, if I had a dream, or if it really happened. It would have been nice to believe Aunt Mary was a magical genie who guided me toward a life changing experience. Who was I to get such special attention? Deep inside, I did believe in ghosts.

We were going to leave for home the next afternoon. Later, I decided to browse through the shops to find the perfect souvenirs for them.

"Are you all right, Madeline?" Bonnie asked. We strolled along the mall and window-shopped.

"I missed Nat last night more than usual," I said. "I'll be fine." I chose not to mention the visit. Bonnie may have thought I was crazy.

"How's your cookbook?"

"It's almost finished, and I think it's pretty good," I said

"Have you got an agent yet?" she asked.

"My next step is to find one. I have a couple of names from a friend of mine, and I might have a chance for a good deal," I said.

Bonnie slipped her arm through mine. "That sounds wonderful. Your cookbook just might make the bestseller list."

I realized how good my life was, and my energy shifted toward a more positive mode.

"I guess I need to remember, I do have a life and remain focused on that, even if it is without Nat."

"Don't forget, this was Nat's choice, not yours," she said. "He's a grown man, and he let you get away," she insisted. "You're a brilliant woman. You'll find someone else one day," she offered.

"Thanks," I said.

"Okay then, let's eat."

We stopped for breakfast in a small café next to the beach.

"It'll all work out," Bonnie said, as she gently placed her hand on my shoulder.

Chapter Twenty-Six

Madeline

On the ride home from the airport, I keep my eyes glued to the road. As we drove past the familiar settings, I sighed. The events of my life raced through my mind.

As we turned down the street to my house, I recalled how the winter months were usually long and lonely for me. The carefree sunny times of spring and summer sped through my mind. The days of winter were short, and by the time I left work, it was dark and gloomy. I realized this could be the perfect time to put the final changes on my cookbook. Bonnie hummed cheerfully to the music on the radio. Desiree's car was parked in the driveway.

"Looks like you have company," Bonnie said. She turned to open her door. "Do you want me help you with your bags?"

"I'll be fine. We've had a long day, you must be tired," I replied. "Come over tomorrow night to see Mother. I'll have the pictures of our trip ready for you."

"I am tired," she said. Bonnie offered me a warm embrace. "Hang in there."

Desiree, Mark, and Jeremy ran to greet me at the door. The fabulous aroma of roasted chicken filled the air. "What's in the oven?" I asked. I opened the door and caught a glimpse inside of a huge brown bird.

"That looks delicious," I said. I put on the oven mitts. I gently pulled out the rack and basted the chicken.

"I even made homemade biscuits, and a custard tart for desert," Desiree added.

"Looks like you really planned this dinner. Is it almost ready? I'm ravenous," I said.

"In a few," Desiree returned.

The table looked beautiful with the fine china, and a pretty floral centerpiece.

Mom sat in her chair and cheerfully sang with her headphones on her head. She wore a silver sweater with white pearls on the front of it. Her hairstyle looked festive. The back was pulled up in a bun, and two curls dangled alongside her cheeks.

I went over to her side and bent over.

"I'm so happy to see you," she said. She gave me a big smile.

I kissed her on the forehead, everyone gathered around me, and made a fuss over my homecoming.

"What have you all been up to today?" I asked.

"We wanted to impress you with a clean house. Desiree even offered to make a welcome home dinner. How was your trip?" Mark asked.

Jeremy wore a linen dress shirt, with perfectly pressed pants. His hair looked neat, combed over to the side. I could not believe my eyes.

"You look really good. Did you change your style?" I asked.

"Well, I'm older now. I might even apply to a university," he said with a quiet confidence. "I might as well dress like a college student."

Jeremy flashed a huge smile. He appeared grown-up and handsome dressed in a more refined style.

"I think you look wonderful," I said, as I reached over to give him a hug. "I'm really impressed Jeremy." I stood back to admire him.

I wondered what motivated him to change. I didn't

complain; miracles do happen I supposed.

Desiree wore her hair down in a carefree style. Her eyes sparkled, when I handed her a gift.

"I bought you a little trinket home from my trip," I said.

"What is it?"

"Open it and see for yourself."

She ripped open the paper. "Mom, this is beautiful."

I found a lovely box filled with French-milled soaps and perfume from an elegant boutique. Inside the box were lilacs and lace.

"You shouldn't have, but I love it," she said.

The boys poked around and tried to find their presents. "You're the best," Mark said. He turned toward Mother who was in her chair.

"I bought you a doll that you wind up," I said. I pulled a chair next to her, and sat down. "It plays your favorite song."

"My goodness, she's so beautiful," she said. She held the doll to her chest.

"I think she resembles you," I added.

"Thank you, my dear, she's wonderful." She pressed her cheek up against the doll.

It didn't take much to make Mom happy. She was so appreciative.

"How was the plane ride, mom?" Jeremy asked.

"It went smoothly until we ran into some turbulence, but overall it was a good flight."

"I'm glad you're home safe," he said.

I slipped into my bedroom to change before dinner, delighted about a special night with my family.

Desiree followed me to my room. She closed the door and down on my bed.

"Have you talked to Nat?" she inquired.

I looked down. "No, not since I talked to him in the coffee shop, before the holidays." I sighed.

"I can't believe him!" she exclaimed, as she raised her arms in the air. "I thought you two were perfect for each other. He really fit in with our family. Oh, don't worry, he'll come back." Desiree assured me. "It won't be long before he realizes how much he loves you. I don't know what his problem is. I'm here for you, just don't weaken."

"How's work?" I asked.

"Great, I may get a bonus soon. I just finished a week of a special assignment. I can finally breathe."

"Is there any other news?" I asked.

"Not really, it's all pretty much the same, I guess," Desiree replied. "I'd like to check out a new car. I just have to find the time," she added.

She had such an ambitious nature. I loved that about her.

"Hurry up, dinner's almost ready," she said. Desiree raced back out to the kitchen.

"I'll be out in a minute." I relaxed for a few minutes alone in my bedroom to reflect on my blessings. I was thankful for the support of my family. I spent the night with my loved ones, and the unexpected welcome home dinner. The next day, I planned to get back on track.

Chapter Twenty-Seven

Madeline

*A*t home the next day, I worked at the dining room table. I pulled the chapters together and went over each recipe to fine tune the ingredients. My concept of sonnets for each recipe worked, and it turned out pretty well. I felt confident I could have it represented by a reputable house. My decision to spend my time on my cookbook left me less time to obsess over Nat.

My time off from work left me a few more weeks, and it came at the ideal time. The trees blossomed with buds once again, and I welcomed the change.

When I took a break a few hours later, I brewed a hot cup of tea, and sat down in the kitchen. A view of the back caught my eye; the signs of spring were all around. The tiny buds shot up through the soil, and I could hear the birds chirp. Spring was the time of year that seemed to signify a fresh start. Happily, I got through the winter with the love and guidance of my family.

Later in the afternoon, I finally wrote a query to send to a group of prospective agents. One of my colleagues gave me a name of a few literary agencies who took e-queries. I sent a letter and a sample of my work to my top choices on the list.

❧

When I received a call from one of the agents the next day, I almost fell over. She called to tell me she would like to work with me and assured me she would be able to get me a good deal. Her interest in my work made me happier then I could ever imagine. It may have seemed childish, but I jumped up and down in my living room. I wondered how I could handle all the excitement. It all seemed dreamlike and somewhat unbelievable to me. The restaurant I worked at was well-known. I realized it helped my book to work in an establishment, which had such popularity. Her name was Ingrid Nelson; she had started as an intern, moving to senior agent, and was interested in my work. My friend had put in a good word for me, and Ingrid liked what I sent her. Ingrid had a special interest in the field of cooking. There were a few best-selling cookbooks represented by her company.

Everything happened so fast. A publishing company she worked with was interested, and I would have to go to New York for a meeting to go over the contract and finalize the illustrations.

When Jeremy came home after school, I greeted him at the door.

"Hey, Mom, why are you at the door? Am I in trouble?" He slid past me as I followed behind him.

"I have good news. But, I have to leave you and Mark with Grandma for a few days."

"For what?" he asked.

I grinned from ear to ear, and jumped up and down. "I have an agent for my cookbook."

Jeremy's eyes opened wide. "Wow, that's cool. Can we celebrate with a pizza?"

"Sure, why not?"

My mother's bus beeped outside, and it surprised me when Jeremy volunteered.

"I got it, you wait here." He rushed to the curb and guided Mother inside.

"Isn't he an angel?" she asked. Jeremy held her arm as he

guided her into the living room.

He helped her take off her coat, and she sat down in her recliner.

"I had a wonderful day. We had a visitor, and we had a birthday party for the aide, Miss Cindy." She grinned like a cat that ate a mouse, as she walked into the bedroom. It puzzled me how Jeremy's behavior switched from arrogant to someone who would to pitch in to help. I shrugged and hurried to order the pizza. Mark called from class and I told him my news. He offered to take care of the house, while I traveled to the city.

A few days later, I packed and, thought about the transition we went through. I was at peace with my decision to take care of myself. I finished sorting through my overnight bag and threw out the old bottles of shampoo and conditioner left behind from the last trip.

Jeremy stayed in his room longer than usual and whispered to someone on the telephone.

I tapped on his door lightly. "Can I come in?" I asked.

"Sure, come in." Jeremy immediately hung up the phone, and jumped up quickly.

"Are you okay?" I inquired. I hoped he wasn't in any trouble.

He shuffled as he straightened his shirt. He threw a couple of books across the bed. "I'm fine," he said.

He seemed a little annoyed with my questions. He scrambled around the room and straightened his clothes that sat in a pile on the floor. His room was so cluttered that sometimes I could not even see the carpet. I was glad it was a dark color.

"Do you have any plans for the weekend?" I asked.

"I'll be home tonight," he answered. "I have an interview for a summer job at the mall tomorrow," he said. "It's at the new sports store, The Mile Run."

"That's great. I hope you get the job," I replied. "I'm so pleased with your behavior lately. You're grown up and have become a responsible young man."

He grinned, as he slicked back his hair. "I was just going through a rough time."

"Remember the time the truant officer called you at work? I'd get off the school bus, and walk right out of the back door at school," he said. Jeremy put his hand over his mouth, and laughed.

"How could I forget?" I returned. "I wanted to send you to a military school."

"I was a kid then. I've grown up a lot since."

A sense of pride filled my heart, when I heard the determination in his voice. "I knew you were a smart guy. I'm so relieved you decided to take a different path."

Jeremy helped me carry my bag to the living room and held his back when he placed them down next to the door.

"What did you put in these bags?" he asked. He frowned. "It feels like you have your whole closet in here."

I laughed, and attempted to lift them. "I always felt it's better to have more."

Jeremy smiled, "Have fun."

I called Desiree to let her know my schedule. I left a brief message on her machine.

Mark arrived home and rushed into the living room. "I'm glad I caught you," he said. "Do you want me to give you a lift?"

"Sure, I think that's a good idea," I replied. "This way I won't have to look for a parking spot."

"Do you have Grandma's pills ready?" he asked. "I noticed her appetite has been poor. I hope she's not sick."

"She looks all right to me. Maybe it's just the weather," I said.

Mark's graduation from Nursing School was coming up. His determination would finally pay off.

"You'll be a wonderful nurse one day," I said.

Mark exuded professionalism. He held the field of nursing in highest esteem.

"I can't wait to graduate. I've already started to look at some hospitals for a job," he said as he flipped through a magazine in the foyer. "I can't believe it has been three years already."

My oldest son was an ambitious young man. I suddenly realized my sons had become responsible adults. I knew they would accomplish their goals, even if I did raise them on my own.

⁓

The train station buzzed with the sound of commuters. I thought it would be better if Mark got back to the house.

"You can have the car while I'm gone," I said. I slipped the keys into his shirt pocket.

"Thanks a lot. Call me when you get there. Good luck," he offered.

"Aunt Bonnie will be over tomorrow to help you with Grandma," I shouted. He made his way down the stairs.

Meeting my agent made me nervous in a good way. I grabbed a quick cup of coffee, from the Dunkin Donuts. The station came alive with noise as I moved up to the platform. I exchanged small talk with the woman who stood next to me. We compared our tickets, and checked the time for arrival. As I made my way down the aisle, I found a seat next to the window, and tried to place my bag above the seat. A nice young man saw me struggle and offered to help. "Thank goodness," I said under my breath. I will travel lighter next time. My eyes connected with a man across the aisle. I found myself surprised to think he looked cute. It was a miracle that I even noticed another man. I was still curious to know how Nat was. I wanted him to be happy, despite our breakup.

The time apart only made me love him more. I added a little prayer every night that he was safe. I struggled with mixed emotions since our last conversation. As time went on, I questioned if I acted hastily. The nights he held me in his arms captured my thoughts, and I could still feel his caress.

The loud announcement overhead startled me. It was my stop, so I hurried to gather my bags. I climbed the stairs. I began to go over the things I would say to promote my cookbook. The nervous energy I felt gave me just what I needed to push through the station. I hailed a cab and was on my way.

The city made me a little jittery. There were cars all over, with hurried drivers that cut each other off on the road. As we neared Central Park, I knew we were almost there. The office was on the West Side. We passed a horse and carriage on the street, and I wished I had time to take a ride through the park. I finally arrived at her office, and took the express elevator. My stomach churned, I think from all the excitement. The nicest woman, who was the secretary, greeted me. She announced me, and I went inside the office with high hopes.

"I'm so glad you could make it," Ms. Nelson said, as she shook my hand. "Have a seat. Make yourself comfortable. I'm really excited about your book. It's got a new great angle, and I think it will sell."

"I'm glad you enjoyed it. I worked on it for a long time to get it just right," I beamed. I was quite impressed with her workspace. The room had lots of windows. The desk was huge with a rich cherry finish. I sat back slowly and took a breath.

"It's nice to finally meet you. I'm confident we've made the right decision," she said.

Her words gave me a sense of accomplishment.

She opened a folder that sat on her desk. She flipped through the pages in-between and looked up at me, with interest. "Our marketing partner will get in touch with you to set up the promo," she said. She offered a polite smile. "I can recommend a place to stay, and I can arrange for a car."

"That's awfully kind of you. I made plans, but thank you for your offer."

We met with the book publisher, and the contract she gave me impressed me as did her professionalism. I signed the contract, which I thought was fair. The publisher loved my work. There were so many opportunities ahead of me now. My determination seemed to all pay off, and I was free for the afternoon. A pizza sounded like a good idea for dinner. There was a brick oven pizzeria with an aroma that reached the sidewalk. I stopped inside ordered a slice with a Diet Coke and jotted down the appointments in my calendar.

As I glanced down at my watch, I realized there was still time before my room at the hotel would be ready, so I browsed through a few shops. Window shopping in the trendy shops made me feel like my life had taken a turn for the better. I had acquired so many new roles in such a short time. It was a challenge, and I was certainly up for it. I eagerly anticipated my book's debut, and I could imagine myself in a studio with my own show. My mind even wandered to the idea of being an owner of a seaside restaurant one day. The realization I might even be able to buy a house on the beach in the future made me feel exhilarated. I could practically smell the salt water. There was no limit to my fantasies now. A world of promise stood behind each step I took.

I called home, to check in with the boys, and I was surprised when there was no answer. My instincts told me the boys would not take Grandma out anywhere. The thought crossed my mind, and I wondered if I left the ringer off. My phone rang, and it was Mark.

"What's wrong?" I asked, afraid of his answer.

"It's terrible, Mom!" he said. He sounded out of breath. "When I came inside after I took the garbage out, I found Grandma unresponsive. I called for an ambulance immediately. She finally woke up when they put her on the stretcher." He paused. "They gave her oxygen; I think that's what helped her. I don't know what happened. She had a big lunch and she got dressed. Mom, she was fine. We're at the hospital, and the doctor is about to come out."

"I'll be right home. Call Bonnie and tell her to meet me at the hospital!" I shouted. My body trembled. I hung up and ran out of the restaurant and grabbed a cab to the station. My insides shook. *What if she dies and I'm not there.* I cried.

"My mother, please God help her." I spoke aloud. The train arrived on time and kept on schedule. It took about twenty minutes. All I could do was pray, and urge the cab driver to hurry. I arrived at the medical center and ran to the emergency room door. I found Mark and Jeremy at the entrance. Desiree straggled behind and she tried to catch up with us.

"Wait for me, Mom. Where's Grandma?" Desiree said. Her voice sounded frantic.

I grabbed Mark's hand and held on to it tightly. "How is she?" I gasped.

"I don't know. No one has told me how she is yet," he said. His hands shook.

"You did a great job with Grandma," I said. I tried to remain calm.

I entered the emergency room and found mother on a stretcher with two nurses and a doctor by her side. She had a mask over her face with IV lines in both arms. Her color looked dusky, and I feared the worst.

The hospital seemed extremely busy. There were noisy machines around and oxygen tanks in the hallway. Mom did not have an advance directive. I had power of attorney, and we decided not to take heroic measures if she took a turn for the worst. Mother told me, when God wants her, she'll be ready. I would allow care, but no CPR or life support. We recently signed the DNR order.

No matter what, I was not prepared to lose her. She was still the elder of the family, and I wanted her to stay with us. I ran to her side, and looked down at her. All at once, she opened her eyes, and I swear she winked at me. The doctor motioned for me to step aside so he could speak to me in private. He informed me that she had a heart attack, and needed to be on a blood thinner. I asked what her chances were. He told me Mother had fluid in her lungs and he would give her a diuretic, and that only time would tell. I went back to her side, held onto the side rail, and gently kissed her forehead. I sat down next to her, and reached for her hand.

Mother turned her head slowly towards me, and tried to speak. "Where am I? What happened?" she asked. Her voice sounded weak. It surprised me to see her so alert.

"You're in the hospital," I answered, overcome with emotion. "We're all here with you. Close your eyes and rest. I'll stay here with you." My whole body relaxed while I breathed a sigh of relief, when I heard her voice.

I watched her chest rise and fall with each breath as she slept. I almost dozed off myself in the corner chair.

The family remained by my side. Bonnie was hysterical when she got there. It took her longer to arrive then I expected. I knew it was difficult for Bonnie to deal with mother when she was sick. She was the first-born, and Mother was still a teenager when she had her.

She hurried over to Mom's side with tears falling down her cheeks. "Is she all right? What happened?"

I handed her a handkerchief. As she dried her eyes, I assisted her to a nearby chair, and waited for her to settle down.

I explained what the doctor told me, and we all waited. Eventually, we moved up to a room. It was easier to be in a place where we could have more privacy. We sat in the family area together, and supported one another. We were a team, and we took turns at her bedside. I tried to remain positive and optimistic, despite Mom's awful color.

I found comfort in a visit to the chapel downstairs in the hospital. It had a few pews, and a book to record your thoughts. There were candles at the altar, if you wanted to light one as a special plea. I wrote in the book, and tried to think of the right words to say. I found a sense of peace and solace in this tiny space. The optimistic quotes from other families who grieved before me, gave me solace. There was a glimmer of hope that surrounded the area. I visited the chapel repeatedly for the next few days.

Mom remained in that condition for two days, when on the

third day she started to improve. Her color came back, and her voice sounded stronger. The staff informed me she even ate breakfast, when I stopped by the desk.

"Mom, you look much better today," I said, relieved by her shift toward recovery. "How do you feel?" I clapped my hands as I entered the room, glad to see her condition improve. I did a little dance for her, and made her laugh aloud.

"I feel good, honey. Where's Daddy? I saw him earlier, and he said he would stay by my side today."

It concerned me when she made that statement. I stopped in my tracks, and slowly advanced over to her bed and sat down. Mother had asked for my father many times before. This time it seemed as if he called for her.

"Don't worry, Dad will be right back," I said, as I gave her a hug.

The little doll I found in the gift shop fell to the floor. I picked it up and placed it on her shoulder. I left it there for her to keep her company.

Mark arrived and handed me a coffee. "How's she today?" he asked. "Grandma, you look really good today." He wore a hopeful smile.

She perked up, and lifted her head from the pillow. "I'm a strong fighter. Don't worry, I'll be all right," she insisted.

We both laughed along with her, while we gave her a bed bath.

"You're a good daughter," she said. Her eyes sparkled.

I felt assured with her progress. I left after lunch with my mind at ease. I knew Desiree would be by after work. I had a few errands to run, before I could stop and return all the calls to friends who had concern for mother. I was optimistic now that she would pull through.

I called Bonnie before anyone else. "She's much better today. She ate breakfast, and even sang a little song for us," I said and breathed easier.

"Thank the Lord," she said. "I'm so glad Mom moved in with you. You've taken such good care of her."

"We all took good care of her, and so did you and Mike," I returned. "You both were there for her, when I couldn't manage. I wasn't able to pitch in much while I was in school. You did a great job."

"I tried," she said in a hesitant tone.

Chapter Twenty-Eight

Nathaniel

Nat parked his car in front of his garage, opened a can of wax and made a circular motion to shine his car. He left the back door open, but Nat usually never heard the doorbell from outback. On this day, he did. He rushed inside, grabbed a towel to wipe the grease from his hands, and opened the front door. A young girl in a frilly dress with a white bow on the top of her head smiled, and handed him a tiny box along with a pamphlet. A young boy stood in back of the girl. All Nat could see were his red sneakers and the rim of his baseball cap.

After he read the pamphlet, Nat thought they were from a religious group. Nat looked up to speak to them, but the mysterious duo were nowhere in sight. The words, "Allow love into your life" were in bold letters on the front page. He swallowed hard and took the message personally. As he hurried down the steps, he scanned both sides of the street. He scratched his head, and thought there must have been a car out front with an adult driver. The wind picked up, and Nat had a weird sense he had lost his mind. It seemed as if they vanished, and Nat became riddled with fright. His teeth chattered, and his heart thumped in his chest.

After he went back inside, he picked up the handout from the floor. He read through it again. The box they carried fell in between two pillows on the foyer bench, and he reached for it. Nat opened the top of the present, and lifted out a tiny charm in the shape of a key. He read the inscription and was shocked to see the message. He held it in the palm of his hand with his mouth open. After he inspected it thoroughly, he took a deep breath. *Maybe the paperwork will have a clue.* He checked it again. Underneath the bold letters he read a moment before, there was a poem that seemed as if it were written especially for him. Nat's eyes opened wide as he absorbed the sentiment it held. He sat down on the couch, and rested his head back. He knew Madeline's mother, Katy, was in the hospital. Jeremy stopped by the day before, and told him she was admitted with a heart condition. Nat and Jeremy kept their friendship a secret. Nat knew it was sneaky behavior and felt bad about it. Jeremy made him promise not to tell his mother. He told Nat he thought his mother would be upset if she knew he kept in touch with him after they broke up. Nat realized Jeremy's position and knew he did not want to take sides.

After the visit, Nat felt compelled to tell Katy about the bizarre visit and the gifts the children left behind. He did not understand why he had the compulsion to do so. Nevertheless, he drove straight to the hospital.

The elderly woman looked peaceful as he stood in the doorway. Her bed rested in an upright position. After Nat knocked gently, he moved to her bedside and had a sudden urge to cry. She turned her head, and caught his gaze.

"I knew you would come," she said. Her words sent a shiver up is spine as he pulled up a chair, and sat down. He felt as if he was in a dream.

❧

Madeline

The family stuck together in a crisis. No matter what differences we had, when someone needed assistance, we were there for one other. I arrived home, and planned to contact the others. Jeremy met me at the door and looked startled.

"I thought you were at the hospital," he said. I sensed he was anxious. He looked away quickly.

"How's Grandma today?" he asked.

"She's better today. It seems like you have a lot on your mind."

"Why do you watch every move I make?" he said. "Haven't I proven to you that I've changed?" Jeremy raised his voice.

"I'm sorry, I'm cranky," I said. "I suppose I'm just tired."

"I have an appointment for a second interview at the sports store, and I plan to visit Grandma when I'm finished," he said, firmly. "Is that all right with you?"

I still detected a little cynicism in his statement.

"I'll see you up there later. Good luck on your interview," I said.

Jeremy amazed me with the total change in his behavior. *A job*, I thought.

The house was quiet, without the sound of Grandma's singing. I took a quick look at Mom's bed. Her dolls remained lined up in a row. Her slippers were at the bedside. The headphones hung over the chair. The room was exactly as she left it. I felt helpless as I showered and dressed. I hurried through my paperwork. I called Ms. Nelson and explained about the emergency, and that I would keep in touch. She was very supportive. I promised I would call her when I knew more.

I hurried back to the hospital as soon as I could. While I advanced down the hall, I heard a familiar voice as I approached Mom's room. I stopped just outside the door, and tried to hear the conversation. I was astounded to see who was next to her. Nat sat at her bedside.

He had his chair pulled up next to her. They both looked so serious like they were involved in a very important discussion. There seemed to be a veil-like haze over Mother's bed. I rubbed my eyes to see more clearly. I noticed a beam of light through the window with tiny particles that shimmered throughout the strands. A cold chill ran through my body. I stood outside the door, and I felt like I was an intruder, so I moved back to be out of sight.

Nat sat back, as if he were under her command.

I swayed a bit and felt the blood leave my head; I thought I would faint. I took a few sips of water from a nearby fountain. I returned to the door, and could hear some their conversation.

Mother held onto Nat's arm. I tried not to move a muscle.

"I know I'm a little absent-minded, but I remember more than you know. If I didn't have the memories of my life with Nick, I wouldn't have made it this long," she said. "That's what kept me strong."

Nat placed his hand on top of hers.

"If it's my time to go, now, I'm ready. The message you received was from two special people. My sister promised me before she died she would be there for me," she confessed. "When we were thirteen, a gypsy cast a spell on us, when we visited her at the county fair. We were joined together in a ceremony by the eldest one of the tribe."

Mother's statement shocked me. I thought she must have had a fever or a nightmare, and she believed it. After knocking to announce myself, I entered the room. I gave Nat a smile and put my hand on Mother's forehead.

"No temperature," I said. "How did you know Mother was here?" I asked, with my eyes on him, then her.

Nat stood up immediately, and hurried toward me. He moved close to me to offer a friendly hug. We embraced for a moment. "I'll tell you later," he said in a whisper. "It's so good to see you."

The scent of his after-shave reminded me how much I still missed him. It made me happy, yet I didn't expect to run into him, especially in my mother's hospital room. Nat must have known how difficult this would be for me. He took his time, before he offered an explanation. Initially I felt lightheaded, and could barely focus. I had to sit down, to collect my thoughts.

The nurse came in with Mom's medication, which gave me the opportunity to leave the room.

Nat followed me out into the hallway. We moved into the waiting area, and sat down in a quiet corner where there were two chairs, and a table with magazines. I became overwhelmed with emotion. I peered out the window to the parking lot, and could not imagine how Nat found out my mother was ill. He didn't speak to any of my friends. I knew I did not discuss my mother's illness with many people, anyway.

"How on earth did you know my mother was here?" I asked. My heart fluttered, and my hands trembled as I searched my purse for a rubber band. I pulled my hair back with both hands.

He looked away at first. It took him a while before he answered.

"Jeremy has kept in touch with me all along," he said. "I've been able to spend time with him. He's been at my place after school to do his homework." He looked down at his lap.

"He's really changed, and now I understand," I admitted. "I don't know what to say."

Nat looked up, turning to face me. "When we first broke up I saw him at the garage downtown. Do you remember? I told you about it," he said.

"I do remember," I said.

"I knew he needed guidance. He's such a great kid. He reminded me of myself when I young."

"After we broke up, he was upset, and he told me, he never wanted to speak to you," I said. "I never knew he was still in touch with you. Now, it all makes more sense."

"Madeline, I have so much to tell you," Nat said. "Please don't be mad."

"I'm not angry, Nat. I'm worn out from all the stress." I gave a sigh and rested my arm on the side of the seat.

"I really must have a serious talk with you soon," he insisted. Nat's tone carried a tone of desperation.

It wasn't clear to me on how to handle the situation. *Be*

strong, you have so much going on in your life. I knew my Mother needed me now, and I did not want to become distracted. Yet, I felt obliged to hear what he had to say. Nat held my heart in his hands, once again. My thoughts became clouded with emotion.

Nat seemed worn out, and his hair was longer than usual. His shirt was wrinkled, and he had a goatee. His hands shook as he tried to get each word across with sincerity. I detected a tear in his eyes.

I tried to resist, but I couldn't. "We can talk tonight, after Mother goes to sleep," I declared.

"Come on, let's go back inside," Nat offered. His tone of voice sounded happier.

The dinner tray arrived on time. I repositioned Mom up in bed, and assisted her with her meal. She rolled her eyes at the meatloaf dinner. She was only able to take a small amount of her entree.

"Don't you like the food?" I asked.

"It's good, I'm just full," she said. She patted her mouth with a napkin.

I opened the vanilla ice cream, and she ate the whole cup in a minute.

"I thought you were full," I said.

I laughed to myself as I snuck over to the pantry and grabbed another cup.

"I let her have whatever she wants," I said. "She's lost so much weight, in just a few days."

"Grandma, don't forget you promised me you would get well and return home soon," Nat said.

"Sure will," she said with a little smirk on her face.

It seemed like they had become a team, just the two of them. I could sense a strong camaraderie between them. I was glad that Nat became a role model to Jeremy. Although, I wished they hadn't chose to hide their relationship from me.

Nat and I moved over to the chairs near the window when Mother fell asleep. We spoke softly, and tried not to disturb mother, or the other patients.

"Did Jeremy tell you I finished my cookbook?"

Nat placed his hand on top of mine. "He did, I'm so proud of your accomplishments," he said.

"I have an agent in New York City," I asserted. "She found me a publisher. Can you believe it? I was in the city when Mother became ill. By the way, how's your business?"

His eyes followed my every move. I stepped over to the window.

"Not bad," he said. "I have a few new accounts, and I've got another builder involved. We've got a big project for a beach hotel project. If it works out it could be a huge boost to my business."

"It sounds wonderful." I sat back down, and turned to face him. "How's the unit at the hospital?" I asked.

Nat folded his arms. "It's got a steady flow. The census has been consistent."

"Do you have enough time to lecture with your new job down at the shore?"

"I make time," he replied.

"The company I'm with is in the planning stage for a beach front vacation community," he said. "There are two and three bedrooms with all the amenities of a fine hotel. They'll all come fully furnished, with water views and luxury accommodations. They are currently for sale, at pretty reasonable prices."

"That sounds like a fantastic opportunity. I hope it all works out for you," I said. "How is the head nurse, Miss Morris? I haven't been there since we split up. I told her I needed to take a break, due to personal reasons."

"It's not the same without you," Nat added. His expression saddened. "The crew still gossips about each other. I'm sure they would love the scoop on us. They ask about you all the time."

"What do you tell them?" I said. I raised an eyebrow.

His tone changed to a shrill pitch. "It's none of their business. I know they're dying to know what happened between us, and I tell them you're great."

It seems like ages ago since I first walked into his lecture. It's funny how our lives turned out. I wanted to stay strong, afraid to take a step backwards. My beliefs did not change. Would Nat be able to change his ways, and commit to a family life? His support came at the right time, since my mother was so sick. I certainly couldn't handle another disappointment, and I did not want to get false hopes.

I looked at Mother so still in the hospital bed. She had the heart monitor attached to her chest, and the IV blood thinner pumped into her arm. I wondered if this was the end for her. I was not ready to accept the fact that one day I might be alone, without the woman that was so important in my life. I moved closer to Nat, and he placed his hand on mine. We remained quiet while we watched her sleep.

Nat's appearance put me in a state of shock. I sunk back into my chair, and tried desperately to relax. So many different thoughts sped through my mind. I remembered Mother's stories of her childhood. All the times she shared the little tales of her parents and their struggles came to my mind. I pictured her by the stove with an apron around her waist, as she prepared dinner night after night for her family. All of a sudden, the years spent with my mother meant so much to me.

I closed my eyes and visualized her in the family photo, the one she held so dear. The photograph was so special to her. I tried to preserve it and kept it away from the sun. The whole family gathered side by side for the portrait. The sisters sat alongside their parents with their hands folded. The girls looked so pretty in their party attire.

Mary succumbed to an infection she developed after a terrible mishap. The girls were out early one Saturday and took a sleigh ride down a neighborhood hill. Mary's sled took off ahead of Katy's and barreled down at a speed that caused her to tip over. The pointed edge of the sleigh punctured her groin. I think Mary's death affected Mother the hardest. Katy and Mary were extremely close; they loved each other unconditionally.

The cycle of life stood before my eyes, and I gained a new

appreciation for all the love she gave me. I cherished her thoughtfulness and her support with my children. We all learned a valuable lesson from Grandma's life. At first, her move to our house was difficult. Later, we learned her presence was truly a gift to us. The family structure gained strength when we pitched in together to help someone in need. Her wisdom was an added gift.

The doctor knocked on the door before he entered. He greeted both of us before he listened to Mom's heart. He sat down at her bedside, and wrote in the chart. I hoped he would be able to give me good news. He told me my mother's heart was still weak. She had completed all the needed tests, and would be released. Her vitals were stable enough to receive physical therapy at home. He added a new cardiac medication that would help her heart pump stronger.

Chapter Twenty-Nine

Madeline

1 felt satisfied with the plan and comfortable enough to leave to spend a few hours with Nat. We drove in separate cars, so I could go home to change. I hoped to see Jeremy before I went out.

I spotted the light on in his room as I pulled in the driveway.

"Hello, where is everyone?" I said as I entered the house. I turned on the lamp in the foyer, and went into the kitchen. I gulped a drink of water with two aspirins.

I heard a voice call out to me. Mark sat at the computer desk in his room. He stared at the screen with such intensity.

"How's Grandma?"

"She'll be home soon," I announced. "I'll have to get a special bed for her, and she'll be on oxygen at home."

"That's great," he said. He gave me a big happy smile. "I have time now to help you. We'll get her back on her feet. Don't worry," he said with confidence. "She's a strong old woman."

He stood up, put his arms around my back, and pulled me close to him. We held onto one another, as I let out a sigh.

Jeremy did not come out of his room. I advanced to his door, and tapped lightly. I peeked inside and saw him on his bed.

"Can I come in?"

He sat up quickly. "I'm sorry I didn't tell you about Nat," he said. His speech was pressured. "I was afraid you would be mad at me. I wanted to tell you the truth, but I didn't know how to. Nat told me he went to see Grandma today, and he would tell you the truth." He rubbed his eyes. "I thought you would be mad if you knew I spent so much time with Nat. Especially since you seemed so upset."

I sat down next to him, and placed my arm around his back. "You shouldn't have kept it from me," I said in a soft, yet firm tone. "I understand that you needed someone to confide in. I've been so proud of your ambition lately. Jeremy, you don't have to hide the truth from me. I love you. Nat is a wonderful man, and whatever happens between us, I won't mind if you stay in touch with him."

"Are you and Nat back together?" he asked with an optimistic grin.

"I don't know what the future holds, but I do know that I will do the best I can," I assured him. I did not want to get his hopes up, and leave him distraught if it didn't work out.

Jeremy had been through so much since his father died, and my break-up with Jon. I could tell he was still feeling vulnerable. I realized the core of our relationship had so much at stake. I saw a completely different perspective when I thought about what Nat had to encounter. He didn't have any children. The commitment to me involved a whole family, and a big step. My heart softened as I realized what Nat had done for Jeremy.

"I'll talk with Nat tonight," I said.

"Great," he replied, with a clap of his hands.

As I looked through my closet and tried to choose an outfit, I noticed a box in the back. It had been in there for months prior, and I forgot about it. I took it out, and placed it on my bed to open it. Inside I found a framed picture of Nat and I at the beach. When I lifted it out of the box, I held it close. Under a pile of papers was a recording that he made of my Mother. He brought over his camcorder one afternoon, and had an idea to interview her. He had footage of an hour conversation with her. I planned to watch it when I got home that night. I peeked at the clock, and saw how late it was, so I hurried to pack the box, and quickly got changed. Nat and I had arranged to meet at his house, where we would have more privacy. As I glanced over to mother's side of the closet, I felt relieved she would be home soon. I sorted out her clothes and put her robe and pajamas on the bed, along with a set of fresh linens.

I eagerly got into my car. I turned on the radio and felt optimistic after my surprise encounter with Nat. There was a few scattered showers predicted, and they had already begun. The neighborhood was quiet. There was an unusual stillness in the air. The early flowers were in bloom. I took a long deep breath and remembered how much I loved the nice weather.

I gave Bonnie a fast call to let her know the good news and gave Desiree a buzz to tell her about Grandma's progress, too.

It disappointed me when Nat called to postpone our get together. He had a big job in upstate New York, and there had been a major problem with the homeowner. He apologized with a sincere approach, and assured me he would call me when he got back. I did believe him, but I was disappointed. At the time, my Mother's condition took priority.

In a few days, we bought her home, and made her a mini hospital in the living room. Mark offered to drive which gave me peace of mind, while I sat with Mom in the back.

We rented a portable oxygen tank from the medical supply store and a hospital bed. This made it easier with her weak condition. She still was not strong enough to walk. You would be surprised how fast an elderly person loses their mobility, even when they are only in bed for a short time. I arranged for her to have physical therapy three days a week at home. I set up a schedule for a nurse to visit. Mark would care for her when he was not at work or school.

Initially, I thought she would make a comeback, and return

to her vibrant self. I suppose I was in denial. I realized later that the doctor sent her home because there was no more he could do for her in the hospital. In other words he sent her home to die. The constant buzz from the oxygen container was the reminder of how our household changed, despite my attempt to push it out of my mind. *She'll be her old self in no time,* I told myself.

At first, mother attempted to recuperate. She ate her breakfast tray of hot oatmeal, a banana, and a nutrition shake every day. I placed her in front of the family photos, and she listened to her favorite music on her headset. I expected her to sing like usual. It never happened.

Her voice sounded weak, and each day it got worse. I kept this up for a few weeks, and hoped it was only temporary. I would toss and turn at night, and check her constantly, to make sure she was still okay. One day I woke up to find her awake and on the edge of the bed. I jumped off the couch, put the side rail of her bed down, and sat down beside her.

"How did you sleep?" I said, as I held her hand.

"I had a wonderful night," she replied.

"What did you say, Mother?" I asked.

She didn't answer me, and I thought I heard her mumble under her breath.

"There's no hurry," she replied.

"I'm going to run to the bathroom to wash my face. I'll be right back to fix you breakfast."

When I returned, I found her slumped over. "Mother, are you all right?" I shouted.

She moaned and opened her eyes. "I'm fine," she whispered in a soft tone.

I immediately called for help. We were at the emergency room in minutes. Mother had a chest x-ray, electrocardiogram, CT scan of the head, and labs drawn. She even gave a urine sample. The tests results were all normal. I could not understand what happened. She convinced me it would be all right to take her home. The doctor wanted to make sure he covered all areas, so he ordered one more lab study. Since I rode in the ambulance to the hospital, I called home to ask if Mark to be at the house when we arrived home. I finally got through to him, and he agreed. The doctor discharged her home with follow up instructions.

We spent two uneventful weeks as we cared for Mother. Her appetite never quite returned, and her singing became less and less. I held onto my plan to nurse her back to health. In the evening, Mark would care for her while I worked. Jeremy never physically cared for her, but he sat with her and read her the gossip magazines. They laughed together at the silly antics.

The restaurant was busy when I received the news. The nurse called from the emergency room. The phone disconnected before I got the details.

As I merged onto the parkway to head to the hospital, I heard the phone again. I swerved away from a car that darted in front of me with my chest tight. I stopped at a red light to return the call. I heard an unfamiliar voice.

"Hello, emergency room. Can I help you?"

"This is Madeline Young. I received a message. What is it?" I said, as I tried to steady myself. "Who is this?" I suddenly felt lightheaded, and my stomach became queasy.

"My name is Carolyn Brown. I'm a nurse at Harbor Bay Hospital."

I felt my heart sink.

"Your mother isn't well. Your son called the ambulance, and I told him I would contact you. He's upset, and I escorted him to our lounge to sit for a while. It all seems a bit too much for him. I think you should come over to the hospital."

"What happened? She was fine earlier in the day," I said. I raised my voice.

"Your mother had respiratory distress. Her blood pressure dropped, and she will be taken to the intensive care unit," she said.

"I'll be right there. Oh, my God, please not again!" I screamed into the phone.

I sped like a racecar driver as I weaved in and out with expert precision. The scenery appeared unfamiliar to me. It was as if the world changed in a second. I stopped for gas and called Nat to tell him what happened. I was not sure if he was back from his trip yet, I simply acted on impulse. I fought back the tears, and did not want to become hysterical. Nat must have sensed that I had bad news.

"What is it?" Nat yelled.

"Mother has taken a turn for the worst. I'm on my way to the hospital." I started to break down.

"Will she be okay?" he asked, as his voice rose.

"I don't know," I shouted.

It seemed like the world was in slow motion.

"Madeline, I'll try to get there. I just have to make a few calls."

"Don't worry, Nat. It's all right. Take care of your business. I can handle it."

I called Bonnie and Desiree before I made my way through the reception area. I ran as fast as I could, and hoped that she would hold on until I got there. We prepared her advanced directive after her last hospitalization. I knew she did not want be placed on a ventilator. I had power of attorney, and we had a DNR. Mom would remind me of how she was ready whenever her time came.

"Are you alone?" Bonnie asked.

"No, Mark is here. Jeremy must be at a friend's house. I'll call a few of them. Desiree is on her way," I replied. "It all happened so fast."

"Stay with Mom, I'll get Jeremy," she insisted.

The area was crowded, but I pushed through, and moved as fast as I could. The security guard stopped and motioned for me to get a visitors' pass. I entered Mom's room, and found her unresponsive with shallow respirations. The nurse adjusted her IV drip while she watched the monitor. I pulled the chair next to her, sat down and gently reached for her hand. Her skin was cool to touch, and I knew she would not make it this time.

In moments, the others were at her bedside. Desiree sobbed

on my shoulder as she trembled.

Mark tried to be brave, but I could sense his concern. His face looked pale, and his eyes were red and swollen

"I'm sorry, Mom. I don't know what happened. She had just finished her snack," he said.

I knew he was upset. His mouth quivered at the corners. He tried to hold himself together.

Bonnie and Mike entered the room and grasped onto one another.

Jeremy walked in behind them, and looked petrified. He sat down and stared into space.

Desiree stood behind me, and placed her hands on my shoulders. We spoke with the intensive care doctor, and he assured us Mother was not in pain.

The doctor explained to us that they gave her morphine to slow her respirations. I appreciated his kind words and he convinced us it would be best to stay, and talk to her. He motioned for us to step outside the room, his words pierced through me like an arrow.

"The ability to hear is the last sense to leave us when a person is toward the end," he said.

He must have said those words to so many families in despair, yet his efforts to support us during our difficult time helped. Strength unknown to me took over, and I was able to maintain my composure.

We all remained by her side as she took her last breath. Nat was not able to get there in time. I called him to let him know, and he apologized for being unable to make it. The woman who started our cycle of life was gone. She would live on in our hearts always. Her gifts remain evident in our strength of character. I only hoped that I could live up to her expectations of me. I wept quietly as I left the hospital, confident that her memory would remain in my heart forever.

We gathered at my house after the funeral. Fortunately, I

was able to prepare the menu myself. It allowed me the opportunity to place my sorrow aside. I wanted to remember the wonderful times we spent with her. Nat came to the funeral, but we never discussed our relationship. It made me feel good to have his support, although I wished we were a couple again. Nevertheless, I kept that information to myself. The family shared our stories that day. We laughed and cried, and I found comfort in the fact that we all spent valuable moments with Mother. Her words remained with me. *"Madeline, he loves you. In time you will see it, too."*

The time after the burial was hectic. Jeremy started his new job at the mall. He was still responsible and even opened a bank account. For the first time in his life, he was able to save a little money. He had a group of colleges picked out, and sent quite a few applications. He made appointments to visit the ones on top of the list.

Mark took summer classes; he was determined now more than ever to begin his career. We sat in the front row at his graduation and cheered when he won an award for clinical and academic excellence. Jeremy put his hands together and clapped. "In four years, you'll be at my graduation. I have my applications in to some good colleges." He held his shoulders back and gave me a proud smile. Desiree and her new boyfriend sat arm-in-arm as they applauded Mark's success. This time I knew Desiree finally found a keeper. He had graduated from Princeton University, and he had the drive and motivation to keep up with my daughter.

Our family took pride in the way we took care of Grandma in her last days. It's funny how we were able to retain the bits of information she gave us. Quite often, people think the comments made by the elderly are eccentric, as if their stories are worthless. On the contrary, their experience from years of living is what makes us understand the meaning of life. It is not until you have fully lived life, that you can reap the rewards when you share your wisdom.

Nathaniel

Nat kept his schedule full to keep him busy. He did not want to feel the pain left behind by his foolish decision. The worse thing he could have done was to push Madeline away. His time with Jeremy was productive, and the teenager's grades had improved immensely. It made him proud to know his time spent with him did some good.

Wednesday night was the day for the antique car show, and he took a walk downtown to check it out. The old relics lined the streets, while fifties music played in the background; Nat bought a pretzel with a mustard topping and took a bite. He wished Madeline was by his side. He stepped into a bar, and grabbed a coke from the freezer.

A raspy voice called his name. "Nat Griffin, is that you?"

It was dark inside, and Nat strained to see the person who called out across the bar. The man walked toward him, and Nat recognized him from a meeting at the hospital.

"How are you doing, John?" Nat said.

A husky man in his early thirties wearing a pair of overalls covered in grease smiled. "Not too bad." He held his head down.

"What's not too bad supposed to mean?" Nat asked.

"Come over here." John pulled Nat by his arm to the side of the room. He leaned in and spoke in a soft tone. "I relapsed a month ago, and I think I'm having DT's."

"What happened? You were so determined," Nat said.

"My wife left me, and I missed meetings."

Nat shook his head, and put his hand on John's shoulder. "My door is open whenever you want to talk. You can get back on track if you choose to."

"Thanks, Nat. I was so ashamed." Nat paid the bartender for his Coke and slipped his card into John's top pocket. "Take it easy," Nat said. "Remember it's up to you."

"I know," John returned.

Nat stepped outside and felt an agonizing guilt. He could not understand how he could counsel so many suffering people, and still make a mockery of his own life. He knew his plan could backfire; nevertheless, he had a plan.

Chapter Thirty

Madeline

I worked nights at the restaurant and finalized the deal for my family cookbook. The promotion kept me busy. The art department designed the jacket beautifully. I anticipated the day when it would finally hit the shelves. The dreams I had came true. I even had a plan for a restaurant of my own. There was a charming old place in Point Pleasant Beach I had my eye on. My realtor showed me multiple places, and they did not need as much work as the place I wanted. My heart was set on the magnificent beach property.

Nat and I never did get together for our talk. My life evolved so quickly, and I hoped when the time was right, he would approach the subject again. My love for him would never change.

The following months seemed to fly by. I was fortunate to receive a good sum of money, from mother's estate. The editing process moved along well. My book was not like the typical cookbook. Sonnets appeared between the recipes with stories about each one. Every verse carried a special meaning behind the meal. Martino's was famous, and I had a sense it would do well. Tony promised me he would let me keep some copies of the cookbook in front of the restaurant next to the other items he sold. He did not want a portion of the money. He was happy for me, and supported me in every way possible.

I had to travel for the next few months on and off due to publicity. As soon as I returned, I looked at the piece of property in Point Pleasant. The realtor let me in, and I immediately knew I had to make this place my own. Bonnie tagged along.

She eagerly encouraged me to take a chance. Ideally, the place was a block from the ocean. Unfortunately, it was not in the best condition. Although, I still saw great potential in the old establishment. The paint was chipped in various areas, and the awnings were faded to a muted shade of red. Nevertheless, the actual structure of the place was beautiful.

As soon as we pulled up in front, Bonnie practically jumped out of the car. "This place is absolutely gorgeous. It's perfect for you!" she exclaimed.

I grabbed her by the hand, and pulled her toward the entry. "Come inside. I have so many great ideas," I said. As I made my way through the dusty corridor to the main room, a fog appeared in front of me. A loud thump startled me, and I could not believe my eyes. A white lace dress hung across the door which led to the back room. It had a satin overlay and a full skirt. It looked awfully familiar, although, I couldn't quite place it. The dress seemed to appear out of nowhere. I closed my eyes and tried to place it.

"What a beautiful old dress," I said. Bonnie grabbed my hand and started to pull me into the kitchen. In the back of the dress, a vision appeared. She floated in and out, so I could not focus.

"Did you see that?" I asked.

"No, what do you see? Do you have a migraine?" Bonnie walked ahead as I stayed behind.

I slowly examined the dress, and I spotted a photo on the

floor. I bent down to pick it up, and brought it over to a window. I could not believe my eyes. It was a snapshot of a young woman in the white dress. She resembled my mother, and I shook in an attempt to understand how it could be. Mary's hair was styled different from my mother's, and it was a way to distinguish them. The girl in the photo had the exact haircut that Mom had, too. I felt lightheaded and reached for the wall. *Could it be?* I knew they lived a few blocks away for a short time when my Grandfather worked on a ship. I took a deep breath, and stuck the photo into my purse. The noise stopped, and the room took on a bright glow. I knew what I had to do. The restaurant would be the one for sure.

"Wow, I can already imagine the restaurant open for business. This spot is ideal for a romantic hideaway," Bonnie said when I caught up with her.

The restaurant had a huge area in front where there must have been a beautiful garden. Although the lawn looked ragged, I could see that in its day it must have been gorgeous. Just outside a large hallway was a frame of the old crew. It took up an entire wall. I loved the way it captured the festive feel of the era. The servers wore starched white shirts, with black aprons. Some of the other personnel were dressed in formal attire. The female patron in the background wore a tea gown with a sheer skirt, and a soft colorful sash. I could feel a sense of the devotion of the staff. There expressions showed their pride.

In the front, there was a huge enclosed porch where I could arrange tables. One of the rooms had a brick fireplace that I thought would create a fabulous private area. The other smaller room had a gorgeous plant filled area that received plenty of sunlight. I thought it would be great for intimate parties. I couldn't wait to place an offer. I arranged a meeting with my lawyer to discuss all the details. The possibilities were endless once I made up my mind.

When we finally closed, I found it hard to believe that I was actually the proud owner of a seashore restaurant. The realtor, along with my lawyer, negotiated a contract that had my best interests in mind. It took two months to finalize the deal. There were a few bumps in the road, due to a previous owner, but in time we worked it out. Hard work and determination put me where I never dreamed I would be.

Desiree and Bonnie helped me pick out the décor, and it turned out superbly. Their enthusiasm made the whole experience a fun challenge. The porch became my favorite room. We furnished it with white tables and chairs, with a tiny vase in the corner of each, which held a single white lily. Bonnie chose stylish table coverings with personalized china. The tablecloths resembled linen, although they were cotton. She thought white would be elegant, yet simple. She placed candles in the center of each table, with a glass holder, and it made the atmosphere warm and intimate. Bonnie spared no expense on the serving ware. The plates were ivory with brown trim, with a large M placed on the top for Madeline. I also found a variety of unique wall fixtures at an exhibit, which fit the room perfectly. The sconces I purchased at an unusual gift shop near the beach were my favorite. They were made of pewter with pink frosted glass. There was only one more area left to complete. I wanted to find a distinctive item to place above the fireplace. I searched quite a few places, with no luck. I wanted the right piece to pull the room together, not an item you would find in every restaurant in the area. It would have to be exceptional. I knew when I found it, I would have no doubts.

Choosing the staff took time, and I had to interview multiple applicants before I chose just the right crew to work by my side. Eventually, I hired a classmate of mine from the culinary academy as my assistant. Her name was Marisol Harris. Marisol's specialty was pastry and desserts. We made the ideal match. Her fabulous creations would top off the menu exquisitely.

Mark, Jeremy, and Desiree worked alongside me whenever they had the time. They put their heart and soul in this investment with me. At first, it was difficult, a new business usually is. With the help of a terrific family and staff, we made it work. I was fortunate to have the opportunity of a lifetime. Bonnie and I shopped for the extra linens and knick-knacks together on the Saturday before the Grand Opening. I realized she had quite a talent for decorating.

"Bonnie, you've certainly missed your calling. You know just where to put the finishing touches," I told her.

"Thanks, I would have loved to have done more in my life," she said. "I suppose it was not in the big plan." She put her hands in the pockets of her smock as she looked around the restaurant. I heard her sigh, as she placed the last table setting.

At that moment, I felt a little sorry for her. Maybe I felt a tad guilty about all my good fortune.

"You're a gifted and talented woman. I would not have made it through all the tough times if I didn't have you by my side. You're a special person that brightens whatever you touch. You raised a wonderful son and managed to make ends meet through the difficult time when Mike was sick," I said. "Your business was a huge success. I'm proud to have you for a sister. You're a wonderful sister." I tilted my head and smiled at her.

Bonnie wiped a tiny tear from the corner of her eye.

I felt a rush of gratitude as I gave her a hug.

The opening day turned out to be more than I ever expected. Many of my friends, business owners, and family members came to wish me the best of success. I hired a local pianist, who became a regular at our establishment. His name was Cole Lance, a tall, handsome Scandinavian man. I met him on a business trip to the city, and I instantly became a huge fan. He put together a record of his songs for the locals, and summer crowd which we gladly agreed to sell. That special evening became one of my most precious memories.

Tony arrived in a black silk suit with a bow tie to match. He held his head high, with his gorgeous bride by his side. His wife was ten years younger than he was, and he adored her.

"I'm so glad you could make it," I said, filled with pride.

"I wouldn't miss this for the world," he said. He opened his arms, and reached for me. He kissed me on the forehead.

"Madeline, I want to give you a gift that is very special to me. It has been in our family for over a century." He handed me an unusual shaped package.

"My goodness, Tony, you didn't have to," I said.

I opened the gift paper, surprised to see what I found. Inside was the beautiful clock he displayed in the entryway of his restaurant. It had been there since the family opened the business. The historical timepiece was in perfect condition. Inscribed on top was 1889. The face was black with gold trim, shaped round, and it had four columns attached to the base.

"This is absolutely perfect for the mantel in the dining area," I said, in amazement. I held the clock out in front of me, and admired its detailing. I knew he treasured it. I could not believe he gave it to me.

"This old clock stands for family, love, and patience." He wore a proud grin. "It has brought good fortune to my life, and now it's time for me to pass it on. I wish all the best for you and your family," he said.

Tony and I advanced through the crowd hand and hand. The night signified the importance of love and kindness. The crowd filled the restaurant with laughter and joy. I kept my eyes on the door, in hopes that somehow Nat would show up.

Cole Lance played a beautiful piece he arranged especially for my first dinner service.

The piano sounded beautiful. Cole soothed our senses with his marvelous gift.

I felt a gentle tap on my shoulder, and I turned quickly to find my girlfriends at my side.

"I'm glad you could make it." I said. I did a little dance, and raised my hands to my face.

"We wouldn't have missed it, no matter what," Anne announced.

I hoped they would all be able to make it. Sometimes our schedules were so difficult to match.

"I'm so happy for you. I knew you would make the restaurant nice, but this place is spectacular," Mara whispered in my ear.

"Thanks so much for sharing this night with me," I said.

They never questioned why Nat never showed up. I placed an ad in the local newspaper, in hopes he would see it.

"Where are the guys?" I asked.

"Over at the bar," Anne said and pointed to their husbands. I waved and glanced over to the door.

"Come with me," I said as I lead the way. "I can't wait to have your reviews on my menu." I sat my special guests at their table, which was the best in the room.

"See you in a few," I said. I turned to greet the rest of the patrons.

Desiree reached for my hand and gave it a squeeze. "The night is magical, congratulations," she said.

Mark and Jeremy offered to valet that night. I bent down to look out of the window, pleased with their enthusiasm. They wore matching white shirts with black vests, and looked so professional. I think they enjoyed the chance to drive the customers' cars.

Toward the end of the evening, I felt a little sad. I wished my Mother could have been with us. I sat back and saw the group of happy faces. She helped me get to that point in my life. *Here's to you, Mom*, as I raised my glass in the air.

Time passed quickly. I was able to live my life with a passion for my work, and it made people happy. I felt alive and vivacious.

Sadly, I would end my day at the restaurant alone. When the sunset and the night ended, I would close my door in the office, and imagine the day Nat would find his way back to me. I still longed for the sound of his laughter, and his boyish sense of adventure.

I reached into my desk drawer and took out an album. I showed Desiree the photos I kept for years. She was old enough to appreciate the triumph I felt over this accomplishment. When she was younger, we used to shop together on Saturday mornings, and later have lunch in upscale places. I saved the cards from the restaurants we visited. I had them pasted in the album.

"You finally got all that you deserve," Desiree said. "Those were some of my favorite memories when I was a little girl."

We would fantasize about the day when I would have a place of my own. Desiree turned the pages slowly, and studied them

"I was a girl that married young and had no career path," I told her. "Who would have ever believed I would have been capable of so much."

Our menu got raves from the patrons. We had a critique in the first year that received four stars.

I attested that the joys in life do come to you, when you believe in yourself. That is really all it takes. I kept a picture of Nat and I under the calendar in my office. Each day when I came to work, I would take it out, and give it a kiss before I started. I said a little prayer for Nat and I to reunite one day.

Chapter Thirty-One

Nathaniel

$\mathcal{T}$he summer flew by, and the cool days of autumn were upon them once again. Nat drove to Madeline's house one evening after a busy Friday at work. Jeremy let him in, and he waited on the couch. He knew how risky it was, to surprise someone. He wondered if Madeline had found someone new. Or maybe her love for him had changed, and she would reject him. He took the chance, despite his fears.

Nat heard the key in the door. Madeline jumped back when she saw him. She held her hand over her mouth. Nat stood up and started toward her.

He bought a new suit for the occasion and had his hair groomed to perfection. He took a deep breath and reveled in the thought of being able to hold her in his arms again. Nat's knees weakened at the sight of her. It was an incredible revelation. Madeline tossed her purse on the table in the foyer and rushed down the hall.

"I'll be right there," she said.

Nat traveled toward her. He swiftly grabbed Madeline and pulled her close to him. As he slowly twirled her around, his heart pounded in his chest. The bedroom door was partially closed, and he kicked it lightly. First, he gently placed her on the bed. Then he moved on top of her and held his chest up, so he could look directly in her eyes. Nat stared at Madeline for a moment before he placed his lips on hers. He felt the warmth of her body against his, and she slowly put her arms around his neck. Madeline sighed when Nat touched both sides of her face.

"Madeline, I love you," he whispered softly in her ear. "My life is nothing without you in it."

She burst into tears. Nat held her close to him, while she cried.

They sat up and straightened their clothes. Nat knew he needed to explain more before she would believe him.

Nat got up, and closed the bedroom door. He took Madeline by the hand and helped her sit up, and he placed the pillows behind her back.

He sat close to her, and held her hand.

"I have so much to tell you," he confessed. "I'm so sorry I waited so long, but I feel now the time is right."

"How did you get into the house?" she asked. Madeline still looked shocked to see him. His complexion turned pale.

"Jeremy let me in before he went to work. I hope you understand what I'm about to tell you," he said. His tone was serious.

"What is it Nat?" she asked. Madeline turned on her side and placed one elbow on the bed.

"About a week before your mother passed away, I heard the doorbell in my house. I was outside waxing my car," he said. Nat spoke softly. "I typically could not hear the bell from the yard. Somehow on this day, I did."

His eyes opened wide. "I opened the door to find a boy and a girl on the front steps. The girl looked angelic in a white lace dress, and the boy had on a baseball cap," he said. "I couldn't see his face. I thought she looked familiar, and then I realized where I saw the girl before. She resembled the little girl in your mom's old photo," he announced. "I swear she looked exactly like your mother's twin sister. She even had the bow in her hair."

Nat shook his head back and forth. "I know it sounds crazy. I stood there with my mouth open. I could not believe it, but she really looked like her. Their faces took on a glow as they handed me a booklet. It read, "Allow love to enter your life." Inside was a poem about love with a little gold key attached. The inscription on it said, "Key to your heart." I got goose bumps when I read it."

"Are you serious?" Madeline asked. Her pitch sounded screechy. He reached into his pocket and handed her the pamphlet.

Nat's voice cracked; his hands were ice cold. "Of course, I'm absolutely serious," he insisted. "It took a while before I looked up again, and when I did I found that they disappeared. When I marched up and down the street, they were nowhere in sight. I thought maybe they wanted a donation of some sort, or were from a church. It all seemed so bizarre." Nat opened the top button on his shirt.

"Are you okay with this?" Nat asked.

"Yes, I'm fine," she said. "Go on, please."

"I thought the visit was supposed to help me accept my past," he continued. "I didn't tell a soul what I saw. I felt disturbed and on edge after they vanished. I asked around the neighborhood. No one else saw them. I even thought it could be my imagination, but I had the booklet to prove it was real," he said.

"I'm so sorry it took so long to come to you. I knew you bought the restaurant, and had so many new challenges in your life. I felt I would only be in the way."

Nat gently touched her hand.

"Madeline, I just couldn't go on like this anymore," he exclaimed.

He inhaled, while his eyes filled with tears. Nat crinkled his forehead as he went on with his story. "Remember when I visited your mother in the hospital?"

"Yes, I sure do," Madeline replied.

"I felt compelled to ask her questions. The visit brought back a day in my life I tried to erase from my memory. I told her the story, and she explained to me that the visitors were especially arranged to give me a message," he said. Nat paused. "Katy told me they were only for me to see. I asked her if she sent them. She winked at me, with a proud smile, and I noticed an extraordinary gleam in her eyes. She explained to me that Mary and Sebastian needed to accomplish one final task. Grandma went on to tell me how you do not have to lose yourself when you commit to another person. She explained how you still keep your own identity, and much more."

"Oh, now I understand," Madeline said.

"She assured me that my world would open up if I allowed another person to share my life," Nat said, "I can still hear her words, especially when I close my eyes."

"'Son, my life would have been empty without my dear Nick,' Grandma said. 'The memories of our life together kept me alive years after he was gone. I did not live in the past, but I was able to fully enjoy the life I had left, with my devoted husband close to my heart.'"

Nat's voice rose with excitement. "Wait, there's more," he said.

Madeline pressed her lips together and stared intently at Nat.

He went on with his story.

"I told Katy how I worked hard to learn to accept who I was," he said. Nat closed his eyes for a moment. "It took years to build up my confidence," he offered. "It all started when I saw the family photo in her bedroom. Remember the night she told us the story about the first day she met your dad?"

"I remember," Madeline admitted.

Nat's words flowed easily as he continued. "When I saw Grandma and her twin sister sitting next to one another, I was reminded of an awful tragedy; one that I was trying so hard to erase from my mind."

Madeline's eyes filled up with tears.

"I had a twin brother, his name was Sebastian," Nat confessed.

He stopped for a moment, and took a deep breath. He placed his hand on his forehead. He rocked back and forth for a few minutes, before he continued.

"He was killed by a drunk driver when he was twelve-years-old," he said. Nat felt instantly relieved. "My mother told me I should have gone for a bike ride with Sebastian that morning. She asked me not to tell my Dad I was playing basketball in the front yard. I wasn't sure why she didn't want Dad to know, and I thought that meant the accident was my fault." Nat took a deep breath. He shifted his eyes toward the floor. "You see, Sebastian wanted to go for a bike ride, and I wanted to practice for the summer basketball league. I made a long shot before the ball rolled into the street. Sebastian rode around the corner at the same time a man in a pickup truck sped down the street. The ball hit the curb, but the truck hit Sebastian. It was dreadful; he died in my mother's arms." He could not hold back the tears.

"Oh, I'm so sorry," Madeline said. She placed both hands on the side of her face.

"When I went to bed, my mother came up into my room, and held her finger to her lips, while she closed the door," Nat said. "She sat down next to me and urged me to keep the secret. I told her that the ball didn't get in the truck's way, but she wouldn't listen. Since my Dad drank too much, I think Mom thought he would be suspicious. I carried the guilt of my brother's death inside me all these years. Her words remained in my head. 'You know your father.'"

"I wasn't sure what she meant by that, but I assumed it was because of me. I never had the ability to grieve," he admitted. "Grandma told me that she knew I had a twin, and that a twin can sense another. Her story reached the deepest corner of my heart."

"'My dear sister Mary left this world when she was far too young,' she told me. 'I carried the guilt of her misfortune around for quite some time,' Grandma said. 'There was really no way for me to save her. Mary and I typically rode our sleds together. It was a usual day. The snow covered the hills perfectly. We made numerous trips down the incline, and screamed with delight. The last time down the slope was when Mary's sleigh headed toward the tree.'"

"Her story amazed me," he whispered.

"'When it first happened, I would cry myself to sleep at night, and pray for her to return,' Grandma said. 'I thought I should have done more to prevent her from harm. You see, my son, it was out of my hands, as Sebastian's fate was out of yours.'"

"She consoled me with her words and assured me that Sebastian was an angel now, who watched over me, and it was time to let go," he proclaimed. "I felt so good to get that story off my chest. It was as if a heavy weight was lifted off my back." Nat gave a sigh.

"My mother is too old now to question her secrecy, and in my heart, I know she meant well. When I went home that night, I searched for the pictures of Sebastian. I held them close to me and wept like a baby," he said, as he reached for Madeline's hand. "I thought about the many years we spent together as young boys. They were the memories I tucked away, and did not think about. That was the first time I cried over his death. I didn't sleep at all that night, but when I woke up, I felt better than I had in years."

Madeline reached for his face and gently touched his cheek. She ran her hand down to his chest.

"I confessed my love for you to her, and she let me know that you loved me, too. She spoke those words to me as if she was aware of the outcome already," Nat said. He sounded more composed. "Katy informed me that your father and her sister Mary needed her, and she was ready. She said that they let her know her job on earth was done."

Madeline clutched her chest in response to his words.

"I wanted to take you in my arms, and tell you how I felt, but I didn't want to interfere with your goals, and then Grandma died. I knew you needed time. I was just scared. I was used to my solitary life for so long. Please, forgive me for my blindness."

"Grandma made me see how I, too, wanted to have the

memories that she spoke of so often," he continued. "At first, the stories made me feel trapped. Somehow, after I read the booklet my fears lifted, and I was able to cast my concerns aside. I knew if I stayed alone I would miss so much. I realize now that our lives can join together, and we can have all that we long for as one," Nat said.

"I've finished the beach project, and I got an offer for a merger with a successful company," he said as he rubbed his chin. "I could never take this step without you and your kids in my life," he persisted. Nat reached in his pocket and took out a gorgeous box.

He handed it to Madeline, and she opened it.

"Will you marry me?" he said.

Perched on top of a velvety red pillow was a beautiful antique ring.

Madeline was in awe. Her eyes sparkled.

"Nat, I still love you, too," she said.

Nat's heart filled with joy. He knew it would not be easy. It would take time for a bachelor to join in, and become a family man. He could not imagine his life without the woman he loved in it.

Madeline looked over to the area where her Mother's bed once sat, and she gave a soft sigh.

A tear rolled down her cheek.

"Yes, Nat, I will marry you."

Nat kissed her and held her in his arms. The night passed, with two people content with the world and with a dream of a life filled with love.

Madeline

I understood completely about the visit from the unusual pair. I wondered if she ever finished her journey. It could just be that Aunt Mary joined with another unsettled spirit to complete the task.

I realized our gang's luncheon approached. I almost canceled due to exhaustion from all the changes in my life. There was so much I wanted to discuss with them. I couldn't wait to tell them about my cookbook. So, I decided to meet with them, anyway. We arranged to meet at our new home's construction site.

Anne was the first to arrive. We blocked off the unfinished areas. The inspector insured me it was safe.

"This may be our new meeting place," Anne said.

"That's a great idea." I agreed.

"Come into the back, the view is great. We moved into a room where we had an ocean view."

"This is absolutely breathtaking," Anne said. She held her hand up to her mouth.

"Isn't it," I said. "It's not finished yet. Anyhow, I wanted you to see it. I'm so happy."

It surprised me to see how Maggie gained about ten pounds. She took such pride in her figure. Although I would never tell her, neither would the other girls. Whenever we get together, it seemed like we were back in school again. We immediately went back to being giddy as we shared our little secrets. One bit of information I held back was the pain I suffered over Nat and my breakup. Especially the way Nat could not seem to commit.

"Let's go to my place for lunch. I think you'll enjoy the spread Marisol helped me with." We drove over in my car.

"It looks even bigger since the opening night. The windows let so much light in during the day," Mara said.

"Sit down everyone," I said. There was a big round table ready in the private dining area the crew set up for us. We were not open on Friday afternoons. I had the place all to myself.

"I think your cookbook sounds marvelous," Anne, said. "I knew you were headed for stardom."

"You're too kind. There's a section with a birthday theme," I said. "I wrote that chapter with you in mind. Remember the time, at your sweet sixteen, when we each consumed an entire pizza by ourselves?"

"How could I forget? My mother had to take out my uniform before our band practice," she added.

"Wasn't the restaurant opening marvelous?" Anne said.

"I'm so proud of you," Mara said. She reached across the table and placed her hand on mine.

Maggie joined in. "That's our girl."

"I'm glad I could share it with you. I can't wait until your wedding." Anne said, "My dress fits perfect, and I love it. It's the ideal style for a beach affair. There's even a hair pin with a flower to match. It makes me look like a flower child." She laughed.

We discussed the plans for the ceremony, and I had the girls' attention, when Maggie changed the subject. Out of the three of them, she was the one who loved to talk the most. Well, Mara kept up with her. "How's the handsome husband-to-be?"

"He's great. Nat and I want to have a big get-together when we move in. It will be sort of a housewarming. Of course, you're all invited."

"We wouldn't miss it," Maggie said. She put her hands together.

"This looks scrumptious, let's eat," Anne said. My assistant set up a marvelous buffet.

Anne winked at me and handed me a plate.

We make our selections, and sat down at a round table with a white linen tablecloth.

"How's your remodeling, Mara?" I asked.

"I can't wait to see it when it's done."

"Wait until you hear what happened," she replied, apparently glad I asked. She began a long story, which lasted halfway through our meal. The luncheon ended with a variety of cheesecake for dessert, and a quick review of the news in our lives. As for me, I enjoyed their company as usual.

Nat and I had a small service on the beach. The mayor of

Point Pleasant agreed to perform the ceremony. The day was marvelous with the sky crystal clear. The temperature was warm, and dry. There was no humidity at all. We marched together down the aisle of white sand. Mark and Jeremy were proud to accompany me, and escort me to Nat's side. The boys selected matching sport jackets, along with sky blue shirts. I had to hold back the tears, afraid to ruin the pictures when I got a glimpse of them. Desiree chose a simple mauve sheath, pleated in the waistline, which made her look beautiful and sophisticated. She stood alongside Bonnie, who was my maid of honor. I gave them each a set of pearls. I think Bonnie was more excited than I was on my wedding day.

I wore an elegant dress, one with satin and lace. I chose an off-white original made by a new designer. The flared shirt made it flow naturally against the gentle winds. In my hand, I carried a bouquet of blush roses. They were so pretty and were complimented with tiny white fillers. It added just the right touch. I'll never forget the way Nat looked at me when I took my place next to him. We invited seventy of our relatives and dearest friends. The restaurant was the perfect place for the reception. We had an unbelievable time on that glorious day. I wore Mother's old necklace, a gem she inherited from her mother. It was a cherished heirloom worn by the senior women in the family. After the ceremony, Desiree gasped as I reached for her hand. I offered her the platinum heart shaped pendant, with a white diamond in the center, surrounded by emerald gems.

"It's time for you to have it," I whispered. I passed along the beautiful piece to my daughter for her wedding day. The look in her eye told me how much she loved it.

Nat and I ran the restaurant together after we were married. We changed the plaque at the doorway to, Owners: Madeline and Nathaniel Griffin. The family worked side-by-side to make the business a success. Six months later, Nat and I moved into our house on the beach. Who would have ever thought my vision would actually come true? Mother knew somehow that I would accomplish my heart's desire. The faith she had in me, assisted me to persevere for all I could be. When you put a thought in your mind, and believe in all that can come from it, it does come to fruition.

September 18, 2009

I sat up in bed awaken by the familiar stream of light. It encircled the far corner of our bedroom. Nat remained fast asleep, and snored as usual. The cool ocean breezes filled the air. A chill ran down my spine. I hoped Aunt Mary was at rest now, since, Mother was gone, and Nat and I were man and wife. It had been such a long time since she came to visit. I blinked, and wiped my eyes. I got up and put on my slippers to search around our room and the hallway. I waited for a while, but no one came. As I crawled back into bed, I said thanks for my good fortune. It was not long before I fell fast asleep. When I woke, a tiny piece of lace and a white ribbon lay on the floor at the foot of my bed. I picked it up and held it to my chest.

Could it be she came to say goodbye? I moved over to the drawer at the side of my bed and opened it. There is where I kept the old calendar from my bedroom, when she gave me the message about Harbor Bay. The memorabilia was precious to me, and I kept it near me for comfort. I held it in my hand and flipped to September. The mark I placed back then remained in the spot for September 18. The date will forever remain in my heart.

~ABOUT THE AUTHOR~

I am a registered nurse who works in an emergency room. On my days off, I spend most of my time writing, and reading, okay and shopping. I am married to the love of my life, Joseph, who has the patience of a saint. We live in Central New Jersey with our dog, Chas, who thinks he's a wolf. I have two wonderful sons, and an amazing daughter, who are all grown. I am blessed with three adorable grandsons. I have been writing since I was a young girl, and had dreams of becoming an actress. My favorite weekend escape is Cape May, New Jersey. I can always dream up a magical tale, while relaxing under an umbrella, on one of their pristine beaches.

Visit Kathleen online at: www.kathleenanngallagher.net

www.ingramcontent.com/pod-product-compliance
Lightning Source LLC
Chambersburg PA
CBHW031257170626
46807CB00001B/186